MW01482983

Art on Fire

Yun Ko-eun was born in Seoul in 1980. In 2004, the year she graduated from university, her short story 'Piercing' won the Daesan Literary Award for College Students. In 2008, she received the Hankyorek Literature Award for her novel *The Zero G Syndrome*. In 2010, she published a collection of short stories entitled *Table for One*, and in 2011 her short story 'The Sea Horse Flies' won the Yi Hyo-seok Literary Award. Her novel *The Disaster Tourist* was published by Serpent's Tail in 2020.

Lizzie Buehler is the translator of *The Disaster Tourist* by Yun Ko-eun and *Korean Teachers* by Seo Su-jin. She holds an MFA in literary translation from the University of Iowa and has studied comparative literature at Princeton and Harvard.

ART ON FIRE

Yun Ko-eun

translated by Lizzie Buehler

SCRIBE

Melbourne | London | Minneapolis

Scribe Publications
18–20 Edward St, Brunswick, Victoria 3056, Australia
2 John St, Clerkenwell, London, WC1N 2ES, United Kingdom
3754 Pleasant Ave, Suite 223w, Minneapolis, Minnesota 55409, USA

First published in Korean as 불타는 작품 by EunHaengNaMu
Publishing Co. in 2023
Published in English by Scribe 2025

Typeset in Adobe Garamond Pro by the publishers

Printed and bound in the UK by CPI Group (UK) Ltd,
Croydon CR0 4YY

Scribe is committed to the sustainable use of natural resources and
the use of paper products made responsibly from those resources.

978 1 915590 90 9 (UK edition)
978 1 964992 19 8 (US edition)
978 1 761386 38 1 (ebook)

Catalogue records for this book are available from the
National Library of Australia and the British Library.

This book is published with the support of the Literature Translation
Institute of Korea (LTI Korea).

LITERATURE TRANSLATION
INSTITUTE OF KOREA

scribepublications.com.au
scribepublications.co.uk
scribepublications.com

1.

Nine years ago, the photo *Canyon Proposal* was taken on Bill Mori's mobile phone.

Bill was a photographer based in Las Vegas, and at the time he was so popular that his clients had to book at least six months in advance. The couple that had scheduled a four-day photo shoot starting 15 June in Grand Circle were his three-hundredth booking. *Canyon Proposal* was shot on 16 June, at four in the morning. For a while, people assumed that this couple were the subject of *Canyon Proposal*. But they couldn't have been — they hadn't even met Bill. Bill Mori's three-hundredth booking, the couple who were supposed to meet him in the Grand Canyon, had cancelled suddenly, right before their scheduled date.

Bill felt a surge of fatigue when he learned about the cancellation, but soon realised that this would allow him to take an unexpected break. His accommodation was paid for, and he'd already driven the five lonely hours to the Grand Canyon's South Rim. The sudden freedom hit him as he was about to wilt under a wave of exhaustion.

Bill went to bed early and woke up before four on 16 June to drive a distance away from the lodge. He wanted to take pictures of the stars. There was a hidden stargazing spot, somewhere that didn't show up on public maps of the park, and Bill was the only person there. He stayed for two hours. The period between 3.00 and 5.00 am is a time for loners — too late for the night owls, too early for even the earliest of risers.

The stars weren't the only thing that made it into Bill's camera frame that morning. Leaning out of his camping chair as he peered into the slowly brightening dawn, he saw a dozen or so elk cross his line of sight. Bill hurriedly snapped pictures of the scene, alternating between his phone and his camera. He was careful not to disturb the elks' secret world. Enthralled by the animals, Bill didn't notice the scene that was unfolding above their antlers.

Only at the end of a relaxing four days did Bill look at the photo he'd taken on his phone and discover unexpected guests within its frame. He thought he'd just taken a picture of a group of elk, but there they were: two people at the edge of a cliff, above the tangled bramble of elk antlers. A woman in a wedding dress and, in front of her, a man on one knee.

It was the kind of photo where, even though you couldn't clearly see their faces, you knew their expressions. The woman's veil hung over her shoulder, fluttering gently in the wind. It looked like a sprinkle of white snow, or silver netting. Moonlight illuminated the couple. The darkness in the picture looked a lot more impressive than it had in reality.

It wasn't unusual for Bill to witness a proposal. He'd seen several in the Grand Canyon alone. He had clapped vigorously in congratulations and even, at one proposal, grabbed a prop that was about to fly away in the wind. As a wedding photographer, he had helped couples plan their proposals, too. But the proposal that Bill had accidentally captured made a strong impression even on him. Later, in an interview, he said:

'If you're awake at 4.00 am, you either haven't gone to sleep yet or you woke up *really* early. I was the latter. I don't know which group these two belonged to, but look at their clothes — that's not something you can put on in a few minutes. They must have been awake all night.'

Bill zoomed in on the couple as much as he could. He'd taken the photo from quite a distance, but the subjects were certain to recognise themselves. Bill uploaded the picture to Instagram with the caption:

'Canyon Proposal, June 16, 4.00 am. Looking for the couple that proposed on the Grand Canyon's most beautiful cliff.'

Within a day, the photo had a huge number of comments. Bill's photos had never before garnered this much attention. Viewers were captivated by the anonymous proposal that took place while they slept. Some went to the place they thought the picture had been taken and snapped copycat photos. The spot was nicknamed 'Shooter's Point'. There were lots of cliffs near the centre of the canyon, but Shooter's Point was no longer just another one of them.

Of course, some people didn't get the photo at all. This was advertising, they said. These people claimed that Bill's photo was staged from the beginning. Bill was a professional photographer, after all. And it was true that he gained many more customers in the aftermath of *Canyon Proposal*. Soon, Bill had to post on his website that he was booked until the end of the following year.

To counter the rumours, he added, 'I don't work *that* hard to promote my business.'

Doubts about the authenticity of the photo were eventually dispelled for an unexpected reason: the scene Bill had captured wasn't a proposal. As it turned out, by the morning of 16 June, the woman in the photo had been missing for a week. Bill learned that the woman was named Lina. She was in her late twenties and ran a wedding dress shop in Los Angeles with a friend, and she'd disappeared while on a business trip to Las Vegas. He learned this, of course, at the same time as everyone else, from the same public sources. But people still asked Bill what else he knew.

It was Lina's friend and business partner who had recognised her upon seeing *Canyon Proposal*. The friend said that there was no reason for Lina to be wearing the wedding dress, but that without the dress she wouldn't have been able to identify her. The friend had designed the dress, and Lina was supposed to be delivering it to a customer. According to CCTV footage from the hotel where Lina was staying, she'd left the premises in a blue romper, carrying two large bags. The dress, which Lina was meant to bring to another hotel only eight hundred metres from her own, reappeared in the Grand Canyon a week later. When the friend saw *Canyon Proposal*, she immediately recognised the clothing, the disappearance of which had sown such confusion: an all-too-familiar dress with a thin veil stretched over the shoulders, out of place in an unfamiliar environment.

The friend submitted dozens of pictures of the dress as evidence to the police, who sprang into action. They obtained records showing that on the afternoon of 13 June, Lina had rented a car just outside the hotel under a false name and entered the Grand Canyon through the North Rim. Someone else had been with her. It was surprising enough that someone meant to deliver a dress in Las Vegas had ended up in a canyon hundreds of kilometres away, but even more unusual was the fact that she'd gone to the North Rim. The South Rim was easier to get to from Las Vegas. Lina may have had a reason to go north, but it was hard to imagine what that might have been, since two days later, at 6.00 pm on 15 June, she was spotted passing through the East Entrance of the South Rim, just as the sky was beginning to turn towards the blue of evening. There weren't many places for people who entered the park at that time to spend the night. The police received several tips about accommodations and campsites in the area where Lina may have stayed, but no useful information. It was impossible to grasp the entirety of Lina's journey within the South Rim. It was as if she'd chosen to travel from one blind spot to another, vanishing in between. Rumours spread about what kind of person Lina was, but no one could confirm the identity of the man on one knee in front of her. They didn't even know if the two had been travelling together.

Canyon Proposal began to be known as 'Canyon Disappearance'. Since he'd taken a photo of a missing person, Bill had unintentionally become a witness to a potential crime. People asked Bill if he was aware of this, demanding that he answer for himself.

'Life is a tragedy when seen in close-up,' Bill wrote in a cryptic response on Instagram, 'but a comedy in long-shot.'

People criticised Bill for plagiarising Charlie Chaplin. As malicious comments piled up, Bill posted again: 'I didn't know anything at the time. I thought it was a proposal — that's what it looks like in the photo. Maybe it isn't really a proposal, but no more information has been revealed. What judgement can you make from a distant silhouette? I didn't even look at the photo on my phone until a few days after I took it — I'm not a witness to anything. Even if I had known it was an emergency, what could I have done? I took the photo at fifteen times magnification — I was at least thirty minutes away from the couple by foot.'

Some viewers sympathised with Bill's statement, but most criticised his weak, indifferent tone. Some people said that it looked like the woman's arms were tied behind her back. The picture kind of did look like that, once you heard the claim, but it also didn't. People listed the actions Bill should have taken, ignoring the fact that he hadn't noticed the couple in his photo until later. He could have called the police, they said, or notified the place where he was staying. He could have honked his horn, turned the lights on and off. 'How could you post something like this?' they asked angrily. 'Did you think about how Lina's friends and family might feel?'

At first, Bill tried hard to defend himself, but after reading several articles about Lina's disappearance, he felt it would be inappropriate to continue talking about the case. Lina's father was revealed to be the founder of the stationery company Waldmann, and apparently a huge amount of time and energy had been put into the case. Detectives contacted Bill, and, under pressure, he deleted his Instagram post. But its contents had spread far enough to evade complete erasure.

The police asked Bill to cooperate with the investigation by coming to the police station as a witness. A few days later, Bill posted again on Instagram: this time, a black square. It was four in the morning, and Bill couldn't sleep.

'It wasn't me,' the caption read. 'Bill Mori did not take that photo.'

In short, Bill claimed that the photograph *had* been taken on his mobile phone at 4.00 am on 16 June, but that it was 'Robert', not Bill, who had taken the picture. Robert was now going to serve as a witness, Bill said, and he would submit his mobile phone as evidence if necessary for the investigation. Bill wasn't his mobile phone, he said, asking his followers to think about the two as separate entities. In his confession, Bill failed to explain why he had pretended to take the photo.

'Did Robert steal your phone?' comments asked. 'Or did you steal his picture?'

Now it wasn't just anonymous social media accounts questioning Bill. Bill's business was in crisis, too. He had to cancel several bookings and give those customers their deposits back. Bill had often used the Grand Circle for his photo shoots, but it had become somewhere completely unfamiliar. He went back to Shooter's Point, but the site was now so overrun by visitors that it required security. Bill stood under the craggy rock and looked at the spot where he had parked his car and taken pictures of the stars and the elk. He stayed at Shooter's Point for nearly two hours before returning to his hotel. That night, he posted, 'Robert the dog will now explain everything.' He stopped updating his website, his Instagram account, and his Facebook page.

Now Robert, not Bill, was in charge.

•

Soon after, a witness to the disappearance appeared at the police station. The police never released the witness's name, but people believed it to be Robert. They said that Robert was Bill's apprentice, that Bill regularly claimed Robert's photos as his own. The identity of someone suspected to be Robert was posted in an online forum and then deleted. Las Vegas police mentioned that they had obtained an additional photo as evidence — the media took this to mean that the second photo proved something definitive. Even so, the police didn't release it to the public.

When the witness appeared at the police station, walking on all fours, tail wagging, no one gave him a second look. They were waiting for Robert. No one at the police station had taken Bill literally when he called Robert a dog. It took them a while to realise that it hadn't been an insult — Robert really was a dog.

The person who came in with Robert introduced himself as an acquaintance.

'Not the owner,' asked the detective in charge, 'but an acquaintance?' The detective was flustered to learn that the witness was a dog. And the person who'd shown up with him wasn't even his owner!

The man introduced himself as the manager of the lodge Bill had stayed at, the closest lodge to Shooter's Point. He had first met Robert half a year earlier. For six months, the manager had fed and more or less housed Robert, but he couldn't say that he was Robert's owner. The detective thought back on what Bill had told him. Hadn't he said that Robert wasn't an 'ordinary man'? Maybe this is what he'd meant. Had this dog really taken the two photos in question? Had Bill lent his mobile phone to a dog — and not even his own dog, but one he didn't know? Had Robert stolen the phone? Later, when the detective asked Bill about this, he said that all he knew was that the dog had touched his phone. The dog had been mingling with all the guests at the lodge; he wasn't being constantly watched.

'Robert is good at communicating,' the manager said. 'People usually aren't saying anything that smart, so he basically understands them. Robert!'

As soon as the manager called his name, Robert ran into his outstretched arms. The detective stared as Robert yawned.

'Let me ask you,' the detective said. 'As someone who knows Robert, do you think it's really possible that he took the picture?'

'Bill already told you,' the manager said. 'Robert took the picture.'

'Doesn't Bill strike you as a little suspicious?'

'I don't know what kind of man Bill is. All I know is that this is definitely the kind of thing Robert would have done. Robert is famous for his photography — at least, he's famous among the guests at our lodge. Of course, he doesn't take a phone out of his pocket and snap a photo right away. But I'm sure he took this picture. The button just has to be in reach of his paws.'

'Well,' the detective said, 'this isn't the first time we've had an animal as a witness. We've had cats and dogs, parrots, iguanas. Their testimony has been very important. But what can Robert testify to in this case?'

He rubbed his jaw with both hands and looked at Robert.

'What can you do, Robert?' the detective asked. 'Is there something you want to tell us?'

Robert glanced at the detective and scratched his ear with one paw.

'Just to confirm,' the detective said to the manager, 'you're saying that this dog took the picture.'

'It's not that difficult for him, as far as I can tell,' the manager said. 'Do you want to see? These are some pictures that Robert took with my mobile phone. Some were taken at night, some are of sunrises, of travellers, campfires.'

'Do you know how many animals there are like Robert in Nevada alone?' the detective asked. 'One hotel has a cat that plays the piano whenever a guest arrives. There's an eagle that cooks meals for its family. An elephant that knows how to drive.'

A colleague walking by joined the conversation.

'My dog will sometimes text suspects in the cases I'm investigating,' she said. 'I have to send them apologies.' When no one laughed, the colleague handed over her mobile phone as proof. The detective rubbed his face again and looked at Robert.

'He's a papillon, right?' the detective asked.

'I'm not sure,' the manager said. 'When I found him, he was injured, so I got him treatment, and after that, he started coming to the lodge to sleep and eat. The park ranger said he's probably not a purebred, but he sure looks like one, right?'

'I heard that papillons are smart,' the detective said. 'The third-smartest breed of dog.'

'That's not the point,' the manager replied. 'Not all papillons can take photos like this.' He pushed his mobile phone towards the detective.

The images were a bit unusual, perhaps thanks to the curious expressions on the faces of some of their subjects — curious or even suspicious of the dog taking their photo. Of course, Robert took pictures of other things, too: candid photos of people looking away from the camera, no particular expression; cracks in the pavement; a dead bird; an abandoned napkin; streetlight shadows; things like that.

Robert didn't have his own phone to take photos with, so he was always jumping into other people's pictures. Some of those pictures had been Bill's. Bill had never changed the factory settings on his phone, so when he deleted a photo, it didn't really get deleted — it just went into the trash. Bill never emptied the trash, so unwanted photos had piled up: detritus that could be restored at any time with the push of a button. One of the photos in his phone's trash can was submitted to the police as further evidence. It came to be known as 'Wide'.

'So it seems that there were initially two versions of *Canyon Proposal*,' the detective said. 'One is a close-up taken at fifteen times magnification, and the other was taken with a wide-angle camera. Bill's phone has a dual camera, so it can take two types of picture at once. Bill had turned the feature off, but Robert must have turned it back on. The close-up picture will save automatically, but if you want to save the wide-angle picture, you have to press another button. In short, we think that Robert turned on the dual-camera feature on Bill's phone, took a picture, and chose to save the close up. Does this seem possible?'

'Bill's phone is a Samsung, right?' the manager asked. 'Mine is an iPhone, but it has a dual camera function, too. Maybe Robert learned by watching me. Or one of our guests. They come from all over the world. Robert knows the differences between phone models.'

'Let's ask Robert,' the detective said, taking his own old iPhone out. He placed it on a tripod and asked, 'Robert, can you take a picture of me?'

Robert moved towards the phone and tapped it with his front paw before tilting his head and turning away.

'He can't do it,' said one of the detective's colleagues, watching from the back of the room, just as the man exclaimed, 'Oh, the touch ID!' and unlocked the mobile phone with his fingerprint. Robert approached the phone again, tilted his head, and tapped the screen lightly. It had been hard for the detectives to believe that Robert could understand them — the whole time they spoke, Robert had only yawned or scratched his ears. His demeanour changed, however, as soon as he saw the unlocked phone. Robert looked at the detective and his surroundings for a moment, then, having completed his reconnaissance, took a picture. One shot, then another.

In the first picture, the detective was on the right side of the screen. There was the orange juice on his desk, the Hawaiian calendar on the wall to the left. It looked like a plumeria flower was blooming out of the juice. In the second picture, the detective was on the left, with a pair of handcuffs and a pile of 'wanted' posters to his right. His expression changed between the two pictures, even though they'd been taken mere seconds apart.

'He's playing with the composition!' said one police officer, handing Robert his phone. 'He thinks before composing a picture. Look, he moved the frame a little bit.'

Robert took pictures on a total of eight mobile phones that day, using the dual camera function on phones that had it and quickly moving the frame between pictures on phones that didn't.

After Robert and the manager left, the detective studied the picture recovered from Bill's phone: the 'Wide' version of *Canyon Proposal*. He couldn't find anything in it that would help with his missing-persons case, but there was slightly more in frame in this picture than in the other *Canyon Proposal*. The side mirror of Bill's car was visible in this version. In the mirror's reflection, you could see a dog pressing his paw on a phone screen. The dog was upright, touching the screen with his front right paw. So this *was* Robert's photo.

The investigation into Lina's whereabouts ended when two bodies were discovered in Joshua Tree National Park. Shooter's Point, the cliff the couple had been photographed on three weeks prior, was more than six hundred kilometres from where their bodies were found. Joshua Tree had been engulfed in a mid-July heatwave much more agonising than usual when Lina and her companion met their bittersweet end. The police reported that they had made an extreme choice after losing their way amid the sweltering heat; one member of the couple had shot the other before turning the gun on themself. Rumours spread that they'd gone to Joshua Tree specifically to take their own lives, that they'd exchanged texts containing the phrase 'lovers' euthanasia' and the sentence, 'Let's do it as elegantly as possible — our last drive together!' Lina's father, the head of the company Waldmann Stationery, had apparently opposed the relationship.

The fact that Lina's father was the chairman of Waldmann, however, wasn't revealed until long after the investigation began. Lina's last name wasn't Waldmann, but that didn't mean she had no relationship with her father. Mr Waldmann had taken Lina on camping trips when she was young; he had roasted marshmallows

with her outside their tent. Once, they'd even stayed the night at
Joshua Tree National Park.

Since his daughter disappeared, Mr Waldmann had been
steadfast in his attempt to find out what Lina's last steps were;
even after her body was discovered, he didn't stop. This was how
he met Robert. According to the detective, when Mr Waldmann
was handed printouts of *Canyon Proposal* and *Robert in the Canyon*
— the picture with Robert reflected in the car's side mirror — he
sank to the ground and cried.

As the summer season reached its peak, the lodge — Robert's
home — was plagued by a surge of guests. Due to the aforementioned pictures, Robert had become a star; everyone wanted to
see him. The manager needed to close the lodge for two months
of renovations, but had to wait until winter for the crowds to die
down. Before the venue entered its hibernation, Mr Waldmann
returned once more, for his third visit. The lodge manager
was surprised to see him; he'd read a recent article about Mr
Waldmann cancelling outside engagements for the foreseeable
future. The eighty-five-year-old chairman spoke slowly. He had
heard about the lodge's renovations, he said, and wondered if he
could spend time with Robert during the winter closure. As soon
as he said this, Robert trotted towards the car parked outside the
lodge, Mr Waldmann's cap dangling from his mouth. It was such
a clear expression of intent that the manager felt disappointed.

Robert did not come back at the end of the winter, nor by
the time spring rolled around. He became a 'permanent guest' at
Mr Waldmann's Palm Springs villa. But Robert didn't forget his
old friend, and when the lodge manager was invited to visit Palm
Springs, Robert dipped his paw in paint and left his autograph on

a copy of *Robert in the Canyon* as a gift. At the lodge, the print with Robert's paw was hung on the wall, and the gift shop began to sell postcards and scarves bearing the image.

It was around this time that Bill Mori began to post screenshots of articles about copyright disputes on his social media accounts. The night that Bill had said, 'It wasn't me. Bill Mori did not take that photo,' he'd chosen to distance himself from *Canyon Proposal*, but at some point he'd begun to draw close again. According to the art world, the photo was 'Robert's', but now Bill wondered if a portion of the rights belonged to him as well.

Bill's first action was to send a message informing the manager of the lodge that a dog could not hold the photos' copyrights, and that he couldn't use the photos to make a profit. The manager said he was selling photos and souvenirs with Robert's permission, but Bill retorted that this was like getting permission from a 'random passerby'. Having previously shunned public attention, Bill went to the press and asked, 'Who placed my mobile phone on the table the morning I took *Canyon Proposal*? You really think it was a dog?

'Dogs, birds, cats, elk, wind — any of them could touch the screen of a mobile phone that's placed in front of them. Just because I didn't press the button, does that mean it's not my picture? If a drop of rain hit the phone, would the resulting photo belong to the raindrop? You have to understand this photo as conceptual art. I set up my phone like a trap, ready to capture any image that happened to come in its way. I put my phone there on purpose. I was the one who named the photo *Canyon Proposal*, posted the picture online, and helped with the investigation. My intention was for the work to be open to all possibilities, including the possibility of a dog passing by and pressing the button.'

From Bill's point of view, there was no difference between the lodge selling *Canyon Proposal* and the lodge selling *Robert in the Canyon*.

'Both pictures were taken on my mobile phone,' he said in frustration. 'It doesn't matter who took them.' But there wasn't much evidence for Bill's purported aesthetic and conceptual rationale.

The statement that came back to bite Bill the most, though, was, 'It wasn't me. Bill Mori did not take that picture.' Bill had denied ownership of the photo because he was worried about getting caught up in a legal dispute. When he changed his mind, the ensuing case lasted over a year, and Bill lost. Bill was on edge the whole time, while the manager of the lodge became more and more relaxed about potential copyright violations. Mr Waldmann and Robert had his back.

That didn't mean, though, that Robert held the copyrights. The results of the case were as follows:

1. Bill Mori does not own the copyright to *Canyon Proposal*.
2. Robert does not own the copyright to *Canyon Proposal*.
3. No one owns the copyright to this photo, so anyone may profit from it. The actions of the lodge manager are not illegal.

Experts stated that it would have been difficult for Bill Mori to obtain the copyright even if he hadn't, as he eventually had, posted that he hadn't taken the picture. Bill would have had to prove that he had planned the photo's composition, which he was unable to do. He gave up fighting.

People naturally listened to the loudest voice in the dispute: the lodge manager. The manager was now selling more photos with Robert's pawprint than ever. Robert no longer lived at the lodge, but in a way, he was ever-present.

More than a year later, Robert appeared alongside Mr Waldmann at an exhibition for the artist Felix Gonzalez Torres. It wasn't the first time they had gone to an art museum together, but that day a particularly large number of people saw them. Mr Waldmann looked more relaxed than before — perhaps due to a change in his facial expression, perhaps a change in his style — and everyone knew it was Robert's influence. Many of the museumgoers stole glances at Robert, but he didn't seem bothered — he was too busy looking at the art, sitting in Mr Waldmann's arms.

The piece they lingered in front of longest was *Untitled (Perfect Lovers)*: two clocks arranged side by side. Mr Waldmann whispered something to Robert; later, an interviewer would ask him what he had said.

'What did I tell Robert? You really want to know? Oh, you're serious. Hmm ... well, I was asking Robert whether he thought I should buy the piece.' (Everyone laughed at Mr Waldmann's facetious grin.) 'But then we found out that the art would be destroyed at the end of the exhibition. So I asked Robert, why don't we make a copy of the clocks to put in our house?'

The interview contained a few follow-up questions about Mr Waldmann's plans to create a knock-off, but he refused to answer them. A few years later, though, he published the following essay in an art magazine.

> When Amatrice was hit with an earthquake, the
> village clock stopped ticking between 3.36 and 3.37.
> The clock in the Banda Aceh Mosque stopped at 8.25
> when the city was hit by a tsunami. In Nagasaki, it
> was 11.02; in Chernobyl, 1.24; in Fukushima, 2.48.
> Analogue clocks don't lie. When the world stops,
> the numbers on digital clocks evaporate instantly;
> the needles on an analogue clock, however, show the
> moment that they stopped moving.
>
> My personal moment of destruction was in
> the summer, sometime between 5.00 and 6.00 pm.
> A desire to run from that moment coexists with a
> simultaneous desire to return, to know the exact
> minute and second it occurred. When Felix Gonzales
> Torres' piece *Untitled (Perfect Lovers)* was destroyed at
> the end of its exhibition, I felt a simultaneous sense
> of pain and freedom. Was it possible for me to do
> something similar? Robert and I decided to copy the
> destruction. We bought two identical round clocks.
> I put them on the floor, so Robert could see them.
> We inserted batteries and set the clocks to the current
> time. The clocks began to move in tandem.
>
> The two clocks were governed by increasingly
> different rhythms, and at some point the time they
> told diverged entirely. One clock stopped, and the
> other continued to tick. I was mesmerised by the

difference, but Robert helped me snap out of it.
Two of his photos saved me. In one photo of the
clocks, their needles are out of step. The left clock
was permanently stuck at three o'clock, and the right
clock was about to reach nine thirty. In another,
Robert is pushing the needle of one of the clocks to
make it align with the other.

In reality, after a while, you realise that one clock
is stopped while the other is moving, but look: the
photo creates a world in which the two clocks show
the same time. You don't need to distinguish between
the clock that's ticking and the one that isn't. They're
like two sets of eyes, meeting each other's gaze for a
brief moment.

There were only two things I could do after
seeing this picture. One, to cry, and two, to create a
world dedicated to him.

Mr Waldmann was dying when he wrote the essay. After
his death, the Robert Foundation was set up with his assets.
According to the executor of his will, Mr Waldmann had decided
that, upon his death, twenty million dollars would be given to
Robert. Separate provisions would be made for Danny, who had
served as Robert's interpreter.

Mr Waldmann's writing was also published at the beginning of a
four-hundred-page book about the Robert Foundation, alongside
Robert's photos. The book was too long to finish during a flight,

but I brought it anyway. It was so large that every time I turned the page, it felt like a gust of wind was blowing out from the spine. The book contained the photos that had made Robert famous. They still weren't copyrighted, but everyone knew them as Robert's pictures. They were arranged in sets of two, the first on one side of the page and the second on the other. The second photo was always a wider version of the first.

Photo 1. A woman sits by the window in a bagel shop, eating a bagel. At the next table, a man in khaki is eating the same type of bagel. The woman cheerfully looks out the window at the blue sky.

Photo 2. The woman's expression remains the same, but in this version, we can see more of the view outside the window. The man in khaki is walking out of the shop. Two cops are pointing a gun at him.

If you turned to the next page, you'd find the title of the work, 'Bagels and Arrest', followed by a few words of commentary:

> It only takes a few seconds for the atmosphere to
> change. That's what Robert was able to capture.

When I flipped to yet another page, I noticed the woman sitting in the aisle seat looking at my book. Pointing, she asked, 'Is that Tanzania?' before quickly correcting herself.

'Oh, sorry,' she said. 'It's an island. I thought it was a bunch of wildebeests. My eyesight isn't very good.'

The picture in question was an aerial shot of a number of islands. I didn't know where Tanzania was. All I knew was Robert had taken the picture. At first glance, it did look like a mass migration of wildebeests.

'Is that a travel magazine?' the woman asked.

'It's a book about ecosystems,' I replied. That was how I felt. The book made me think of things like the deep sea, or deep space. It contained worlds that I'd never otherwise encounter, but that still somehow affected me. If I was a shallow-water fish, the Robert Foundation was a deep-sea creature. These two beings were unlikely to meet, but sometimes seawaters got mixed up.

The pilot announced over the intercom that we were heading into a bout of turbulence. Suddenly the islands on the page really felt like wildebeests on the move. How many of them would get eaten by crocodiles? The young and sick were in the greatest danger. I looked at one of the smallest islands and, in the next moment, looking at the next picture, realised that it had disappeared. Like a lie, like it never had existed. I blinked. There were so many islands that I couldn't even tell which one had vanished. I knew that that this was photo 1. On the next page was something entirely different.

2.

One year earlier, I had received a call from the Robert Foundation. It was the same day I delivered a Shake Shack burger to apartment 1903. I had met all sorts of people while working as a delivery person, but none as perplexing as this man. At the time, I'd been working for the delivery app Bballi for about a month. It was so easy to get hired there that it barely took any time at all to start making deliveries. A lot of people signed up thinking that they'd begin working the next day, maybe even the next week, but orders would come in so suddenly that they were able to start immediately.

The Shake Shack order came in at 5.00 pm, and the delivery was complete at 5.08. The app told me that, in eight minutes, I had traversed a radius of six hundred metres. However, it didn't take into account what was road and what wasn't, so the actual distance I had travelled was much greater. When I reached my destination, bag in hand, a man already standing in the hallway greeted me curtly.

'My hamburger must already be cold,' he said. 'And I bet my shake is melted, too.'

I didn't know how to respond. The man repeated that his burger had to be cold, and his shake had to be melted, as I stroked the bag with my gloved hand. Were my hand movements provoking him? He looked out the window and grumbled that he could hardly believe I was a delivery person.

'Walking up with your hair fluttering in the wind,' he said. 'Were you out on a leisurely stroll? What about my hamburger?'

I could feel his eyes on my shoes, as if he were going to report me for not wearing sneakers. I wanted to tell the man that I was a pedestrian delivery person, that it was natural for me to walk to my destinations, but I shut my mouth and held out my phone to show that it had only taken eight minutes for his order to arrive.

'Even on foot, Shake Shack can't be more than four minutes away,' the man said. 'You went too far! I can't believe it. You went to 107 first. I can see it all on the screen!'

He held out his mobile phone to show me, but all I could see was a dot. Car, motorcycle, bike, feet … no matter how I travelled, on the app, I was nothing more than a round blue dot. Would this man have reacted differently if the map showed the locked back door, the footpath closure, the tree disinfection trucks on the street, the broken elevator — everything that made it difficult for me to get to his apartment? I didn't want to explain myself to someone who was treating me as if I were useless, a broken computer mouse. It would be best just to apologise and leave. But an apology wasn't what came out of my mouth.

'Your hamburger was going to get cold at some point,' I said. 'And your shake was going to melt. If you wanted a piping-hot hamburger and an ice-cold shake, you should have gone to the store yourself.'

The man flushed violently; even his neck was red. He looked so threatening, I wished I could take back what I'd said. What would have happened if he hadn't opened the front door to the building and gestured for me to leave? Thirty minutes later, I got a notification on the Bballi platform informing me that I'd received the lowest possible rating for my delivery. It was Mr 1903's right to give me whatever rating he wanted, but it was also my right not to put up with his nonsense, so I called the Bballi support centre and asked for my rating to be corrected. The voice on the line told me that the company wasn't able to change ratings.

'But I was so fast,' I said. 'I was basically running. I got there in eight minutes — why did I get the lowest possible rating?'

The employee's voice grew a little clearer.

'The delivery speed wasn't the issue,' she said. 'The problem was your attitude.'

My *attitude*? I kept protesting, but to no avail. As soon as I hung up, my phone buzzed with a notification informing me that there was a 'special offer' for delivery people. My phone was still ready to go; I hadn't bothered to turn off Bballi notifications.

I didn't want to move, but it turned out the delivery request was from a Chinese restaurant only fifty metres from where I was standing. Was it that building over there? My fingers automatically accepted the request. At the entrance to the restaurant, the hostess asked, 'How many in your party?' When I said that I was there to pick up a delivery order, she asked me to wait outside. The food came out three minutes later. Assigning a jjajangmyeon delivery to a pedestrian delivery person must have been a system error, I thought, resisting the urge to run. My pace grew faster and faster until I gave in. It was jjajangmyeon — I needed to hurry, or the noodles would get soggy.

I left the food at the entrance of the apartment building and sent the customer a text, as requested. Over the next two hours, I took four more orders. I hadn't planned on doing this, but the orders were always nearby. Just a slight distance from me, then a little bit farther, then a little farther than that, until I was getting requests from three hundred metres away, and found myself quite far from where I'd started. I was getting paid a higher rate than normal due to the cold; I just couldn't stop making money. Despite the temperature, sweat dripped down my back and was slow to evaporate. From the street, I could see apartment lights turn on one by one. Streetlights, LED signs, lights I hadn't noticed before — suddenly they were all flashing. I saw someone carrying an insulated delivery backpack. Would the hamburger from earlier have stayed hotter if I had one of those? I turned off Bballi notifications, but I wasn't living in an on/off world. That was the moment I got the call from the Robert Foundation.

'Is this the writer An Yiji?' asked a polite voice. It was Director Choi, the Korean head of the Robert Foundation. At the time, I didn't really know what the Robert Foundation was, so I listened to Director Choi suspiciously, as if he might be a spam caller. After hanging up and doing a few Google searches, though, I realised my dream had come true.

It was raining heavily the day I was supposed to meet him. Director Choi had heard that I worked at an art school and offered to meet me there, but I'd quit that job several months earlier. When I said I was happy to travel to meet him, the farther the better, Director Choi suggested a restaurant two hours from my house.

It wasn't rush hour, but the subway was full of people in black puffer coats. I was one of them. I played Tetris in my head while swaying to the rhythm of the ten-car hunk of metal transporting us. When people wearing the same colour of clothing stood next to one another — poof!

'What do you mean, *poof*?' Director Choi asked. The game wasn't anything special, but since he'd asked, I had to explain, and he listened to my answer so intently that I didn't know when to stop. I kept talking.

'You know how when you play Tetris, if you get a complete line of tiles, those tiles disappear? What I do is make people on the subway disappear. In my mind, of course. If I erase other people, I create a space that's all my own. There's a cheat code, too. In the winter, ninety per cent of people are wearing black — poof!'

My explanation ended just as the menu arrived. Director Choi seemed to be the same age as my father. Maybe it was his slow and polite manner of speaking. He ordered a two-hour multiple-course meal for us.

When the bread arrived, he picked up a roll and said, 'I come here for the bread. That's life, isn't it? The main course isn't everything. Sometimes you make decisions based on the bread rolls … Eat up while it's still warm.'

When he cut the dark, pebble-like roll in half, hot steam rose up from the middle.

'Right after you graduated from college,' Director Choi continued, 'you were one of the four winners of the Young Artists of the Year Award. That year was really competitive. And you've all been quite active since then, haven't you?'

'Everyone except for me,' I replied.

'Do you know why you haven't been working?'

'Well, my lack of talent.'

'You've had bad luck,' Director Choi said.

'Really?' I said saltily. 'I wasn't aware.'

'The organisation supporting you went under, didn't it?' the director said.

'It was a difficult time for everyone. A bunch of companies went bankrupt. I just didn't realise it was going to affect my ability to exhibit my art.'

'If the organisation hadn't gone bankrupt, you'd be making art like we all expected.'

At that moment, the first course came out: a beautiful plate of pink prawns covered with bright-yellow flowers and green sauce. After briefly admiring the food, I returned to our discussion of my unfortunate history.

'I suppose that's true,' I said. 'But the past is the past.'

'The organisation was shut down when it was acquired. The financial problems it was facing kept getting worse, and the acquiring firm decided it wasn't worth the expense,' Director Choi said. 'But do you know what company acquired it?'

'Uh, I'm not sure …'

'Waldmann Stationery.'

'Okay.'

'They're the owners of the Robert Foundation,' the director added.

There weren't any open windows nearby, but it felt like a cold wind was blowing over us. Plates from the first course disappeared, and the second course arrived: colourful cold pasta.

'This means that the Robert Foundation has been influencing your life for a long time,' Director Choi said.

'In a negative way, right?'

After we shared an awkward laugh, I reached for some bread. He did, too, and our hands collided. We both gestured for the other to take a roll first, but neither of us ended up taking any, distracted by the arrival of the third course.

'It was just like this,' the director said. 'Your situation at the time. We both forgot about the bread because of the third course. It was a timing issue: for you and for the bread.'

By now, I was starting to feel irritated, in part thanks to the way Director Choi was talking. He spoke slowly, inserting frequent pauses between words, and considering that he was likening me to bread, who'd be able to stay calm for long?

'So you're not here to apologise to me, a stale bread roll?' I asked.

'Give us the chance to make it up to you,' the director said. 'Give the Robert Foundation a chance.'

I was the one setting boundaries here. Maybe I was just small fry to them, but it felt like this kind of thing happened to me too often. The world didn't work like this, did it? Someone who hurt me tells me to smile, and then everything's alright?

'Of course, that's not the only reason,' Director Choi continued. 'The Robert Foundation is careful. It takes a very long time for us to choose which artists to sponsor. We consider the whole person. We are looking to sponsor artists around the world … Anyway, I'm rambling. Let's eat while the food is still warm.'

'I'm still thinking about how you view artists like bread,'

I said. 'What happens if the artists get hard and crusty?'

The director laughed loudly and said, 'There are a lot of ways to salvage old bread. That's what the Robert Foundation does.'

He handed me a picture. It was of my most recent painting, *Hangover Relief,* which I'd posted online two months earlier. This wasn't my past — this was my present.

'Robert left you a heart,' the director said.

'Robert?'

'Our president.'

Director Choi pointed to the image of a dog on his business card. I laughed, thinking it was some kind of joke, that the director was mocking his boss. Of course, I know now that the director was just telling the truth.

'Robert is interested in your work,' he said. 'I myself was intrigued when I read an interview you did nine or ten years ago; the way you talked about your situation then was quite similar to how you describe it now. You said you were waiting for a life where you had a backyard and a dog. Do you remember the interview I'm talking about?'

'I think they were asking me if I liked animals,' I said. 'So I said it would be nice to have a yard, with a dog.'

'It's funny, because, you know, Robert is a dog with a yard. You've been invited in by a dog with a yard. Your words planted the seeds for reality. Was there a particular reason you answered the way you did?'

'Well, at the time, my biggest concern was buying a house. Nothing's really changed since then …'

My answers to the questions from the interview were as follows:

1. I'd like to have a dog.
2. With a yard, if possible.
3. I'd treat the dog well and live there with him.

When I pulled up the words in my mind, they transformed into the following:

1. A house with a yard was my dream, but there's no hope for it now.
2. If I had a dog in the yard, what if the dog liked me?
3. I would have succeeded earlier if I'd had the kind of life that included a dog and a yard.
4. I can't tell if it's a dog running around in my yard, or me running around in the dog's yard.

I was twenty-six, twelve years ago, when I became one of the four nominees for the Young Artists of the Year Award. At the time, I believed that the story of my life was going in a completely different direction. But when I look back, I can see that I'd already passed the final page of good luck. Like there was some misprint on the paper, I was thrust into a dull sense of anxiety and uneasiness.

I didn't realise at the time that I'd already reached the limits of my success. I only knew where I stood in comparison to my fellow artists — friends I'd known since we were teenagers. When I started an art school, my friends began to call me Director An, but running the school drove me further from the world of my dreams. When I closed the school after seven years, my friends told me it was time to spend the money I'd made and focus on painting again, but I'd barely saved anything. I wanted to make art, but I still needed to earn a living. At one point, I was afraid that everyone except me would become a famous artist, but that wasn't the most nerve-wracking thing. The real shocker was when one of my friends — supremely talented, with big dreams for himself — suddenly announced that he was preparing for the civil-service exam. This sent shockwaves through our friend group. Everyone started to lay down roots at jobs that had formerly been part-time. So few of us even identified as artists anymore. As we all grew busier, I almost forgot that I was a painter. I had started to casually work on my own projects again a year before my art school went under, but was posting them online without any real expectations. That was how the Robert Foundation took notice of my work.

It was only after our two-hour, ten-course meal that I realised I was being interviewed. According to Director Choi, Robert liked to eat multiple courses, and including conversation, his meals ended up taking an hour and a half, if not longer.

'How painful the meal would have been,' Director Choi said, 'if you were the kind of artist who's so stingy you put leftovers into Tupperware containers as soon as you finish eating. Or if sitting for this long made your back hurt.'

The Robert Foundation's guidebook included the motto 'Robert: embarking on a search for a pawprint that will transform a world of darkness, one inch at a time.' The book spent multiple pages explaining the Robert Foundation's efforts to discover unique artists. I was one of the pawprints they had supposedly 'discovered'. Honestly, it was hard to believe. Why me?

Director Choi told me to trust Robert's discerning eye. The Robert Foundation had supported a total of twenty artists over the past seven years, most of whom described their four months at the Robert Museum of Art in Palm Springs as a 'significant opportunity'. The Robert Foundation remained one of the most impressive lines in their resumes, and its influence continued to radiate throughout their careers. Seed money, a ladder that had helped them climb down from the edge of a cliff, a turning point, divine intervention, winning the lottery ... This was how artists described the program.

I was the first Korean artist to participate, and they had translated the long guidebook for me. The most important part was found on pages nineteen to twenty-three.

Financial Support

- Necessary travel, including round-trip airfare and car rentals
- Comfortable accommodations, independent studio
- Unlimited meals
- Weekly stipend of five hundred dollars over sixteen weeks (total of eight thousand dollars)
- Materials (up to two thousand dollars)
- Interpretation, translation, and exhibition planning services

Artist Expectations

- First twelve weeks: creation of at least one work of art inspired by Q City, located near the Robert Foundation's headquarters
- Weeks thirteen through sixteen: exhibition of artist's work
- Last day of exhibition: incineration of one piece by artist, to be chosen by the Robert Foundation

Incineration?

I wondered if 'sale' had somehow been mistranslated as 'incineration', or maybe there'd been a printing error. But no — they really did mean that the art was to be burned. It wasn't a metaphor.

There have been intermittent cases of deliberate art burning. A museum in Naples was burning one piece a day at one point to protest the government's indifference towards arts and culture. Artists have incinerated their own work for similar reasons. Some even burned originals after turning their art into NFTs. However, I had never heard of art being burned in a program that supported artists. I had assumed, of course, that the Robert Foundation would purchase the artwork to be burned before destroying it, but Director Choi said that the Foundation did not purchase art.

'So will I be donating my work?' I asked.

'Not exactly,' the director said. 'Rights for the work belong to the artist, and the art is burned with that understanding. Burning art is an important part of the program, so we ask for our artists' voluntary participation. You have to agree in order to take part in the program. Do you?'

'Hmm ...' I said. 'This is interesting. And a bit distressing. A while ago, I was an artist in residence in the Netherlands. Participants were supposed to donate a work at the end. Of course, I chose which piece I donated. But we don't get to choose which piece burns?'

Director Choi said that he understood my concerns, but that the artist's distress was the point of the burning. Such distress, he said, kept the exhibitions going. The fact that a newly created piece of art was to be burned by the artist upon the conclusion of the exhibition excited even the most unenthusiastic museum-goers. Some of the Robert Foundation's artists had cried. Their process remained in video form, and in memory, but the art itself disappeared.

'Your residency in the Netherlands was three weeks, you said? How much art did you make during that time?' the director asked.

'Maybe twenty pieces?'

'And you got two hundred dollars for materials.'

'How do you know that?'

'We're always doing research on other residencies,' the director said. 'The program you were in was great. But the Robert Foundation operates on a much larger scale. Our program is much longer, with better space for artists to work in; the piece that gets burned is just one of many created during the residency. But I don't know if it makes sense to compare. All I can say is that the Robert Foundation's residency will help your career.'

As Director Choi said, unless I only created a single piece of art during my entire stay, the piece that would be burned would be one of many. It was sad to call a unique piece of art 'one of many', but comparing what would be lost if I took part versus what I would lose if I *didn't*, I knew what I had to do. This wasn't an offer I could turn down. I would just have to work as diligently as possible.

I agreed to the conditions. One of my first tasks was to complete the Robert Foundation's online safety training. It looked just like Bballi's employee training, as if designed by the same company, but instead of learning about the ten types of traffic accidents that could occur during a delivery, I learned about twelve types of incidents that might occur during an artist residency. Plagiarism, sexual harassment, giving the Foundation false information, etc. When I logged onto both the residency training and the delivery training sites, my internet browser warned me that the site I was about to enter was 'not secure', which I found amusing. To be a safe delivery person, to work in a safe creative environment, I had to expose myself to an unsafe website — for three hours.

The rainy season began two days before I left for the US. On the way back from buying things I'd need for my trip, walking through a combination of rain, lightning, and thunder, an idea struck me. With this weather and traffic, Bballi would almost certainly be paying delivery people special rates. I wanted to do something to commemorate my departure from the world I knew. I was on my way home, I was hungry, and I'd already thought about ordering food, so I decided to open up the Bballi app and play the role of both a customer and a delivery person. If I gave myself five stars, I'd have a perfect last delivery.

I could see the pasta restaurant I had in mind. I quickly placed an order. But before I could accept the delivery request that popped up on my phone, someone else did it first and ruined my plan. I wanted to at least get a look at the person who'd stolen the job from me, but surprisingly, by the time I made it through the rain and arrived at my doorstep, the food was already there. It was warm to the touch. This wasn't the departure I'd envisioned, but I carried the warm pasta inside. Two days later, I was on a plane to Los Angeles.

My mood peaked when my seat was upgraded; then it sank with the plane's landing. When I picked up my luggage and entered the arrivals hall, no one was waiting for me, holding a sign with my name on it, and neither Director Choi nor the person designated to pick me up answered the phone. I sat at a café in the airport for an hour, but no one called me back.

At first, I just thought that the driver was late. But after two hours, I started to think that he or she might have forgotten about me. After waiting a bit longer, I checked to make sure I hadn't misunderstood anything. I made sure my phone was working. I looked around to ensure I was in the right terminal. Another hour passed.

I went to the bathroom, washed my face with cold water, and glanced at the mirror. The person I saw reflected back at me looked like she was trying to hide her nerves. I wiped the water off my face with determined strokes, applied lotion, and was unzipping a green pouch to pull out my lipstick when the person next to me asked, 'Do you have any lipstick?'

She was much taller than me, and I was so nervous that I could feel myself leaning away from her. There was something strange about her. She already had a grotesque amount of make-up on her face, and she wanted more? I had my lipstick in hand and didn't know how to refuse, so I passed it over. I watched the woman adding several layers of colour, even covering the inside of her lips, and when she handed the tube back to me, I grabbed it so protectively that I almost dropped it. I had only just bought the lipstick at the duty-free shop, but as soon as the woman left the bathroom, I threw it in the rubbish.

My plane had landed at 5.00 pm, and I got to the arrival hall by six, but now it was after nine, and I still hadn't left the airport. I started to see more and more suspicious-looking people, like the lipstick woman. I probably looked suspicious myself.

If things had gone according to schedule, I would already

be in Palm Springs, but for some reason, I was still waiting in the airport. This situation hadn't appeared anywhere in my five sessions of online safety training. I opened Uber and typed in the Robert Foundation's address. How much would it cost to Uber there? What if I couldn't find the Uber driver either? Would it be rude to give up on waiting for someone from the Robert Foundation? While weighing my possibilities, I hoped that my assigned chaperone would appear, and I wouldn't have to make a decision.

Until that point, I thought I was facing only one problem, but then I realised I couldn't find my credit card. I searched every pocket on my clothes and in my bag, but the card wasn't there. I mentally retraced my path through the airport. I had used my credit card at both of the cafés I'd patronised. The only other time I had taken the green pouch that contained my credit card out of my bag was in the bathroom. Had that bizarre woman distracted me to steal my card? Oh, and my phone! Where was that? I saw it sticking out of my jacket pocket, as if it were hiding from me.

Fortunately, my bank hadn't reported any unknown purchases that would require I block my card. But this was the only credit card I'd brought. I had five hundred dollars in cash, but was that enough? The Robert Foundation was supposed to provide everything I needed, but I couldn't even find the person meant to pick me up.

It grew dark outside. People had begun to flock to the airport, seemingly to spend the night there. Only then did I notice the news stories about forest fires playing on the airport's TV screens. I'd known about the California wildfires before leaving Korea, but the problem didn't have the same valence from such a distance.

I smelled something acrid at the tip of my nose. The damage had spread during the hours I was on the plane.

I opened a hotel reservation app and looked for a place that would allow me to pay with cash. The hotel closest to the airport was fully booked. So was the second-closest. The hotels downtown were almost all full, too. Maybe it was because of the fires, but an available room was hard to find. I didn't have many options since I'd lost my credit card. One older hotel in Hollywood said it would accept payment upon arrival. However, not all the rooms had bathrooms. You could choose a private bathroom, a room that shared a bathroom with one neighbour, or a room where you had to use a public bathroom down the hall. The room-to-toilet ratio was either 1:1, 2:1, or n:1. The 1:1 rooms were all booked. It was almost comical, having to decide between a 2:1 room and an n:1 room. As I read user reviews on my phone, part of me still waited for someone to show up, holding a sign with my name on it, saying, 'I'm so sorry I'm late.'

I chose an n:1 room because I thought it would be better to use the bathroom in the hallway than to share a bathroom with an unknown neighbour. But when I got there, the woman at the front desk told me I had been 'upgraded', then talked at length about a red button I would need to press while using the bathroom. I only realised what she meant when I entered my suite: I'd been put in a 2:1, the kind I had deliberately tried to avoid. The room had a large balcony, but all I could see beyond it was darkness.

A sign on the bathroom door stated that guests should refrain from showering after 11.00 pm and instructed that they press the red button inside to lock the door to the neighbouring room. The bathroom was square and larger than necessary. When I opened the door and went inside, I saw a shower and toilet on the left, and a towel rack and mirror on the right. Next to the toilet was a door leading to my neighbour's room.

Nothing happened when I pressed the red button, so I wasn't sure if the door had locked properly. When I used the bathroom a second time, I realised that I had previously left myself vulnerable. After completely closing the door to my room, I had to press the red button until it lit up and made a buzzing sound.

Even without the red light or the buzz, an unspoken lock existed on the two doors. I wasn't sure if the whole hotel was like this or if I'd just been given an unfortunate room, but the sound-proofing was awful. The bathroom seemed to amplify noise; you knew when someone was entering or leaving. You could hear how many steps they were taking, when they lifted and closed the toilet lid, when they removed their clothes. At exactly 3.00 am, my neighbour decided to take a shower. *Shhhhhhhhhhh. Badadadada. Shhhhhh. Badadada.* I knew the *shhhh* was the sound of water droplets, but I had no idea what the *badadadada* was. Amid the noise, I collapsed into sleep, and the situation repeated the next night. In other words, I didn't check out of the hotel in the morning.

When I opened my eyes after the first night in my unfamiliar room, I sensed an effervescent energy from the light outside, threatening to break through the curtains. It seemed like a good sign. When I pulled open the curtains, the light streaming in seemed to disinfect all of yesterday's misfortunes. I wanted to take the shower I'd skipped the night before, but I had only just heard someone leave the bathroom. I wanted to wait until the soap or shampoo scent, the condensation on the mirror — traces of someone else — had vanished.

I knew that sharing a bathroom meant you shared the towel rack or the shelf above the sink, but I also saw someone else's body cleanser on the shelf. The whole time I was showering, I didn't have anywhere in particular to fix my gaze, so I read the cleanser's ingredients list. It was in Korean. So the person next to me was Korean, or at least knew Korean, unless they just happened to be using a Korean product. I noticed the date written on the bottle. It had been expired for fifteen years! After I finished showering, I took my possessions and left the bathroom.

While I was sleeping, I had received a number of calls from unfamiliar numbers, none of whom were answering now. I finally got in touch with one of them at 10.00 am, as I was trying to decide whether to return to the airport or go to the Robert Foundation on my own. I heard a familiar voice through the phone. It was Director Choi. He asked if I was still at the airport. He was relieved to hear that I had found somewhere to stay. Only a few hours earlier, the Foundation had contacted Director Choi to tell him that there'd been an unavoidable mistake, and he said that the person in charge would get in touch soon. He kept asking me if I was surprised, but it seemed to me like Director Choi was the one who was most surprised. He insisted on trying to comfort me, as if he thought that was his duty, and spoke in a disorganised manner, saying things like, 'Nothing like this has ever happened before, not since the beginning of the Robert Foundation's residency program, but it's not a big deal.' I was a little tired from having to assure Director Choi that I was indeed fine, but still, I felt lucky that I'd finally reached him.

Conscious of my phone, assuming that the Robert Foundation would call at any minute, I went to a nearby café for a bagel and americano, but even after I'd returned to my room, no one had called. Losing my credit card was nerve-wracking, especially as I only had a bit of cash on me. I wanted to go to the bank and figure out how to withdraw more cash, but it was Sunday. As I began to despair about how I could do nothing but wait, my phone finally rang.

'This is the Robert Foundation. Is this An Yiji?'

When I confirmed that it was, the person on the phone quickly mumbled something in a language that didn't sound like English at all. The Robert Foundation had promised me an interpreter, but only after I arrived on the premises.

'Is there someone there who speaks English?' I asked, to which the voice replied, 'This is English. English is the only language I've ever spoken.' My request helped regardless. The young woman on the phone began to speak more clearly. According to her, the problem wasn't that they'd had the wrong number for me, as I'd initially feared, it was that the road between the Robert Foundation and the LA airport was blocked due to an emergency. Perhaps because I didn't reply immediately, the woman asked, 'Have you seen the news?'

'Yes,' I said. 'I'm watching it right now.'

The woman seemed relieved to hear that I knew about the fires. She asked for my current location.

'The Orange Tree Hotel,' I said.

I was worried there might be two Orange Tree Hotels, so I gave her the exact address twice, but she kept repeating, 'Orange Hotel.'

When Director Choi called me soon after, he, too, asked if I'd seen the news about the wildfires.

'Yes, yes,' I said. 'I've been watching the news.'

According to him, the fires had blocked several major roads throughout California, which left the person in charge of picking me up stranded. Another driver had been sent to the airport instead, but there had been a misunderstanding, and someone with a name similar to mine had been picked up instead.

'So now An Young is at the Robert Foundation. Seriously,' Director Choi said.

'Who's An Young?'

'The person they thought was you.'

'That's a completely different name!' I said. 'An Young and An Yiji. They don't even sound similar.'

'You're right,' Director Choi said. 'My apologies. I'm really sorry. It seems like the person meant to pick you up was inexperienced, and he couldn't handle the job. He made a huge mistake. Coincidentally, An Young is in the same situation. He had a layover in LA, and things got messy because he accidentally left the airport. He was waiting for a driver when this ridiculous situation happened. You guys were mistaken for each other. He must be just as frustrated as you. He was supposed to go to Mexico but ended up in Palm Springs.'

'Director Choi,' I said. 'I don't care about An Young. I want to know what's going to happen with *my* situation.'

'Ma'am, you have nothing to worry about now. We'll pay for your hotel, so you can stay at the nicest place you'd like. The Robert Foundation will pick you up in two days, max. Just wait until the day after tomorrow, please.'

'The day *after* tomorrow? Not tomorrow? You just said you were coming tomorrow.'

'We're trying our best, but the evacuation zone is getting bigger and bigger. We'll come the day after tomorrow at the latest. Robert's banquet is that night, and you can't miss that.'

Irritation surged at the fact that, despite the chaos of my pick-up, they could still confidently assure me that the time of Robert's banquet would remain unchanged, but I just listened quietly.

The Robert Foundation staff seemed to have misheard my location, so they kept asking me to confirm the name of my hotel, even as they urged me to move elsewhere.

'Orange, Orange Tree — it doesn't matter, ma'am. Just move to a better hotel. Oh, you lost your credit card? How terrible. Are you carrying cash? Thank goodness. Don't worry, we'll make sure the Foundation pays for your hotel move. Ma'am, are you there?'

'I'm right here — what about the Robert Foundation?'

'Huh?'

'Nothing.'

I felt like a food delivery order that had ended up at the wrong address, or an umbrella that had fallen into the gap between a train and the platform, but I had no need to be anxious. Calm down, calm down, I told myself. An hour later, someone else from the Robert Foundation called. He confirmed what I already knew: that all the hotels in the area were fully booked. Not just the best hotels, but the second-best ones, too.

'I'm sorry, ma'am,' he said. 'We'll move you to the best room at the Orange Tee Hotel.'

'Orange Tree,' I corrected.

'Yes, that. Where you're staying now.'

Did they know that the best rooms in this hotel, with a 1:1 bathroom-to-room ratio, were also all booked? The best place for me, then, was where I already found myself. After I hung up, I continued to lie in bed, trying to gather strength for my next move.

It existed, right? The Robert Foundation — it wasn't a scam, was it? I felt more perturbed knowing that it wasn't.

I wondered if the Foundation had withdrawn my invitation. When I told a college friend about getting in to the residency program, her reaction was extreme — she said they were crazy. When I asked who was crazy, she equivocated and replied, 'I mean they're awesome!' Now, I was ready to agree.

How did I get this kind of opportunity? I'd thought it was the chance of a lifetime, but they couldn't even pick me up? I was afraid of being forgotten. I mocked myself, resigned to the fact that nothing came easy to me, and as that feeling began to lose its edge, I got a notification — the Robert Foundation had sent me an email.

'We have been informed about your missing credit card,' the email read. 'Please see the attached list of companies with which we have partnered. If you tell them that you are with the Robert Foundation, you can use their services free of charge. Additionally, we have covered your lodging and breakfast at the hotel you are currently staying at, so please enjoy the next few days there. Your driver will pick you up from the hotel as soon as he can.'

As soon as he can? Where was he? Had he followed An Young to Mexico?

Feeling defeated, I stuffed my belongings in a small bag and left the room — I needed to do something, regardless of whether I extended my stay at the hotel.

Two things then happened in quick succession: I found out that the guest next to me was Korean (we opened our doors at the same moment and greeted one another with '*Annyeonghaseyo*?') and that the Robert Foundation really had already paid for my hotel stay.

The staff at the front desk looked at me and said, 'Your bill has been taken care of. As requested, we'll move you to a room with a private bath as soon as one opens up. It'll be in two days. There's a concert tomorrow, which is why we're so booked up.'

Two days? It was baffling to think that I could end up spending six nights at this hotel. The text I'd got from the Robert Foundation had assured me that I would only be here for a 'couple of days', but they had paid for an entire week's stay. Was I being overly suspicious? 'One day' had become 'two days at most' and now 'one week' had been paid for. What did it mean? I felt uncomfortable. I was stuck, with no promise of getting out.

3.

Some of the restaurants the Robert Foundation had partnered with were within walking distance of the hotel. I asked the concierge at the front desk to make a reservation at one of them. Determined to enjoy myself as much as possible in spite of the circumstances, I went around Hollywood and Beverly Hills like an eager tourist. I waited in lines, I bought a hot dog, I took pictures of the murals in Beverly Hills, and I bought an Oscar trophy at a souvenir shop for ten dollars and change. I chose the Oscar for 'Best Artist'. I'd considered 'Best Tourist', too, but when I pulled the trophy out of my bag, I realised that I had taken 'Best Person'. Mistakes continued to follow me.

When I got to the restaurant … well, I realised I hadn't needed a reservation. That's how shabby the place was. There were only three tables, one of which was covered with piles of napkins and straws. A few customers were collecting food to take away, but no one sat down to eat. It didn't seem like the kind of restaurant that would even take reservations, and the food was just alright. Still, when I gave them the name of the Robert Foundation, they said the meal was covered.

I had filled my stomach, but felt the urge to eat somewhere else anyway. Another restaurant on the list was only two blocks away. It was an impulsive visit, but when I got there it looked big enough to require a reservation. When I said that I was alone and hadn't made a reservation, that I was an artist with the Robert Foundation, the waiter asked if I'd like a seat at the outdoor terrace. There was one remaining seat with a view of the HOLLYWOOD sign and today, he said, it was particularly worth seeing. I followed the waiter to my table and was surprised by what I saw. Instead of reading HOLLYWOOD, the sign read HQLLYWQQD, with all the Os replaced with Qs. The waiter told me that the change had happened overnight. Then he asked me if I knew what it meant.

'I've never seen anything like it before,' I said. 'Do *you* know what it means?'

'No, that's why I'm asking. Every customer today has given me a different answer.'

'It's illegal, right?' I asked.

'It's illegal, but people usually do it to mark an event of some kind.'

The waiter pointed to the wall of the restaurant, which was covered with Hollywood signs, but if you looked closely, you could see they were all slightly off. HOLLYWEED, HOLYWOOD, BOLLYWOOD: some of them took advantage of the sign's existing letters, while other arrangements used different letters entirely.

The waiter handed me a menu and took a photo of me in front of a HQLLYWQQD sign painted on the wall. I repeated that I was an artist with the Robert Foundation.

'Oooh, the Robert Foundation,' the waiter said. 'That's a great place.'

'Do people from there come to this restaurant a lot?' I asked.

'Yes, and they often eat this dish.'

The waiter turned to a page at the back of the menu, displaying various options for three-course meals, and with his help I chose the restaurant's signature 'Seafood Crunch'. He confirmed that drinks were not included, but at his recommendation, I ordered a glass of white wine.

I liked the restaurant's music. There were only a few plants placed between me and passersby on the street, and sitting here gave me a sense of comfortable belonging. I watched the stores bustling with evening business, the people on their way somewhere, then suddenly it hit me: I was in Los Angeles — in Hollywood. Even though this wasn't my destination — just a longer-than-expected stopover — I wouldn't have been able to see the HQLLYWQQD sign at any other time.

The presence of the Qs seemed significant. My residency was part of a program the Robert Foundation had started to revitalise boring urban areas, and the city I'd been assigned to enjoy, physically and spiritually — to depict in my art — was called Q. I wasn't sure if the sign was referring to *that* Q, but the image intrigued me. I thought about how I was always one step behind — *I* should have come up with an idea like this. Anyway, now I could send a photo of the sign to Director Choi.

Unlike the previous restaurant, this one had a number of customers, all of whom looked great. The food was tasty, too. The bill, brought over by the waiter, came to $210. The wine I'd chosen only cost twenty dollars — how could the bill, even with tax, be $210?

'Everything is included,' the waiter said. 'A three-course meal and a glass of wine.'

He pointed to minuscule letters at the bottom of the menu that read 'Market Price' and said that the cost today reflected the presence of the HQLLYWQQD sign.

'I think there's been a mistake,' I said. 'I'm with the Robert Foundation. Can you bring me a bill with the Foundation discount?'

The waiter didn't seem to understand.

'Your restaurant has a partnership with the Robert Foundation,' I added.

'What's the Robert Foundation?'

'Didn't you say you knew it?'

He smiled lightly and pointed to his T-shirt.

'I know Under Armor, I know Nike, I know Samsung. And I know the Robert Foundation.'

When I showed him the email I'd received with the list of partner businesses, he gave me a puzzled look and said, 'I'll check to see if there's some sort of relationship between our restaurant and the Robert Foundation that I wasn't aware of.'

He came back shortly after and said that there was no such partnership.

'Are you sure it's our restaurant?' he asked. 'Not one in Hollywood? As you can see, we're not in Hollywood.'

He pointed to the HQLLYWQQD sign out the window, but I wasn't in the mood to humour his joke. I could feel glances from the people at the table next to me. Finally, I pulled out my wallet and was, as expected, short on cash. When I added the twenty-five per cent tip the waiter urged, I didn't have enough money to cover everything. I changed the tip percentage. The waiter coolly brought me a revised bill, but I still didn't have enough money.

Half my cash was in the safe in my hotel room, and I hadn't expected to spend nearly $250 today.

'Ma'am, you're thirteen dollars short.' The waiter said this twice. When I said, with an embarrassed look on my face, that I would have to go back to my hotel to get the money, he completely gave up the perfunctory kindness he'd shown me previously. In a slightly more domineering tone, he told me to pay right now. Another employee approached me. The people at the table next to me no longer hid the fact that they were staring ... then I noticed someone walking down the street. It was the man staying in the room next to me — the person who shared my bathroom. He had looked so different this morning, when we greeted each other, that I didn't recognise him at first.

'Hello!'

'Oh, hello.'

'Where are you going?'

'A launch party.'

'Sorry, but could I borrow thirteen dollars from you?'

He entered the restaurant and helped me pay the bill, mumbling, 'Market price? This is a scam,' while smiling at the waiter as he brought us the receipt. The man kept adjusting his glasses and looking around at the surroundings. He was trying to avoid the paparazzi — an occupational hazard, he said. The man was an actor, on his way to the launch party for a TV series, and he'd dressed up for the event.

'If you don't have any other plans, would you like to come with me?' he asked. 'It's just over there.'

He gestured to a crowd of people. Camera flashes burst onto a street darkening to dusk.

•

An actor? Back at the hotel, I zoomed in on a photo I'd taken from a distance, of him posing in front of a red-carpet backdrop and saw written in tiny letters 'Hunting or Gathering'. When I went to the show's website to find out more about it, I didn't see his face.

There was a photo by Willy Ronis hanging next to the elevator in the hotel lobby, and seeing it made me think about what I'd left behind. A child was running, holding a baguette as long as he was tall, looking like a delivery person. I turned Bballi notifications back on. My location was still set to Gyeonggi-do, Korea, and requests for deliveries there started to come in immediately. When I changed my location to the US, I got a call. I assumed it was the Robert Foundation, but it was Bballi, which I had left behind in Korea.

'Are you a rider?' the caller asked.

'Huh?'

'There's food near you now — could you pick it up?'

'Oh, but … I'm in the US right now.'

'Yes, I can see that. 1765 North Orange Drive, Los Angeles.'

They could track me? I didn't remember agreeing to that, but it must have been one of the countless terms and conditions I'd agreed to. Puzzled, I continued to listen to the voice coming from my phone.

'There's a pick-up forty metres from you. Can you do that?'

'Forty metres? Alright.'

'Please pick up the food from the listed location and deal with it yourself.'

'What do you mean, deal with it myself?'

'Deal with it at your convenience.'

'Oh … Do you mean I should throw it away?'

'Many riders eat the food.'

'So you want me to eat it?'

'You can do that. After picking up the food, deal with it in whatever way you see fit.'

I got a text message explaining that the pick-up address was 'secret'. Not 'special', but 'secret'. I'd already left the hotel. I had heard about Bballi expanding to the US, but who would have thought that I'd experience it firsthand? My destination was a small shop in the building next to my hotel. On the counter was a shopping bag marked '35'. I faltered, unsure if I should just pick it up; when I did, someone came up to me and asked, 'Bballi?'

'Bballi,' I said in response. That was it. I didn't need to send a photo of the delivery to the Bballi app. I'd already got a message.

'Thank you for picking up the order. A secret amount will be deposited shortly into your rider account.'

Then I got nineteen dollars. The currency was displayed in dollars now that I was in the US. It was a pretty good rate for just going to the building next door. There was a familiar hot dog in the '35' bag.

I received a text message from Director Choi.

'That's so cool!' he wrote. 'The Hollywood sign covered with Qs is amazing. It bodes well for your creative success.'

The message concluded with an excited dancing emoji.
I sighed. I wasn't just experiencing a time difference between
Korea and the US; it was like being on a different planet. I
placed the hot dog in the fridge, put thirteen dollars in a ziplock
bag and placed it on the shelf above the toilet, and pulled a thin
hoodie out of my suitcase. That was when I found my credit card
— in the hoodie's side pocket. As soon as I told my bank and
they unfroze my card, all strength left my body and I couldn't
do a thing. I took a shower, feeling like I'd been possessed by
something, and only after a while did I realise that I'd used the
old body wash.

My sleep kept getting interrupted that night, as if I needed
intermissions between dreams. The air conditioner wasn't cool
enough, its noise incessant. The sounds of dripping water and
switches going on and off next door were amplified by the hotel's
thin walls and shared bathroom. When I started to hear thumping
and the sound of someone vomiting up their guts, I crushed my
ears under my pillow. Only after my neighbour had thrown up a
few more times did I get absorbed back into sleep.

I met Robert in my dream. He looked like what I'd seen in
pictures. A white and dark brown papillon, with an expression
so arrogant it looked cute. Robert told me he would give me his
personal phone number, so I had my phone open, ready to save
the information. Zero one zero, three seven four four, ha ha ha ha.

'Zero one zero, three seven four four — hahahaha? Can you,
um, repeat those last four digits?'

'Zero one zero, three seven four four, ha, ha, ha, ha.'

It was a strange number, but I wrote it down in a hurry. After
several more dreams, the one in which Robert had appeared

became hazy, but when I got up in the morning, I found a scrawled note by my head.

010-3744-hahahaha.

It was written in sloppy handwriting on a memo pad embossed with the hotel's name in small letters. The memo felt like a metaphor for the past few days. This was the situation I found myself in. I had a number, but I couldn't call anyone with it. Was this a test? A test of patience? Was it Robert — mischievous Robert — who'd put me in this situation? I'd already searched 'Robert Foundation, artist, cancellation' the night before. Thinking too far into the future was an old habit of mine. As soon as I start something, I worry about how it might end, and even when I succeed, all I can think about is my failures. But no matter how many unsavoury words I typed into the search bar, no comparable situations came up. I wanted to believe that this adventure wasn't a misfired bullet. There was no reason that a mistake, a cancellation of an artist's application, or an endless delay would have made it into the news, but I couldn't stop searching, and because I couldn't find the results I feared, I alternated between short-lived relief and anxiety. I tried to remind myself that there were uncontrollable variables everywhere — that waiting a few days was no big deal. But hadn't I woken up from a dream and written down '010-3744-hahahaha'? That was a rift between the two worlds I was fighting to squeeze together.

'Robert Art Foundation Advances Urban Cultural Revitalization', 'New Changes to Traditional Artist Residency', 'Number One City Q', 'Q: A Short Distance Between Artistic Inspiration and the Marketplace' ... When my persistent searches led me to these articles, I felt further relief, and I wondered if I was making too big a deal of a simple delay. Well, you couldn't call it a *simple* delay — everything had a margin of error, but if that was the only problem with my airport pick-up, things should have been fixed within a couple of days, tops. Of course, I was aware of the unprecedented emergency. Yesterday a neighbourhood in Los Angeles had recorded a temperature of 119 degrees Fahrenheit. In Celsius, that was over forty-eight degrees.

I turned the air conditioner off and on again, but it still wasn't working properly. The refrigerator wasn't staying cold either. When I opened its door, I saw that the hot dog inside had aged ten years overnight. Its wrapping paper was soggy, the inside of the fridge lukewarm. I felt the urge to throw the hot dog outside, but as soon as I opened the window, stale air flowed into the room. It wasn't even 8.00 am. Everything was stagnant, inside and out. Moored at sea for three days before reaching my destination. The sky was yellower than it had been upon my arrival, and it smelled increasingly acrid.

The hotel lobby was chaotic that morning. More than a few guests said their air conditioners hadn't been working, and each time someone complained, the employee at the front desk pointed to the same words on an iPad screen: 'Lightning has hit the area over ten thousand times in the past few days.'

A mobile map indicated current wildfire hotspots but, in contrast to the severity of the situation, the fire icons on the map looked almost dainty. The fire's origin was above a national freeway, but it had been migrating west and would soon reach San Bernardino National Forest. People were concerned about the blaze running into small, regional fires. That had already happened in some places, and the new conflagrations had veered onto entirely unexpected routes. One town on the map was so surrounded by fire icons, it looked like it was under siege. Humans and nature, playing a deadly board game.

The disaster was unfolding on a huge TV in the lobby, but I couldn't hear the anchor's voice. I wasn't sure if the volume was off or if the music in the lobby was drowning it out. The reason the lobby was so crowded was that, unlike in the forests depicted on screen, engulfed in flames, underlined with correspondingly serious text, it was fairly cool here. Strangers conversed; one would say that the situation was more severe last week, that the fires were under control, and someone else would refute that statement.

One woman, who said that if it was like this in the summer, she couldn't imagine how bad things would be by autumn, when fire season would be at its worst, turned to me and said, 'My mom always fantasised about coming to California — especially because of the weather — but now it's on fire!'

A silver-haired woman sitting next to us said, 'Let's go home. Let's pack our bags.'

'But Mom,' her daughter responded, 'we just got here.'

Then, to me, she said, 'The airport is on the verge of being shut down. We only just managed to get out of it.'

'The airport is closed? In Los Angeles?'

'Yeah, we left and then they shut the doors.'

I had tried to call the Robert Foundation so many times, to no avail, that by the time my call was finally answered, I had almost

resigned myself to another day of waiting, and forgot why I'd
called them. When I heard the woman on the other side say,
'Robert Foundation,' I came to my senses. It was a familiar voice.
Maybe we'd spoken before. Regardless, she wasn't the person
meant to pick me up. She asked if I was calling about personal
business, and when I said no, she replied with a list of mysterious
words and asked which of the aforementioned projects I was
calling about.

When I asked the woman to run through the projects again,
she did so at extreme speed. I quickly realised these projects had
nothing to do with me, but the woman continued speaking. In
the end, I had no choice but to cut her off. Maybe I'd be misunderstood as impatient and rude, but there was a problem with
speaking so fast and for so long that people had to cut you off.

'Sorry, I don't know what those are,' I said. 'My name is An
Yiji. I came from Korea to participate in the residency program. I
landed four days ago, but I'm still waiting to be picked up.'

I emphasised 'still'. The woman asked me to wait a moment,
and then I heard what sounded like something collapsing. What
the heck? At least she hadn't hung up.

'You said your name is An Yiji, right?' the woman asked when
she returned. After I confirmed, she told me that my project was
briefly on hold due to the absence of a driver to pick me up.

'On hold? What do you mean?'

'That's its current status.'

But what did that mean for me? When I asked if someone was
still coming to pick me up today or tomorrow, she said, 'That's to
be determined. For now, everything is on hold.'

'You picked up the phone, you've heard about my situation,'

I said. 'What's your name?'

She told me her name was Sam.

'Sam, can you help me, please? Just take charge!'

Sam said in a low, uncomfortable voice, 'I'm an intern,' then, 'I'm still in my probation period, so I don't have any authority. I can't be in charge of this.'

'Can you tell me the name of the person who is in charge, then?'

'They're on their way, so I'll leave a note for them.'

'No, I want to know their name.'

'Oh, I can't give you that. To be honest, this is my job.'

'Huh? It's your job to annoy me?'

'No. This person is busy. It's my job to tell people when they're too busy to answer. I want to do my job right.'

'But you haven't told me that, and you haven't told the person in charge, either.'

'Telling you that they're temporarily unavailable — that's my job. I told you that.'

'It's not temporary … There's no one in charge of my case, is there?'

Did no one want to take charge? I was about to ask. Fortunately, I swallowed my words and spit out something else instead.

'I'll take a taxi.'

'You'll arrive by taxi? Alright.'

Her tone was a little bit gentler than before, and I lost steam. I was starting to think they had been waiting for me to do this all along. It didn't seem possible that she'd care about when I arrived, but I assured her that I would get there as quickly as possible. She had already hung up, though.

Now all I had to do was take a taxi … but no matter how many times I tried, I couldn't get one. Uber, Lyft, another rideshare app I'd never heard of before — none of them had cars available. When I went to the hotel front desk and asked if the concierge could call me a taxi to Palm Springs, he said that would be difficult due to road closures. And even though not all the roads were closed, the chances of having to return without another passenger were so high that taxi drivers wouldn't want to take me, he said. When I asked if there was another way to get there, the employee just reiterated that lightning had struck the area ten thousand times in the past few days.

'I guess I should just go to the airport,' I said.

The employee gave me a pitying look. 'The domestic terminal is closed.'

'Then I'll go to the international terminal and fly home.'

I was serious, but she took it as a joke. She told me to wait, that my friend had said they were coming to pick me up. I asked if the person she'd spoken to on the phone had sounded trustworthy, and she took that as a joke, too.

I went to the breakfast buffet and put a piece of bread in the toaster. The mother and daughter I had spoken to earlier, who said everything was on fire, saw me and asked me to remember them. 'Everything is on fire, but remember us, please.'

I asked them to remember me, too. It was a breakfast before the end of the world, and I knew that I wouldn't be able to forget them. The daughter was beautiful, with long hair. Every time she leaned over to talk to me, her hair would brush against my arm. She didn't seem to notice that I kept leaning away from her (in spite of my efforts to make it clear), but I got some useful information from them. Behind the hotel, there were several small travel agencies and rental-car companies.

After breakfast, I spent three hours, in the midst of the heatwave, searching for anything — bus, train, plane, taxi — to travel by, to no avail. Almost everyone told me that the roads were closed due to the fires, and the most optimistic among them said it would be at least two days until I could go anywhere.

As long as I found some form of transportation, I didn't care if I had to stuff myself in the luggage compartment, but every time I came close to finding one, something went wrong. One taxi-company employee, holding the car keys in his hand, asked, 'Just you?' I couldn't bring myself to answer. He might have been a driver, but he was also the type of person I intuitively wanted to avoid. When I said I was just shopping around, he offered to lower the price, but after I left, I ran into him again at another place, offering me a higher price. I was told I'd be shown a 'sincere, professional driver', and it turned out to be him. By then, my will to keep searching had halved.

For the next two days, I continued my search and — for absurd contrast — I did two more deliveries for Bballi. No one was getting in touch with the artist An Yiji, but there was regular contact with the delivery person An Yiji.

On the fifth day of my stay at the hotel, I heard that the man in the room next to me had acquired a car and was going to drive to Las Vegas. This was my chance! But when I asked if I could come along, he said no.

'Song Jun, help me, please,' I said.

Surprised, he asked, 'How do you know my name?'

'I like the movie you were in, *Zero G Syndrome*.'

The movie had come out five years earlier, but I'd watched it the day before, so I was able to talk more concretely about why I liked it. Jun had played the role of 'real-estate employee two', something I'd discovered after several layers of searching. When I'd looked up the name of the series having a launch party, several articles had come up, and there I'd seen comments congratulating the actor 'Song Jun'. That was the guy in the room next to mine. If you looked at his filmography, you'd see that he mostly played bit parts, but he'd held an important supporting role in *Zero G Syndrome*. He'd played a man who didn't believe in gravity, who couldn't believe that the earth was round. His lines were memorable — his character insisted that you had to drink, because that was the only time you could step on the curved parts of the earth. Of course, there was no need to tell him about the entire process. It would take too long to explain why solving this puzzle that had nothing to do with me gave me a sense of comfort.

Jun seemed flattered and told me that we could take a picture together if I wanted. It seemed like he was going to give me a ride, but in the end he refused.

'I'm not actually sure if I'm going to leave tomorrow or not, and riding in a car with another person is a bit …' he trailed off, then said, as if looking for my agreement, 'It's self-care, you know?'

'No …' I replied. 'Aren't you a celebrity?'

'Gosh, thank you.'

'I'll pay for the petrol,' I said. 'I'll even pay you extra for going through the fire zones!'

'I'm sorry. I'm just being cautious to avoid unnecessary mis-understandings. This is why I haven't had a single scandal since the beginning of my career.'

He listened as I explained my situation and asked if I'd face some sort of penalty for not arriving quickly. When I told him no, he said this was a first-world problem. He didn't understand why I was anxious about waiting a few more days. If it were him, he said, he'd just sit in comfort at the hotel. I wanted to be like that, too, but the next day brought further woes.

Throughout the early morning, I could hear sirens shrieking like wild beasts. By the time I went down to the lobby at 6.00 am, a violent storm had already come and gone. The classical music that had droned on had been turned off. The lobby looked as haggard as a deflated ball, and without the music playing, it felt too big. Someone — I wasn't sure if they were a guest or a passerby — told me there had been a murder. The eighty-three-year-old mother from Ohio and her daughter had been attacked by a stranger in front of the hotel. The mother had been taken away on a stretcher, unconscious, but her daughter had died. It didn't feel real — I remembered the feeling of the daughter's long hair brushing against me as we sat by the breakfast buffet, and how they'd asked me to remember them. I touched my arm. The perpetrator had been caught at the scene. He wasn't targeting the mother and daughter, it was just a random act of violence. They'd never met him before.

The hotel employee who'd discovered the two victims kept apologising to guests, who were hurrying to pack their bags and check out. She said that she understood, that she didn't want to stay in this city anymore, either. I will never forget what she said when I made eye contact with her: 'As you can see, it's now extremely possible for me to move you to a 1:1 room. If you want, I'll move you.'

When I told her that I intended to check out today, too, she reminded me that my stay was fully paid for. I knew that, but I was still going to leave. I didn't have a plan, but I couldn't stay. It wasn't just about switching hotels; I needed to get to where I had to be. My head throbbed.

'Are you still looking for a car?'

It was Jun. Yesterday, he hadn't displayed the slightest desire to take me with him, but now he seemed different.

'I'm about to take off,' he said. 'If you want to come, I'll give you a ride.'

I packed my bags in ten minutes and went down to the lobby.

On our way out of the city, I saw the Hollywood sign restored to its original lettering. HQLLYWQQD had returned to HOLLYWOOD. It hadn't taken long. Maybe I'd even noticed it belatedly. I felt like I'd seen a misprint on the pages that made up this city.

An Young, who'd met my driver several days earlier at the LA airport, must have got onto Interstate 10 after leaving the airport and sped passed Riverside, Morongo, and the Yucca Valley before reaching my destination, the Robert Foundation. While the wrong person arrived at my destination, I had been waiting vacantly at the airport. Finally, I'd found someone to take me.

An Young's route was very different from the path we ended up taking, as we had to detour to avoid the blazing mountains. We were forced to choose between a road that would take us to the north of the Robert Foundation or one that went to the south. To the north lay the Pearblossom Highway. When I said it was the inspiration for one of David Hockney's photo collages, Jun seemed interested. He said he'd heard the highway was in some music video, too. The STOP sign in Hockney's collage had long since been changed to traffic lights, but for the music video, Jun said, they'd changed it back to STOP. We decided to take the Pearblossom Highway ourselves.

'Yiji, you're not answering your phone. Call me as soon as you get this. I see that you've taken a taxi.'

The text from Director Choi arrived two hours after we'd left. He wanted me to call him so he could find another way for me to get to the Robert Foundation, but I was already in transit, using the only means possible. When we'd left, our expected arrival time was two in the afternoon. It was a generous calculation that included breaks, but variables kept changing. Three hours into the drive, the cars on the road were at a complete standstill.

'A tour bus and a cargo truck collided. The bus overturned and it's blocked the road like a barricade. There are injured people, and police are patrolling the area.'

That's what Jun said when he came back to the car after checking out the situation. It didn't seem like the flow of traffic would resume anytime soon, so people were getting out of their cars and then returning to them, opening the doors with ruddy faces. When I searched the name of this area online, live news stories popped up. There was even a picture of the scene ahead, which I couldn't see in real life. Helicopters had been mobilised, and people were being carried away on stretchers. As vast a country as the US was, the roads here were narrow. I saw a car attempting to go back the way it came, but it couldn't. We could only go east. The only good thing about being trapped here was that there was a shopping mall a five-minute walk away.

Some people, like us, left their cars on the road and went to the mall. It was a fully constructed three-storey building, but the shop windows all had 'For Rent' signs, as if no one had moved in yet. At the entrance, several people were handing out long black umbrellas. I wondered if they were emergency supplies, but it turned out that they were 'grand opening' gifts. Since we were already here, we figured we might as well eat lunch at the mall. From the window of a pizza restaurant, we could see the road chock-full of cars. At the other tables, we heard people in the same situation as us talking about the accident. I didn't know if what they were saying was true, but according to them, the hand of a child on the overturned bus had been severed. The child was the first person to be carried away by stretcher to a helicopter, and there were other injured people, too. There were also several tons of eels from a cargo truck scattered on the road.

Road conditions didn't improve until after we'd eaten pizza, gone to the bathroom, and slowly walked around the building. I noticed that all the needles in the shopping mall seemed to be broken — the hands on the clocks didn't move, the needles on scales in the hallways didn't weigh anything. Much of the mall was at a standstill, so when I found an elevator that clearly went up to an observation deck, I wasn't sure whether I should take it.

'If we go, we'll be able to see farther along the road, won't we?' Jun asked. 'I'm curious about the future. Our short-term future.'

'But is the elevator working?' I asked.

When Jun pressed a button, the elevator door opened without

a sound. The floor inside became level with our feet. Because there was a sign that read 'check elevator floor' affixed to the front of the door, I poked at it with my umbrella.

'This is like a slapstick comedy.'

'What is?'

'You poke at the floor with your umbrella, then the next moment we fall through the elevator.'

'Why would you say that?'

'Can you really ensure our safety with an umbrella?'

'It's not a weight check, it's a knock. Can I come in? That's what I'm asking.'

The site of the accident was farther ahead of us than we'd thought. This was the best place to see the future, but since there was no roof, I felt like my scalp was burning. Still, at the end of the road, I noticed that cars had begun to move. Traffic had started flowing again.

Jun imitated me when we got back to the car. Tapping the hood with his umbrella, he asked, 'Can we ride?'

Cars set off, one after another. We passed the section of road slippery with eels, and in the midst of it all we realised at some point that we'd bypassed Pearblossom Highway. Jun had wanted to take a picture there, so he was disappointed, but then another view unfolded in front of us like a new world. The cars that had covered the road had scattered, and now it was just us.

Jun was on his way to Las Vegas for an audition. Someone else had been chosen for the role originally, but they had dropped out at the last minute, so now Jun had his chance. Despite the fires, this was such an opportunity that Jun said he had to go. When he asked what my reason for coming was, I had to think about how to answer. Fear of exclusion? Doubt? If so, doubt about what? Anxiety about myself? I said, 'Because I'm curious.' If Jun had asked about what, it would have again taken me a while to choose my words, but he didn't ask any further questions. I told him what the Robert Foundation did, how they discovered artists. I had started talking because it seemed like Jun was fighting against drowsiness, but it put my mind in order, too.

'What you're saying reminds me of this song,' he said.

Jun played 'A Day in the Life' on his phone. He said that the silent part of the song wasn't actually silent, that it was audible to dogs, that the music was at an entirely different frequency. I wanted to keep listening to the song while Jun had the radio on, so he handed me his earphones. We continued along, listening to different songs and occasionally talking. He couldn't believe that Robert was a dog. I said that I hadn't either at first. But the more I'd learned about the Robert Foundation's history and traditions, the more comfortable with the idea I had become. This unfamiliar world, like an image in a frame, was now only thirty minutes away. The road stretched out narrowly below the low, cloudy sky, surrounded by light-olive-coloured fields, as if just briefly permitting two new tenants. It wasn't that narrow, but amid the vast nature it looked like a thin line. Sometimes we would pass a parked car, but they were only ever there for one of two reasons: the car had broken down, or it had run into wildlife. Neither applied to us, but at one point we, too, had no choice but to slow down. What looked like dead animals littered the road.

At first I thought they were roadkill, but as we got closer I recognised them as tyre marks. I saw tyres in the distance. The car slowed down further. As the field covered in tyres stretched out on our right side, we turned off the road to see.

When I opened the car door and climbed out, a feverish heat hit me. The air was breathtakingly heavy. As soon as I put my feet on the ground, I could hear the parched earth collecting moisture from my body. Everywhere I stood was an extension of a crack. The ground was made up of countless puzzle pieces the size of my hand. Upon closer inspection, I realised that some of the black shapes I'd thought were tyres were in fact bumpers. And they weren't the only things that melted when they touched the ground here. After standing for a while, it became clear that my brain was melting, too. When I looked around, I saw the black shapes rolling around here and there. If I fixed my gaze in one specific spot, I could see even more.

'It looks like the skin of a tyre has been peeled off,' I said. 'I've never seen anything like this.'

'It's like when the sole of your shoe comes off. The heat separates out the layer that touched the ground. It happens at extremely high heat and velocity. As the centrifugal force increased, the rubber detached. It gets soft when it's hot. That's how the rubber grew weak and came off.'

'Oh, you played a tyre repairman, didn't you? In a Korean drama?'

'You really are a fan.'

Jun counted me as his sixth fan.

'Actually, I worked at a tyre factory for a long time,' he said.

'Did you know tyres aren't round at the start? That's just the shape they take after all the trimming. You shave the surface of a freshly extruded tyre with a Y-shaped knife. Like this.'

Many speculated about the cause of the wildfires: lightning, firecrackers from a party, even tyres from a truck. Supposedly, when a tyre came off the vehicle, the wheel was exposed directly to asphalt, and that caused a spark. Sparks could emerge from anything to cause fires that spread uncontrollably. We passed ten lost tyres, one hundred wind turbines, and a thousand puzzle pieces of cracked land. Finally we reached our destination: the Robert Foundation. It was four in the afternoon, seven hours after our departure.

The first thing to catch my eye when I got out of the car was the clear sky; it was as if the yellow filter had been removed. The acrid smell had gone away a while ago, but now the visual landscape, too, returned to its state before the fires. The air felt buoyant and fresh, as if it had been transported from the morning I'd left for Incheon Airport. Seeing such a blue sky after all the sluggishness that had been in the air since my arrival, it felt like I'd entered a completely different world.

The Robert Foundation sign looked fairly old. Regardless of whether it was faded by the sun or hit by soot from the infernos, it looked pretty dismal. A tremendous silence accompanied the heat. At 4.00 pm, the zenith of the day had passed, but rays of sunlight still poured down, and the surroundings were silent, as if sound couldn't travel in this temperature. Like in water. I rang the doorbell once. A thin chime continued for several seconds, but I didn't hear a reply. I pressed a little harder, but there was still no reply. When Jun got out of his car and rang the doorbell, it was the same.

'What do you do as a delivery person in situations like this?' Jun asked. 'When no one answers the door.'

'I double-check my options,' I said. 'There are several. Ring the doorbell again and leave the package by the door, don't ring the doorbell and leave it by the door, don't ring the doorbell and send a text after leaving the package by the door, ring the doorbell and send a photo of the package by the door, send a photo without ringing the doorbell, call the recipient … there are so many options.'

'Which one is your favourite? Leaving the package at the door?'

'Leaving the package and ringing the doorbell. I feel uncomfortable leaving the package otherwise; I get nervous not knowing if the recipient got their delivery. Sending a photo is okay, too. I take the pictures right away.'

'Then that's what we'll do,' Jun said. 'The item is in front of the door now — we just need a picture!' Jun handed me his phone.

He refused to take the money I was trying to give him, but he did accept the coupon I'd made, scribbled on the pizza restaurant napkin. It read: 'Coupon — Help whenever you need it. — Fan #6, Yiji An'. The coupon was valid for four months, the length of my stay in the US.

The door still hadn't opened. The Robert Foundation hadn't selected any options for my delivery. I briefly envisioned a scene in which a crude voice came streaming out of the speakers to say, 'We didn't order anything!' Jun pretended to tap on the door with the end of his umbrella.

All I could see over the thick iron gate was a straight path. I didn't see any of the Joshua trees that were so common around here, nor any signs of life. I felt like a blundering tourist who'd shown up at a movie set after filming was over, right before it was about to be disassembled. If not for the nameplate on the gate, I wouldn't have known this was the Robert Foundation. Unless they were all asleep, how could they not have heard three separate doorbell rings? The delivery was complete, and we were ready to leave, but we couldn't start the engine.

I rang the doorbell once more, and finally the gate opened. Jun got back into the car, and I did too. We drove for a while. After we passed through another iron gate (thankfully, this one opened automatically), I began to detect signs of life. To our left was a large swimming pool. The walls of the pool were a bright sky blue, full of water, flamingo floaties bobbing, sunbeds all around, towels rolled up beside them like kimbap. The scene relieved me. Five hundred metres past the swimming pool, a building emerged like an enormous roll of toilet paper. The Robert Museum of Art! I'd seen it on the Foundation's website.

Jun pulled over in an area that said 'Guest Parking'. He completed the delivery safely, leaving with excessive faith in the power of the coupon I'd given him. Now separated from him, I walked alone towards the museum through a long covered walkway. The late afternoon light hit the ground at an angle, so half of the walkway was illuminated and the other half was cold and dark grey. As I followed it, I saw an array of attractions to my left. I passed a fountain gushing with water, a sculpture of a rabbit with two erect ears, and even a pond with stepping stones. I think I walked for ten minutes and still hadn't reached the end of it. It wasn't leading to the building I'd seen in the guidebook, but I didn't know if it would make sense to leave it, because there were Robert Foundation notices posted along the path.

It was surprising that I hadn't run into anyone yet. They had to know I was here, considering that the gate had opened for us, so why had no one come to greet me? The nerves and exhaustion that had been buried for a while slowly awakened, threatening to devour the sense of calm I'd finally reached. And then, at the end of the corridor, something disturbed the light. I heard a low whistle, then a sound like horse hooves fast approaching. As I turned my head towards the sound, I saw a black shadow running towards me at full speed. It came at me like a bullet. I had no time to assess the situation. I froze.

An umbrella opened in front of me like a shield. If it hadn't unfolded in front of me, the dog would have hit me, and I would have fallen. Luckily, the umbrella protected me. An umbrella big enough to cover two people. The familiar smell of sweat hit me.

4.

The day I arrived, the heat had been merciless, extorting energy from every pedestrian, car, small tree — everything under the sun. The Robert Foundation was in the middle of it all. A vacant figure, yawning slowly.

Maybe no one had heard me ring the doorbell because it was the hottest day of the year? With that level of heat and fires, there was no way I could stay sane. In fact, if I weren't a little bit crazy, I wouldn't have made it to where I was. So even if the Robert Foundation's staff were slow, defying norms and common sense, I felt like I'd made an implicit commitment to understanding their actions as human nature. Despite holding myself to this, only a few hours after arrival, I found myself questioning whether it was the right choice.

The black umbrella had only been unfurled once that first day, to protect me, but it kept opening in my dreams at night. In the hazy world of dreams, Jun appeared from behind me, shielding me with the umbrella. The dog bounced off it.

'Oh, you're a guard dog, not a genius dog,' Jun said.

In my dream, I stood at the beginning of the corridor and the dog rushed towards me as the umbrella opened, then I turned the corner and stood at the beginning of another straight path, and the dog ran towards me as the umbrella opened, then I turned another corner … then an unfamiliar image came into view. High ceiling, crown moulding, walls with vertical mint-coloured stripes, and a black umbrella resting modestly beneath me.

It was now morning.

Thanks to that umbrella, now rolled up and leaning against the wall, I had survived the previous day's attack. A few minutes before the incident, Jun and I had said our goodbyes and headed in opposite directions. After parting, Jun had realised that my umbrella was still in his hand, so he ran after me and discovered the dog. If Jun hadn't run up and unfurled the umbrella, the dog would have kept ferociously charging at me. The speed at which the umbrella unfolded was also the speed of my dream last night. The smell of Jun's sweat, the sound of my heart pounding … clearest was the image of the dog changing direction just as the umbrella opened. The dog suddenly stopped and disappeared in the opposite direction.

Two employees were chasing after the dog, but had no control over him. After he ran off, one of them went to look for him and the other asked if I was okay, but she didn't look okay herself. Her face was so white, it looked like her soul had left her body. Her name was Sam — the Sam I'd spoken with on the phone.

Sam was cold, acting as though I was an uninvited guest, an intruder. But I'd told her that I would be arriving today, so they should have been expecting me. Regardless, Sam seemed to be at a loss, as if I were some unforeseen variable she had come up against. Who on earth was to blame? I was just one person, but everyone at the Foundation seemed to be at a loss as to how to deal with me.

Sam told me she'd been worried because the Foundation couldn't get through to me all day, but she said it in a cool tone of voice that didn't hide the embarrassment layered underneath. She apologised an hour later, but she couldn't erase what had already been said. She treated me as though I had dug a trap to ensnare her, asking why I hadn't waited for their driver to pick me up, if I wanted to get her in trouble. My fear of the dog gave way to disappointment and fatigue, but then Sam began to cry. She wept like a child overwhelmed by confusion. It was much better than a formal apology. I realised that Sam was very unstable and had a thin skin, which made it easier to deal with her. Feeling some compassion for her helped reduce my frustration a little bit.

It was Sam who walked me to my room on the first night. After a good cry, she regained her senses and told me that the person responsible for collecting me had not arrived yet. She told me that this person had gone to Los Angeles to pick me up. We'd missed each other, in the end. However, she'd got through to them and said that we'd be able to meet tomorrow.

A short distance from the museum sat a long, low building about the length of six subway cars. Inside, down a hallway and past a small living room and study, was my room. The walls of the hallway were completely covered with photos. They were all of Robert the dog alongside different people. There was also a bunch of alphabet blocks, arranged to form the words: I AM INDEX. Running alongside the wall, over a metre off the ground, was a fifty-centimetre-wide ledge. It was clearly for Robert. It had no railing and was covered with an antique patterned carpet, and curved down to the ground wherever it met a doorway. Papillons are small dogs, so Robert's eyes were inevitably below my knees, but using this walkway, his gaze was level with, or even above, mine.

I thought that my room would be ready by now, but it wasn't. I was puzzled to see several staff members come in and make the bed. I asked Sam if artists always stayed in this room, mainly to confirm that I was, in fact, one of the residency's artists and not an unwanted guest. 'You have to use this room,' Sam replied. She thought I was asking to stay elsewhere.

The room was quite spacious. There were windows on two sides, and a print of *Canyon Proposal* on the wall. I'd never seen it so big. The size was overwhelming. The moonlight, the Grand Canyon's heavy silhouette, the lovers on the cliff. If you were familiar with the wide version of the photo, *Robert in the Canyon*, you couldn't help but think about the photographer just outside the frame. Reflected in the side mirror of the car — hidden in this version — was Robert's gaze. It almost felt like someone was outside staring at me, watching me as I entered the room. Next to *Canyon Proposal* was a black acrylic panel, the same size as the print, and if you looked closely, you could see that the name 'Robert' was embossed on the plastic in a subtly different colour, like a constellation of stars. I could have slid the panel to the left to cover *Canyon Proposal*, but I kept it as it was. I was lucky to lie in bed and look up at two lovers under the moonlight.

The room had everything I needed. There were two windows, four adjustable lights, four different types of chairs, and four pillows on a king-sized bed. The closet contained additional pillows of varied firmness and filling type, labelled 1 to 5. A note said that I could request more pillows if I wanted. There was nothing ordinary about the room: the fancy closet, a real chest of drawers, even the notepad and pen laid out on the desk. Everything felt deliberately placed. It felt like I had to stay in place, too.

When I set my cross-body bag on the table, Sam picked it up and said, 'I'll put that on the bag hanger.' I looked around, wondering where I was supposed to put my other things.

Pointing to a hook on the wall, I asked, 'Is this where I put my hat?'

Sam replied, 'Yes, that's why it's there. The hook is there for you to hang your hat.' Her answer made me feel a little embarrassed.

'We clean your bedroom every day,' Sam explained. 'We do your laundry every day, too. If you don't want us to do that, put a check here. These are the pyjamas we provide for guests at the Robert Foundation. You have three sets, so don't worry about getting them dirty.'

The pyjama set consisted of a button-down shirt and pants with a drawstring. The thick cotton fabric looked sturdy. The collar appeared to have been ironed flat, but later I realised it was sewn to the body of the shirt. Even the collar and seams of my pyjamas were required to stay in order.

Everything had its place, but I wasn't clear about my own. I felt as if the room was trying to spit me out. There were trivial (but really not so trivial) signs of indifference everywhere. Like the desk calendar. Months had passed since November 4 — the last date circled. I flipped forward several pages until this month was showing. If you invited someone to your residency program and set up a desk calendar like this, weren't you supposed to make sure that the right date was showing? Compared to the level of detail they'd invested in my pillow options, this was so apathetic, it almost seemed rude.

I was told that my luggage had to be checked by security outside the building. The process took more than three hours. How was I supposed to believe that security here took longer than in the Los Angeles airport when the only bag they were looking through was mine? Sam explained that there had been a recent bombing in this area, but I was doubtful. It was only after I had a dinner of Mexican food, showered, and changed into the pyjamas provided for me that the bag returned, looking like a fallen soldier. It wasn't just the bag — my reflection in the room's beautiful mirror looked worn-out, too. Compared to when I had left the airport a few days earlier, I'd aged.

By the next morning, things were running more smoothly, which made me think that I'd just had a brief nightmare, that whatever was haunting me the previous night had passed by. The biggest difference was in Sam. When she rang the doorbell to my room and I opened it, she greeted me with 'Good morning!' in a voice a whole octave higher than the day before. Her facial expression was similarly cheery.

'Breakfast is until ten o'clock,' Sam said. 'Come down to the cafeteria whenever you want.'

She then placed a shiny silver tray on the table. Of course, she didn't forget to add, 'This is where the silver tray goes!' but because her voice was so much brighter than the previous day, it sounded like she was announcing the rules of a fun game. On the tray was an envelope with a red seal and a placard that read

'Today's Weather', folded up like a little tent.

'Is your friend from yesterday okay?' Sam asked.

She even felt relaxed enough to ask how Jun was doing. There was something reassuring about her confidence today. The person responsible for me was finally back, she said. I asked for the wi-fi password. Sam flipped to the last page of the guest manual on the desk and showed me the longest password I'd ever seen in my life. The meaningless combination of letters and numbers was so long that I wanted to give up typing. I had to make sure each letter and number was in the right place. After failing twice, I finally managed to connect to the wi-fi. As soon as I did, a message Jun had sent me the night before flew in as if it had been waiting.

'It's too long to use as earphones.'

A photo followed, depicting a long, thin piece of dental floss coming out of a round white case. At first, I wasn't sure what he meant, but later understood when I found an identical-looking earphone case inside my toiletry bag where I was supposed to have floss. I'd accidentally given Jun my floss rather than my earphone case. It was just like the mix-up between An Young and An Yiji. I'd never considered it before, but wireless earphone cases and plastic floss dispensers bore a surprising resemblance to one another in colour, shape, and even texture. An umbrella was not the only thing Jun and I had exchanged as we parted ways. Jun video-called me. He jokingly placed the ends of a stretched-out piece of floss in each ear as he hummed a line from 'A Day in the Life'. It seemed that the real reason for his call was to check that I was okay.

'You're still alive?' he asked.

'For now!'

Jun said that he hadn't made it to Las Vegas yet, that his fatigue and all the dry lightning strikes had forced him to stop at a small hotel adjacent to the freeway. I was impressed by the antique decorations visible behind him.

The envelope on the silver tray was sealed with red wax that made a crackling sound when I opened it. There was a thick sheet of paper decorated with gold leaf inside, and on it an extensive letter was typed in tiny letters. Font size seven? Six? That's how small the letters were.

> Dear Ms An Yiji,
> I would like to express my deep gratitude to you
> for coming all the way here, through the fierce and
> beautiful heatwave and spectacular wildfires. It was
> only a few years ago that the largest lake in this area
> dried up and exposed its rough floor.
>   Recently, cracks have appeared in the dried
> surface, one of which contained a small hardened
> fish. The fish had multiple heads, so we took it from
> the lake and contacted an agency that could study it.
> They said they would retrieve the fish promptly, but
> they didn't, and the fish remains in my freezer.
>   Yes, it's because of the forest fires. The spread
> of the fires has left us almost completely isolated.
> Fortunately, they seem to be getting under control.
>   This is, of course, a relief. I have to say, though,
> when the wildfires were raging, I could smell in

the smoke the fragrance of roasting chestnuts.
The whirlwind of flames sometimes gave off the
concentrated sweetness of melting marshmallows.
Now that's all a dream I've woken up from.

It doesn't take long to get here from Los Angeles,
but crossing through fire is another thing entirely. I'm
astonished that you made it. In fact, you rendered the
efforts of our Robert Foundation workforce useless.
Our employees went to fetch you yesterday but were
confused to learn that you had already left your hotel.

Another residency participant was similarly
trapped due to a magnificent hurricane, but she
graciously waited for us, with an artist's optimism and
understanding of disaster.

We of course expected you to do the same, but
that was a mistake on our part. You are surprising.
I heard you've worked as a delivery person — is
that why you arrived with precision? Unanticipated
precision — faster even than the pizza we ordered
for dinner. And so, unintentionally, we caused you
trouble.

We miscalculated you, and your actions took us
aback. If only you had contacted the Foundation,
or been a little more patient. But the bed of the
largest lake in the area was even drier than usual on
the morning of your arrival, its cracks legible like
the lines in the palm of a hand, and in them I saw
infinite possibilities, new possibilities, due to your
unannounced arrival.

Even though you violated our rules against arriving with an outsider, I'm glad to know that you got here safely, and I welcome you.

We're in the midst of a heatwave. Things are not normal. There's a crazed sense of beauty in the air.

Oh, and there's a bit of a problem with your paperwork. We had to redo the documents two or three times because the ones we received from our Korean director weren't right, and there was never any follow-up, because no one would admit to wrongdoing. But this is now bygone meandering. I have no doubt that, having overcome this ordeal and finally made it to the Foundation, you will do great work here.

Early this morning, one of my roses dropped all its remaining petals. It was a light-yellow rose, named Rococo. Rococo's finale was beautiful. Its petals were like tears, or raindrops, announcing an unexpected new start. I sincerely welcome this start, Rococo! I've decided to give the name Rococo to yet another being, to the fish from the lake that's long convalesced in my freezer. The act of naming this fish means that it's now mine. You contributed to its name, too.

When I saw how far you've come despite this incredible situation, I thought about the research organisation I've been waiting on for weeks. They have no intention of coming; otherwise, why wouldn't they have made it here when you did?

I've now closed my mind to the possibility of
meeting them and instead have taken the fish out
of the freezer and named it Rococo. Today, the fish
became Rococo.

I'd like to discuss with you where to put the fish.
What's certain is that, while Rococo can no longer
swim, it has become an immortal being by nature of
possessing a name. Immortality: that's why we love
art.

I hope that Rococo will be an inspiration to you
over the next four months.

Well, then, I'll see you this evening — an evening
that will come to pass only once. An evening where
the orange flames of our lonely fireplace dance as they
burn.

Robert

The letter ended with Robert's pawprint, stamped in gold
ink. It was about twice the size of my fingerprint. After reading
the tiny, beautiful English text before me once, I went through
it again, carefully, using a translation app on my phone to check
the strangest sections. I was hoping I had misunderstood something. This was supposed to be a welcome letter? These sentences,
which seem to have been mistranslated on their way from dog to
human? Robert's letter rebuked me in the most arrogant, sarcastic
tone. The ultimate victim-blamer, that's what he was.

It seemed as if Robert had forgotten mid-letter that he was
addressing me — like a dog sniffing everything while on a walk.

The letter had started with an elegant salutation, but then, sloppy as a 'No Parking' or 'No Dumping' sign marred with spelling errors, it unveiled the disorganised emotional upheaval hiding beneath the surface. I hadn't noticed it at first, but as I reread Robert's words, I saw a tonal shift towards indignance throughout the letter. Robert seemed to swell with irritation, to hurl himself off a cliff of anger. I was confused by the 'beauty' he intermittently referenced. Had he understood what he was writing? The letter was close to nonsense. Why had he mentioned a fireplace at a time when a heatwave and forest fires were causing such a mess? As I contemplated whether the letter I'd received was an invitation, a warning, or a drunken screed, I looked closer at the 'Today's Weather' card. The smiling sun illustration looked like it was mocking me.

'You need a special kind of literacy to read Robert's letter,' said Danny, the person who was responsible for my wellbeing. He'd finally shown up. 'Robert literacy.'

'Robert literacy?'

'He writes these long, classic sentences because he values formal beauty. You don't have to assign meaning to every word. They're just decorative elements.'

But presumably Robert hadn't written this very human letter word by word, right? Wasn't it a group effort? By experts who had long observed the dog's eyes, nose, ears, tail, vocalisations, posture, expressions, and response speed, and added human subtitles to his canine communication? That was, until now, how I'd assumed Robert could communicate. But Danny said the translation wasn't interpretation. Robert chose each word himself, down to the punctuation marks.

'We do say there's something magical about Robert's use of language, but that magic is born from discipline and unbelievable effort. Robert spent four hours in the middle of the night working on this letter.'

'I heard there's a translator,' I said. 'A huge one, the size of a dresser.'

'The black box,' Danny replied. 'It's often said that Robert's words go into the black box and come out as human language. But it's not that simple. Certainly, in the case of letters, he revises his work in a very formalised manner. A human reads several versions of the letter out loud while Robert listens carefully and chooses his favourite. The dog has an amazing ability to distinguish between intonations. He unwittingly senses the delicate nuances of the mind. He's not a typical dog, of course.'

'So he does this over and over again? Sentence by sentence? They were all chosen by Robert? Then how am I supposed to respond when he says things like this?'

I tried to list some of the letter's more offensive lines, but Danny raised his hand to stop me.

'He has a sharp tongue. Just focus on the gist of the message. Normally he wouldn't have written it in the middle of the night, but since you arrived without forewarning, he was strapped for time. Robert's fatigue might have been reflected in his words.'

'I have a sharp tongue, too,' I said.

'You don't have to reply. He won't read it anyway.'

The best thing about the Robert Foundation employees I'd met so far was that they were all humbler than Robert. Was Director

Choi different? He'd seemed a bit slow. He was still sending me
messages asking if I had made it to the Foundation. Danny, who'd
shown up late without so much as a formal apology for his mistakes or the confusion he'd sown, was Robert's closest aide — the
one who appeared in Mr Waldmann's will. He was an intimidating
man, with his deep voice and sharp eyes. He was tall and didn't
not smile, but there was something expressionless about his face.

I was a bit surprised when, accompanying me to my studio,
he gave me the choice to walk down a 'beautiful' path that ran
alongside a pond, or use the covered walkway, which would get us
there faster. It was only later that I learned Foundation employees
habitually used the word 'beautiful'. I chose the faster path. Not
because of the speed — because of the walkway. I needed to go
back to the place the dog had charged at me.

'Is Robert alright?' I asked. 'Considering what happened
yesterday.'

'What do you mean?'

'Honestly, I think Robert owes me an apology. As soon as I
arrived, he jumped at me.'

Danny listened and then called someone on the phone before
apologising to me, but the whole gesture seemed like an evasion
of responsibility. Was he not going to report the incident?

'That was Marty,' Danny said, 'not Robert. Marty's such a rascal, Robert can barely handle him, either. He's just too aggressive.
Marty is particularly sensitive about things, and he tends to get
hostile. Had you eaten pizza last night, by any chance? Marty can
smell pizza on you even if you digested it days earlier. Apparently,
he was hit by a pizza deliveryman as a puppy, and ever since then
he's hated pizza.'

When I said that I felt unsettled, Danny stressed that I wouldn't see Marty again, that the most important thing wasn't Marty, but rather my relationship with Robert — the dog who'd invited me here.

'So is Robert aware of yesterday's situation?' I asked.

If he were, the letter should have at least mentioned it. As my host, it was his job to apologise. But Danny's response suggested that he did not deem it necessary to report such trivial matters to Robert. He changed the subject.

'It's not easy for dogs to overcome their sensitivity to smells,' Danny said, 'but Robert is experienced. He understands that you have to play it cool. But even with him, you must avoid certain types of perfume. When we searched your luggage, we found a perfume whose base scents are on the list of items banned by the Foundation. We took it from your bag.'

'I didn't realise perfume wasn't allowed.'

'If you completed the safety training properly, you'd know. Perfume is one of the prohibited items. It could endanger Robert's life.'

My perfume was being stored in a ziplock bag. It would be returned to me when I left.

As we spoke, we reached the site of the prior day's incident, where an A-frame sign read, 'Maintenance Request: Floor Damage.' The sign hadn't been there yesterday, and there was no way I'd damaged the floor.

'Lots of places around here need repairs,' Danny said, diluting the incident into nothingness. 'We do our best.'

As we turned the corner, an artist's studio appeared. Somewhat obscured by the tall grasses surrounding it, the small circular

building resembled the art museum. When I tapped my card key
against the door of my new creative hideout, it opened slowly. A
pillar of light extended from a rounded skylight down to the floor.
The ceiling was so high that I felt as if I'd entered the ruins of an
ancient temple, of which nothing but the foundational columns
— these beams of light — remained.

'It's so beautiful!' I exclaimed. Danny smiled.

The studio had several smaller skylights that I could open
and shut as I desired. There was a huge workbench, too. On it,
a variety of tools were neatly arranged alongside a sealed gift box
stamped with Robert's pawprint. When I opened the box, the gift
inside made me scream and look away. It was Rococo, the fish
with two heads. Why was it here? Had Danny known about this?
He quickly closed the box.

'Do I need Robert literacy to understand this, too?' I asked.

'Please understand Robert's sincerity,' he said. I mustn't forget
that Robert was a dog. Wondering if this was supposed to be a
welcome gift, I thought once again about the letter in my room.

'The welcome gift is always changing. For a while it was
flowers — light-yellow roses. This time, it's a fish.'

'A dead fish,' I said. 'It's not exactly a standard gift, is it?'

'Robert doesn't see much difference between roses and this
dead fish, especially considering that they have the same name.'

'What should I do with it?' I asked. 'Am I supposed to keep
it?'

'Well, when you give someone flowers, you can't control what
the recipient does with them. The recipient might dry the flowers,
put them in a vase, take a photo and then discard them. It's no
different with a fish.'

'If I'd got flowers, I would know what to do with them. Robert mentioned Rococo in his letter, but I didn't expect to come face-to-face with it.'

'Once he gifted someone a mothball named Rococo,' Danny said. 'The artist who received it used the evaporating naphthalene from the mothball in his work. The rose named Rococo became a piece of art, too. The piece was made up of Rococo's petals.'

Was I supposed to dip Rococo the fish into formaldehyde or something? I didn't feel like doing that. After taking a picture of my Rococo, I decided that it should be put it back in a freezer. I couldn't think of anywhere else to put it for now.

Danny ordered one to be sent from the cafeteria to the studio. I hadn't expected my first activity upon arriving at my new work-space to be waiting on a freezer delivery, but so be it.

Finally, the freezer came and Robert's gift was put in it, and the excitement I'd initially felt upon entering the studio was quickly forgotten. I wanted to go back to bed and lie down.

When Danny and I left the studio, though, there were people waiting for us. Danny introduced me to them. They were all citizen representatives of Q City.

I received a lot of business cards from people as soon as I met them, but I couldn't tell my new acquaintances apart. They were nothing more than their various titles within the local govern-ment hierarchy.

One exclaimed, '*Hangover Relief*! You're the artist. That paint-ing was the best!' and asked to shake my hand. I was surprised that they knew my latest work and, in a moment of defencelessness, promised them an artist talk. I felt a bit coerced into offering it, but Danny said to expect many more of these requests in the future.

'Q City is very interested in our residency program. This is the first time that the Robert Foundation is working with a local government, so it's a challenge for us as well. It may become tiresome for you. If their requests start to disturb your work, you can turn them down.'

Danny looked at the clock and said that it was time to go to the banquet hall. We needed to rehearse for my dinner with Robert. The banquet hall was its own building, and from the outside I had no idea what the interior would look like. When I opened the door and peeked inside, my first impression of the room's design was: anything goes, as long as it's dramatic. The door was interesting, too — very small. Maybe a metre high? Robert could pass through it gracefully, but his guests could not. Danny managed to squeeze his large body through, and I had to crouch as well. Inside the banquet hall was a rectangular table about five metres in length. Danny pulled out a chair at one end and said, 'This is your seat.' He walked to the other side of the table, pulled out another chair, and sat down.

'This is Robert's seat,' he said.

The tabletop was completely coated with white and blue candle wax. It looked like a sugar glaze or fat drippings from meat had been applied to the surface. Originally, the tabletop been black marble, Danny said, but after Robert saw an exhibition organised by the artists Colin Nightingale and Stephen Dobbie, he'd transformed the table into its current state. Mr Waldmann and Robert had enjoyed taking inspiration from art exhibits as they designed the banquet hall's interior. After seeing one exhibit featuring phosphorescent pigments, they'd had the walls of the banquet hall painted to glow in the dark. The walls were supposed to lose some of their phosphorescence and grow dimmer over time. At the end of one 'season' of illumination, as Danny called it, you could restore their brilliance by shining a light on the paint. At the moment, visibility in the room depended on how recently the walls' brightness had been touched up, but the Foundation was planning to add lights to the room, so Danny assured me that I didn't need to worry. From my seat, Robert's chair looked like the vanishing point on a horizon line. Danny sat there for a moment, looking at me, before coming over to raise the height of my chair.

'You're too nervous,' he said. 'Let's adjust this so that you and Robert can meet each other's gaze at a comfortable angle. Oh, that's much better. Robert can smell fear. He reads body language. Sit confidently, with your shoulders back, and look straight ahead — but don't stare at him.'

Look straight ahead but don't stare? That was a confusing statement.

'Robert has a lot of experience with these kinds of meals, but you don't need to make trouble on purpose. There are things on the table you can look at. These beautiful objects — look at them.'

First the vase, then the silver candlesticks, then the right side of Robert's chair, then the *left* side of Robert's chair. Finally, I should defocus my gaze, and when necessary, I was to move my gaze from the vase to the left side of the chair. Vase, candles, right, left — was that four-four time? It was like some sort of vision exercise. I'd never prepared for a meal in this way before.

'Robert will look at whatever you look at,' Danny said. 'It's not good to look like you're trying to avoid him, but it's also rude to make overly intense eye contact, so you want to continually shift your gaze.'

Eye contact was rude? Did they even know what rude meant?

'What happens if I keep looking at him?' I asked.

'It'll be uncomfortable.'

'For Robert?'

'For you, too.'

Apparently, Robert had refused to meet a guest who showed up to a banquet dinner in jeans. I was wearing an orange dress and teal sandals. I had read somewhere that Robert liked complementary colours, which was why I'd brought this outfit, but now that I was in the US, one day out from the welcome dinner, I wasn't sure I still wanted to impress Robert. When the rehearsal was over, I wondered if Robert would even be able to tell the difference between the teal and orange. I'd always heard that dogs weren't as sensitive to colour as humans. Of course, the Robert Foundation's response to that would be that Robert was different from the average dog.

Since meeting Robert, Mr Waldmann had come to favour olive-coloured clothing, because whenever he wore that colour, Robert would jump into his arms. He had wondered if the colour reminded Robert of the Grand Canyon. Not everyone agreed with him. What was the colour olive supposed to mean to dogs when they saw the greenery of a garden as yellow? Grass, snow, marble — they all looked the same to dogs. Dogs could only distinguish between two or three colours, people said. Yet supposedly Robert could pick out the colour olive. When someone pointed this out during an interview, Mr Waldmann stopped talking — only momentarily, but it long enough for the interviewer to feel a gulf widening between them. As time went on, the people around Mr Waldmann took it for granted that Robert was different. They had a certain level of faith. 'Dogs are colourblind,' they said to themselves, 'but Robert isn't a normal dog. We don't know exactly what Robert sees. We can only guess.'

According to those who'd met him, Robert was aristocratic, elegant, and graceful. I hadn't heard anyone say he was considerate or kind. If I changed my perspective a little, maybe I'd see him as charming. I didn't expect him to have a good personality — he was a dog, anyway. Why was I expecting something from him that was rare to encounter even in humans? I repeated this sentiment, trying to convince myself that it was true.

Danny had parked his car in front of the banquet hall. It wasn't even a twenty-minute walk from my accommodations, but we drove. He seemed to be trying to figure out whether there was anything dangerous about me, but there was nothing to find. The problem was with them, not me. Danny said I might encounter some issues at the dinner. There was an issue with the interpreter. They'd put in great efforts to find a Korean interpreter for me, Danny said, but since I had arrived so suddenly, the Foundation hadn't been able to book the interpreter they'd intended to hire.

'But I didn't arrive suddenly,' I said. 'I got here late.'

'Not everyone can pass through a forest fire like you did. The interpreter we chose was supposed to come from Los Angeles, too, but he wasn't able to make it because of the fires. We wanted to invite you here after we'd set everything up. Once everything was perfect — Robert-style. That's why I asked you to wait at your hotel longer, but then you arrived yesterday. I hired another Korean interpreter, but he's not a professional in the field of art. I hope you'll be understanding, even if the interpretation is a bit rough.'

'I'm talking to you in English, though,' I said.

Until then, I had been wondering how I'd be able to talk with Robert. Presumably there was a limit to human–dog communication. But we would have a Korean interpreter, right?

The dining room seemed to be ablaze. It wasn't that bright inside, but somehow it still felt that way. The candlesticks on the table-top were designed to look as though they were melting just like the candles they held, and scarlet lights dangled from the ends of the table. With the lights swaying, a dimness in the air, and an utter lack of sound — much less music — I felt like I would get drunk just sitting in my seat drinking water. Robert and I faced one another at opposite ends of a table that could fit ten. I already knew that he was a dog, and I'd spent the past few days dwelling on the fact that I'd come here as his guest. Even though nothing about this situation was a surprise, sitting here with Robert felt stranger than I had imagined.

Robert sat as motionless as a doll, dressed as if he were human; only the sound of his breathing signalled that he was alive. Because the room was so silent, I could hear the tension in his nostrils. He was busy figuring me out. It was a tenacious endeavour that made me feel as if he were chasing me. I was trying to look straight ahead, but not directly at Robert. He must have understood this.

It looked as if he were resisting the urge to come down from his chair and sniff me.

Maybe he wasn't. I wondered what Robert was thinking. He hadn't said anything since we first greeted one another. Everything was so calm that I could hear the candle wicks burning, and the low hum of the light bulbs. I wondered if things looked the same from Robert's end. Dogs could see much better in the dark than humans, after all, so perhaps Robert could see more in the intricate layers of twilight surrounding us. Was I being arrogant, calling the silence of the room silence?

I was fortunate to have many points to stare at — metaphorical trees bordering the path of my anxious gaze. Vases, silver candlesticks, the right and left side of the chair opposite me. They were my natural refuges. They weren't just props, but beautiful pieces of art in and of themselves. Still, I couldn't help but look at Robert. The lights on the table were arranged such that it was impossible to avoid the figure opposite me. A mix of brown and black fur, a white torso. I was particularly fascinated by the way Robert's dark-brown ears moved. I had heard that papillons had ears that fluttered like the wings of a butterfly, but Robert's ears weren't butterfly-like. They were more like … a phoenix? Like a phoenix's wings.

I remembered reading that the first step of Robert's communication with humans involved a device attached to his body that displayed his thoughts externally. Some people said the device looked like a headband, others said it was in the shape of a necklace, and still others said it was like a crown. Was that it? I could see that there was an odd hornlike object hanging from Robert's ears. As I couldn't see it directly, I tried to use its shadow to guess its shape.

As the light in the banquet hall grew dimmer and dimmer, everything about Robert unexpectedly increased in size, even his shadow. Robert was sitting motionless. I realised that what I had thought was his leg was actually the frame of his chair, and what I'd thought to be the frame of the chair was the unfamiliar object connected to his ear. It was impossible to tell whether it was decorative or had a use. On second thought, the black cube in front of Robert looked suspicious, too. Was that the black box? Could this cube read Robert's consciousness? The person sitting closest to the box was Danny.

Our conversation was made possible by four separate stages of translation: Robert → black box → Danny → English–English interpreter → English–Korean interpreter → me. Even if I spoke English completely fluently, Sam later told me, they would have hired an interpreter. Interpreters considered more than just the flow of language; they provided a certain security. For safety reasons, Robert's words passed through several checkpoints before reaching me. If I were a native English speaker, that would have removed only one of the checkpoints. Multiple stops existed between artist and patron.

'What was your first impression of me?' Robert began. At least, that's what I was told he said. He didn't utter the words in an audible language, but they reached me in a comprehensible form after passing through the many interpreters.

'You reminded me of a phoenix,' I said in Korean.

The Korean interpreter uttered the Korean word for phoenix — *bonghwang* — to the English interpreter, who asked, quietly,

'What does that mean?'

The Korean interpreter said, 'It's a type of bird. It symbolises many things,' to which the English interpreter replied, 'A pigeon?'

The Korean interpreter stressed the symbolic nature of phoenixes so heavily that he forgot other pertinent details, and as a result, Robert was told that he reminded me of 'a mythical Korean pigeon'. That was it.

A Korean pigeon? Considering that I could understand English, how could I not intervene? I said in Korean that a phoenix was not a pigeon, then I repeated the sentiment in English. I added — again in both Korean and English — that phoenixes symbolise royalty. When I heard my words transformed into 'It's the king of Korean pigeons', I wanted to explode, but there was a rule against mobile phone use during dinners with Robert, so I couldn't look up the right word in English. I asked the Korean interpreter what the English word for *bonghwang* was, but he couldn't think of it. Then we heard a voice in the darkness say 'phoenix'. I assumed it was Danny, but I couldn't be sure.

Other than the surface of the dining table, everything was so dark; it was hard to see. The tabletop was a stage. Did that mean our foods were actors? No, it was our conversation leading the performance. Our words. I had to check to make sure everything that departed from my mouth was transported correctly.

After all my words had made it to Robert, he responded with the following: 'The symbol of Arizona is the phoenix. Since you're finally here, you should take advantage of the opportunity to visit nearby states as well.'

I found the word 'finally' jarring. I wasn't sure if this was another floral addition to Robert's speech, or an awkward translation. It was definitely preferable for me to believe that his phrasing had just got tangled up during the multi-stage translation process.

The dinner lasted for two hours. It unfolded like scenes from a dream, starting with gazpacho and ending with grapefruit pudding. Before each course, we were told about the ingredients that had gone into our food. The 'golden grapefruit pudding' was topped with a sprinkling of Arizona cactus powder — a specialty from Q City, the place that was supposed to be inspiring my art. I remembered receiving a business card. The pudding was surprisingly hard to eat; it was firm, as if alive, and my spoon had no points with which to poke at it. The pudding kept running away, so even once I'd got it onto the spoon, I had to be careful not to spill it on the way to my mouth. It felt like completing a stunt. When I looked up, I found that Robert had already polished off his dessert. Apparently, he had the same dessert as me, just in a different shape. This meant that, unlike me, he could gracefully swallow the small, round bites with just a flick of his tongue. Robert stared at me as I watched his long, prosciutto-like tongue emerge from his mouth before going back in. I quickly moved my gaze to the upper-left corner of his chair, before looking straight ahead again.

'That colour suits you. I like orange very much,' Robert said. Or, his interpreters did. I said that his clothes looked good on him as well.

'It goes well with your teal shoes,' Robert added. When had he seen my shoes? I'd been sitting when he arrived.

'The colour combination also looks good against your irises,' he said. 'They're golden, like an ale beer.'

I knew that dogs could see better than humans at night, but when he described the colour of my irises accurately, despite the distance and the dark, I became extremely nervous. Come to think of it, Robert's eyes were located more to the sides of his head than was typical for dogs. Perhaps this gave him a wider range of vision. Or maybe it was the additional pairs of eyes around him. Robert's crew of interpreters, there to reduce his misunderstandings and blind spots, might have heightened his already above-average vision. Robert's language existed in the number of times he scratched at his fur, the angle at which he did so, and of course in his sneezes, hiccups, coughs, and the movements of his paws. After looking at Robert's actions from all angles, Danny used the black box and two interpreters to convey his thoughts to me. They expressed Robert's feelings so carefully that if they weren't perfect translators, they were perfect actors, or perfect lunatics. Even though it seemed as though Robert and I were sitting alone at this dark, grand dining table, that wasn't the case.

Compared to the Robert Foundation employees, I *was* alone. When I arrived at the Foundation, I'd planned to tell them jokingly about my weird hahahaha dream, but I didn't feel like doing that anymore. They seemed to think, no matter what I said, that I was blaming them. They were defensive. When I told Robert that the food I'd eaten the night before — on my brief sojourn to Mexico — was delicious, the Korean–English interpreter didn't seem to convey the sentiment properly, so I asked him to interpret the sentence again. The mood soured after that.

'You mean when we mistook someone else for you,' Robert said in response. 'I think I've already explained myself enough.'

When Robert's words finally reached me, moving from dog to box to human to human to human to human, they were not what I had expected. He seemed to have already forgotten about my supposed doppelganger. He wasn't being sarcastic about their incompetent pick-up service. I added that it was just a dumb joke and said a few more things to change the energy in the room, but no one laughed. Perhaps the problem was that Robert and I were using interpreters rather than communicating directly. Speed was important when telling a joke, so by the time mine got to Robert, it had lost its punch.

If communication between Korean and English was like traversing the Pacific Ocean, then I would have assumed communication between a human and a dog was like leaving the Earth's atmosphere.

There was a border collie named Rico that supposedly knew over two hundred words, and another dog, Chaser, that knew more than a thousand. Before meeting him, I thought that Robert might be around that level. Maybe this reflected my own hubris, since I knew a lot about the subject, but I didn't think you needed that large a vocabulary to discuss art. Now that I was sitting before Robert, though, he didn't seem to be communicating at the level of words or grammar. Robert was simply scanning me.

Over the course of dinner, I was growing smaller. Danny had talked about the importance of posture, but no matter how confidently or upright I tried to sit, my posture still began to flag. Robert and I needed to have a deeper conversation, yet I couldn't help but wonder if my impatience — showing up at the Foundation so hurriedly ('hurriedly' being a relative term), participating in this dinner without any real preparation — had ruined this opportunity.

More challenging than communication between dog and human was overcoming the barriers between our native languages. That is, if you could call English Robert's native language. I had expected the interpreters to narrow the distance. However, the Korean–English interpreter didn't seem to like me very much and kept filtering out my words. At least, that was what I had been able to pick up on. There might have been even more omissions than I'd realised. It was as if I had ordered jjajangmyeon, jjamppong, and sweet-and-sour pork, but the jjamppong wasn't delivered. Had the jjajangmyeon and pork arrived? There was no way to confirm. Eventually, I asked the interpreter to deliver my sentences as is, rather than cutting things out, and he replied, 'We need to edit them.'

He said this with a kind expression and gentle tone of voice I hadn't yet observed.

'That's how we've been able to keep the meal going,' he added. 'Otherwise things get awkward — like when you made the comment about Mexican food.'

My request wasn't completely in vain. The interpreter started to add helpful supplementary explanations after translating Robert's words. He noted that Robert used the word 'plantation' instead of 'farm' when referring, for example, to orange farms, date farms, and even wind farms. There were a few words that Robert really liked, one of them being 'plantation'. He referred to the wind farm I'd seen on my way here as a 'windmill plantation'.

This was part of the conversation that made it through the four tollgates separating me and Robert:

'What's the most memorable art exhibit you've seen recently?'

'I saw the Michael Craig-Martin exhibit before I came to America.'

'What struck you about it?'

'The whole space felt like a Costco. There were all these things you'd see in a supermarket: a pepper grinder, an electric toothbrush, a mobile phone. In the context of an art exhibit, these commonplace objects were like exotic creatures. It was like seeing a deep-sea creature in a museum. I was watching wine openers and tape measures move like living creatures, with tongues and tentacles and skeletons. That kind of hit me over the head.'

I'd felt the same way when I saw Robert. I was sitting right across from a creature I had no reason to encounter. Or, five metres across from him.

'Interesting,' Robert replied. 'I saw that exhibit, too. A few years ago, with Mr Waldmann. We especially liked the homage to Velázquez's *Las Meninas*. Remember that? Michael Craig-Martin replaced the human figures in *Las Meninas* with household items. Sunglasses for the princess, a fire extinguisher for the artist. There's also a dog in *Las Meninas*. Do you remember what Michael Craig-Martin put in the dog's place?'

'I don't.'

'A belt. He replaced the dog with a belt. I was so engrossed by it that I had a dream about a belt that night. It was a teal belt, slithering down a road. The belt looked like a snake, yes. I dream a lot. Recently, I saw a piece by Charwei Tsai. It was a video of a Buddhist mantra being written repeatedly in tiny letters on a piece of tofu until the tofu shrivelled up and caved in. The imagery repeated itself over and over again in my dream.'

'Did you become the tofu in your dream?'

'I was one of the letters in the mantra, about to be written on the piece of tofu. I desperately wanted to exist, but my dream ended before the artist could inscribe me. In short, it was a dream of indefinite waiting, of worrying that my turn would not come. Whenever I go to an exhibit, it takes a long time to leave. It feels like I've reached the end, but then there's more to see. Have you ever experienced this? I think that's what art is like. It's a spirit that, in reality, is a dead end, but it crosses over into our dreams and tells us to keep talking. That's the light that the artist instils in us. I will be living inside your work even after your exhibition ends, Ms An Yiji. I look forward to your cooperation.'

I briefly defied the warnings not to look directly at Robert and peeked at his expression. Robert was watching me. Maybe I was imagining things, but it seemed like he was smiling. I felt possessed. How was this happening? This substantial conversation. After several up and downs on this roller-coaster ride, I had finally reached a marvellous destination.

After dessert, Robert wished me a good night from his end of the table. 'I enjoyed our meal tonight,' he said, 'and hope to have many more.' We said goodbye at a distance of five metres. I remained seated at the long, desolate table and leaned back. The chandelier above me looked like a spider stretching its black legs.

When I lowered my head, the chair across from me was empty. I was still a little confused. I imagined the real Robert showing up all of a sudden — the real Robert, too shy or too busy to eat with me, or maybe too mischievous, watching a recording of this meal in some far-off place. I was as mystified as the detectives who'd first encountered Robert long ago. But the Robert they had met

was different to the Robert I had just had dinner with. At that
time, Robert had to prove his uniqueness to strangers, but no
longer. Now *I* had to prove myself.

'The editing seems to have been successful. That was such
a beautiful conversation,' my interpreter-slash-editor brazenly
whispered.

He told me he'd simply changed my words to those Robert
particularly liked. 'You don't have to thank me,' he added.

Then, to Danny, he said, 'I missed the word "phoenix" —
how did you know that one?'

Danny replied, 'Harry Potter.'

I had read about another artist getting an upset stomach after
their meal with Robert, so I was worried the same would happen
to me, but it didn't. Maybe I'd talked too much, though, because
two hours after the dinner, I started to feel hungry again. I ate a
bag of potato chips, but they weren't enough. I took some instant
rice I had stored in my purse in case of emergency and went to
the kitchen, where Sam showed me the microwave.

'Have any other artists eaten instant rice after a full-course
dinner with Robert?' I asked.

'Don't worry, Ms An,' Sam said in reply. 'Things like this
happen. It was your first meal with Robert — you worked hard!'

I looked around for two minutes as the instant rice rotated
inside the microwave. It was night, but the cafeteria was bright
as day. I noticed that, in the study, Robert and Mr Waldmann
had taken design inspiration from artworks they'd seen. Two
analogue clocks hung side by side. At first glance, they seemed

to indicate the same time, then you realised that one was at three o'clock and the other at nine-thirty. Their hands were at the same angle, though, because one of the clocks was turned upside-down. These were the clocks I'd read about. The clocks that had made Mr Waldmann cry. Sam told me something that hadn't been in the article: Mr Waldmann had actually removed the batteries from both clocks. Now they would point to the same time forever.

Two minutes passed, and my rice was warm.

Three days after our first meal, Robert suggested another. He could have skipped the formality, since by now we were acquainted, but that morning, he sent another handwritten invitation sealed with red wax. I don't particularly wish to recall the contents, but I did feel significantly less humiliated by the second letter than I had by the first. It was less that his expressions had softened and more that my expectations had lowered. He had written about how I, as an artist, determined whether or not I struggled to create new work, and if I couldn't deal with that pain, then why had I come all the way here? It felt crazy to use the phrase, but now that I had some level of 'Robert literacy', I understood that the arrogance and reproach in Robert's letters were simply a literary style. A style with a lot of unnecessary decoration.

I was curious about past Robert Foundation artists; according to Sam, most of them ate with Robert once or twice while they were here. They only received a letter at the beginning or end of their stay, but I received another strange, formulaic missive three days after the first. It might have been because Robert was on the

Foundation grounds more often than he used to be, due first to the pandemic and then to the wildfires.

Every morning, Sam placed 'Today's Weather' on a silver platter, which she set either on the table inside my room or a small table outside the door. She drew a mark next to one of five weather icons, like something from a child's diary. The five icons were sun, clouds with sun, clouds, rain, and snow, with boxes to indicate the high and low for the day, as well as sunrise and sunset. I began to collect these weather reports rather than throw them away. I knew that some hotels diligently informed their guests of the daily weather, but the Robert Foundation wasn't a hotel. I was the only visitor here — what kind of weather-specific activities would I be undertaking?

'It's important for you to know the weather,' Sam said. 'You're a painter!'

Sam informed me that I wouldn't have to worry about the dress code when dining with Robert this time. Robert had suggested lunch, and we would be eating under a canopy on the outdoor terrace, so I could dress comfortably.

'You'll be protected by a cool fan, so don't worry too much.'

It was a strange thing to say, but Sam seemed to think that I was a preternaturally fearful person. I kept replaying the image of the black umbrella unfurling to protect me, with Sam rushing over one moment too late.

We met at 1.00 pm at an outdoor table under an orange canopy. Robert was wearing more on his body than I was. When he saw me, the first thing he uttered was, 'You look good in olive.'

The second thing he said was, 'What's the most memorable art exhibit you've seen recently?'

I was a little puzzled and wondered what exhibitions I might have seen between dinner three nights ago and today. I mentioned an exhibit I'd seen in Korea, then one I'd seen in Hollywood, but Robert kept waiting for me to say more. As if I hadn't given the right answer.

'Uh … well, I mentioned it already, but the Michael Craig-Martin exhibit was very impressive. The most impressive, actually. It was his first time in Korea.'

Robert finally responded.

'Interesting,' he said. 'I saw that exhibit, too. A few years ago, with Mr Waldmann. We especially liked the homage to Velázquez's *Las Meninas*. Remember that? Michael Craig-Martin replaced the human figures in *Las Meninas* with household items. Sunglasses for the princess, a fire extinguisher for the artist … There's also a dog in *Las Meninas*. Do you remember what Michael Craig-Martin put in the dog's place?'

The words he spoke were almost the same as the last time. Almost, I thought — or maybe they were exactly the same. Now I was supposed to answer. I could have said that the dog was replaced by a belt, but I couldn't bring myself to, and as I equivocated, Robert said the following:

'A belt. I was so engrossed by it that I had a dream about a belt that night. The belt looked like a snake in my dream. I dream a lot. Recently, I saw a piece by Charwei Tsai. It was a video of a Buddhist mantra being written repeatedly in tiny letters on a piece of tofu. The imagery repeated itself over and over again in my dream.'

I couldn't decide on how to react, so I nodded slowly. Wasn't this almost the same as last time, too? Robert seemed to be waiting for me to say something, but I couldn't remember my lines. It was obvious: I had no lines. I could have said anything, but for some reason, I felt the pressure to give the right answer. I managed to open my mouth and ask, 'What kind of dream was it?' then added, 'You didn't become tofu, did you?'

Predictably, Robert said that he'd become one of the letters to be written on the tofu.

Was this conversation that interesting? No matter how engrossing, you couldn't act out the same conversation over and over, could you? Conversations didn't just disappear after they happened. When we conversed, the words accumulated in our minds, turning into flesh and blood. It was inevitable that we chose subjects of conversation according to our interests, but if we'd already talked about an exhibition, there was some level of implicit abbreviation and omission required when bringing up the same topic three days later. We have to tread lightly on common ground, but Robert did no such thing. Was it true what people said, that time for dogs consisted only of the present? No. As far as I knew, dogs remembered the past. So did Robert enjoy this conversation?

Between Robert and I sat one box and three humans. We were in broad daylight, so I could see the interpreters' expressions. I grew more confused when I realised that everyone, not just Robert, seemed new to this conversation.

According to our script, it was now Robert's turn to say this: 'I think that's what art is like. It's a spirit that, in reality, is a dead end, but it crosses over into our dreams and tells us to keep talking. That's the light that the artist instils in us.' Which was exactly what he'd said the other day.

I remembered everything I had eaten at our first meal, but I couldn't deal with such a drawn-out conversation again. When dessert came out, Robert again asked the question, 'What's the most memorable art exhibit you've seen recently?'

I wanted to cry. I tried to bring up a few other exhibitions, but the conversation was set. When I mentioned Michael Craig-Martin, Robert guided us through a slightly abbreviated version of the same conversation. Was Robert actually curious to know my answers again? How could he have the same conversation three times in a row? He repeated it again before the meal was over. This time, he didn't even ask me about any memorable exhibits I'd seen, he just repeated his prior statements, condensed to half their original length. When he finished, Robert said the same thing again, condensed further. It took five minutes. Then he cut it in half again, to two minutes. By the end, he'd shortened his speech to a single line: 'I think that's what art is.'

After this, Robert ended the conversation. He looked sated. I just nodded, absentmindedly folding my napkin into a paper boat as I listened. One more fold, and the boat would turn into a crane. Paper boats and paper cranes had the same starting point. Four boats wobbled on my lap before some of them fell to the ground like dead leaves.

The same story, folded in half again and again until it was a single line. It was such a bizarre way of speaking that it seemed like a kind of compulsion. I wondered if our conversation had the same function as one of Robert's chew toys, but Danny said that Robert held this rhetorical technique in high esteem.

Anyway, there was an unexpected effect to this conversation style. It relieved my tension somewhat. As Robert's lines decreased in number, my hunched shoulders straightened, my neck gained strength, and I found myself wondering if his language skills were nothing more than a few set patterns. 'What's the most memorable art exhibit you've seen recently?' was an easy question for Robert to ask anyone he met.

Still, there was no denying that Robert and I had had a 'conversation' about Michael Craig-Martin's work. If Robert's questions were fixed, how would he have known how to respond to my answers? But maybe he'd seen my posts about the exhibit on social media. Maybe I was predictable.

Four days later, I got another invitation, this time for dinner. I wondered if I had the right to refuse. Did Robert even consider that possibility? Sam brought the letter in the morning. It contained the same biting lines as always.

5.

Compared to what I'd face in the real world after my time at the Robert Foundation, I had assumed that long and frequent meals with the Foundation's president would be manageable. The problem was that these meals were more boring than I could have imagined. I remembered how the residency guidebook had mentioned that the Foundation provided participants with 'unlimited meals'. What did they mean by unlimited? Several times, I tried to break out of Robert's preferred conversational structure. I attempted to change the subject when he finished the second iteration of one of his monologues. It would have been rude to butt in mid-speech, so I needed to speak up as soon as Robert was done with one of his summaries. If I missed that brief interval, I'd have to wait for another chance. Thanks to my hesitation, though, I often missed it. Robert would throw himself headfirst into his next monologue, and I would feel even more exhausted than before.

My agony reached its zenith at my fifth meal with Robert, by which point he'd stopped asking me about art exhibits. During our third and fourth conversations, he didn't even bring up his

increasingly abbreviated story about Victorian lemon squeez-
ers. There was no longer any reason to play around with such
detail, as everything Robert had to say could be summed up in
a single line. Silence followed. I almost missed the origami-like
folding, the consecutive reductions, of Robert's prior utterances.
Six people — or rather, five people and a dog — sat around a
circular table inside a glamorous greenhouse, clinging to our
respective seats as if any divergence would cause the set-up to
collapse. No matter what questions I asked, Robert failed to
respond, making me wonder if he was in a bad mood. A similar
pattern continued during our sixth meal. Forced to sit through
multiple long courses, I had to watch as silence flowed around
us. It was so quiet that during the meal, a button the size of a
bean fell onto the floor, and the staccato tapping sound it made
as it bounced off the ground four times in a row put me on edge.
My heart skipped a beat; I initially thought that a tooth, rather
than a button, had fallen. The button was the size of a tooth
and ivory in colour. The group was so unrealistically calm, so
lacking in reaction, that I felt sick. What if it *had* fallen out of
my mouth?

I would have felt less on edge if Robert had stopped seeking
me out. Our two-hour dinners stole my energy, and sometimes
I found myself eating cup noodles or a whole package of cookies
alone in my studio afterwards. Even when Robert wasn't around,
reminders of his presence followed me. The cafeteria staff were
obsessed with seating. They asked me to let them know in advance
if I wanted to eat something specific at the daily buffet-style
breakfast; they could cater the menu to my tastes. But I didn't
want different food, I wanted to request a different table set-up.

Despite my repeated pleas that the staff stop cleaning up after me, they wouldn't stop. Things they removed from my table included a salad I'd just brought over from the buffet, an omelette, still warm and uneaten, and a cup of coffee from which I'd drunk a single sip. I had only left my salad bowl on the table while I went to get some yoghurt, but when I returned, the salad had disappeared. Foods were removed ruthlessly, without exception — even if I hadn't taken a single bite. If I got up from my seat after setting down a cup of coffee, it would be gone upon my return. The fate of paper napkins was the same. It sapped me of my desire to eat.

'Coffee cups are a bit much,' one of the interpreters said. 'They usually don't go that far.'

I'd been a bit more careless this time — since I knew he could see my table from where he was sitting, I figured my meal was safe. But when I went to get a plate of fruit, my coffee disappeared.

'I only had one sip,' I said. 'Can you ask them not to remove my dishes?'

'You have to copy the way we do things here. This is all Robert — he's not going to change.'

Were empty table places a part of Robert's aesthetic? The interpreter said that Robert didn't like the sight of unattended dishes.

'Robert doesn't even use this cafeteria, does he?' I asked.

'Well, air circulates. You have to respect the energy in the air here.'

Later, when I pleaded with the interpreter to translate what I said directly during our meals with Robert, he replied, 'That's a very arrogant thought, imposing human language on Robert.'

While humans communicated with one another line by line, he explained, Robert saved the entire space-time of a conversation in his head, like an enormous file transfer system. Talking to Robert required a lot of stamina, so the interpreter had to eat well. Technically, though, he was the interpreter furthest from Robert in our chain of communication, so he didn't speak to Robert directly. He had been hired specifically for my sake, moving between Korean and English. When I mentioned this, the interpreter became irritated and seemed not to understand.

'You think Korean–English interpreters are a rare breed? There's a reason I was chosen over everybody else. I know what words Robert likes. When you two were speaking, I purposefully said "strike" instead of "hit". I said that because he's particularly fond of the word "strike". Do you realise how much this sophistication contributes to a positive atmosphere? It's specialised knowledge. Know that it requires a lot of energy for me to stand on the front line between you and Robert. That's why I'm eating these mountainous piles of food.'

Another translator — the one who stood even closer to the front line — walked over. Danny was the first gate through which every word had to pass on its way from Robert to me, and how he turned Robert's words into human language remained a mystery. He had three tools: the black box; his animal behaviourist background, as a former sheepdog handler; and all the time he spent with Robert. But presumably the latter two were less useful when it came to discussions about art. Everyone wondered how the black box worked. From what I'd heard, the device had been developed by Danny and Mr Waldmann. It was extremely expensive and tailored to Robert. You couldn't just buy one, even if you had the money. The black box looked like a tissue box, or a speaker, but you couldn't see what was inside. Its appearance reminded me of a phone conversation I'd overheard on the bus one day.

The woman behind me, on the verge of tears, had yelled into her phone, 'It's a black cabinet. Yes, the files are inside, but we don't have the key.' During the thirty minutes I was on the bus, which was entirely silent other than her shouting, I had no choice but to listen along as she tried to solve the conundrum she'd found herself in.

'Yes, break it, please,' she had said. 'That's okay. Break it and get the files out.'

I hadn't thought that there was anything unusual about my bread until Danny pointed at it and asked, 'Did you pick that on purpose?'

I had accidentally placed a piece of plastic display bread onto my plate, which made both him and the interpreter laugh.

What do you mean? I thought to myself. The model bread was in the breadbasket — it looked the same as the real thing. When I picked it up with tongs, I just thought it was a bit crusty, not that it was fake. As I returned the bread to the basket, Danny finished his meal and left his seat. I saw him outside the window, walking with Robert. Between the two of them, the black box wasn't necessary. Danny's body looked much larger than normal. He looked solid, his frame large but without excess. Danny's muscles moved gently as he spoke with Robert. I almost felt like I could hear the distant conversation, but sound can't travel that far, so I just watched them, observing Danny's graceful steps. Surprisingly, it was Danny rather than Robert upon whom my gaze lingered.

Upon arriving at the Robert Foundation, I had received three keys: one for my bedroom, one for my studio, and one for my car. The car was an orange Lamborghini with fewer than sixteen thousand kilometres on it and a full tank of petrol, kept in a shady parking garage. I had got an international driver's licence, thinking that it might come in handy someday, but at this point I hadn't driven in so long, the beautiful vehicle was useless to me. I liked how when I started the engine, the ground below the car turned orange, like a personalised carpet, so sometimes I sat quietly in the driver's seat just for fun. Sitting there in the early hours of morning, I saw palm trees short and tall swaying silently. Long like dinosaur necks, these trees weren't native to the local climate. But here they were.

In the three weeks since I'd arrived here at the beginning of July, I had only left the Foundation grounds to buy art supplies with Danny. Outside the walls of the Robert Foundation, things continued to ignite for no reason. With the fires, I didn't dare venture outside in the middle of the day. But maybe the fires weren't the only reason. I was too busy adjusting to life at the Foundation.

That being said, it wasn't like I spent all day holed up in my studio. I ran outside in the early morning and at sunset. There were a total of sixteen trails on the Foundation grounds. Technically only three crossed the property, but if you went down them, forks in the road appeared, making for sixteen different paths. They looked the same, though, so it was hard to tell them apart. Not to mention that they were all under some degree of construction. Q City was a place that differed each time you woke up from a night of sleep.

I often saw police officers on the trails. In the middle of the day, heat stroke was a risk, so they patrolled several points to ensure hikers were carrying water. Despite the forty-five-degree heat, inside the Foundation walls it was cool. The grounds were kept at ideal humidity levels and temperature. Not too hot, not too dry, it was like a temperature-controlled terrarium protecting arctic foliage brought to a tropical climate. The nearby artificial lake had run dry, but the pond at the Foundation was always fresh. I walked across the stepping-stone path that crossed the pond. Two stones in the middle were a slightly different colour, like they'd recently been replaced.

The Robert Foundation's enormous yard was lovely. Its architects had taken light and shadow into account, but since some of the expansive garden wasn't covered by an awning, energy had to be expended to keep the outdoor space comfortable. Sam had told me that the Foundation used two thousand tons of water each day to support their young artists. I was so visibly shocked by this statement that she had to tell me not to repeat this information. When I did the calculations, the Robert Foundation was consuming more water than a nearby luxury resort. And the Foundation didn't house that many people, so when you calculated water consumption per-person, it was even worse.

Robert and I now went for walks through this lush garden before and after our meals. Robert showed off the Foundation's basic facilities and landscaping to guests, but there were so many hidden spaces on the grounds that you wouldn't see them all even if you spent the entirety of your four-month residency walking around. Just because I was also taking walks with Robert didn't mean our meals were any shorter. Sometimes we would end up spending a total of four hours together.

July came to an end, and I still hadn't started work on my paintings. It was as if my only goal had been to get here. There were so many things I had wanted to do as soon as I arrived, but now when I looked over my to-do list, I couldn't muster the motivation. I was so frustrated that I started to take the Lamborghini on short drives around the area. My friends in Korea said that even if I didn't make any new art, at least I'd get driving practice. They were joking, but I was afraid that's what would really happen.

In August, once I'd acclimatised, I had to attend several meetings each week to show just how well I'd acclimatised. Danny introduced me to several affiliates of the art museum. The group included a legendary art auctioneer, a famous art collector, a museum curator, and a critic. They were curious about my current projects. The problem was that I didn't have any current projects. I still talked as if I was in the midst of something. My rambles almost made me feel sorry for myself, but fortunately I only met these people once. Although Robert wasn't present at the meetings, I could feel him in the air. After an hourlong teatime with our guests, I felt like a dusty piece of clothing that had been beaten into cleanliness.

The most hostile group I met with consisted of people interested in the 'reconstruction' of Q City. They used the word 'reconstruction' a lot, specifically in their motto: 'The journey from inspiration to influence, shorter and faster thanks to the

reconstruction of Art Highway Q.' The artist talk I'd sponta-
neously agreed to didn't make me feel like I was being beaten
clean; it felt like being tossed into an oven. The audience didn't
like my clumsy speech. As soon as I mentioned my recent painting *Hangover Relief,* one belligerent member of the Q group said,
'We want to be the subjects of your work, Ms An,' and burst into
applause. *Hangover Relief,* which Robert had graced with one of
his footprint hearts, was meaningful to me, too, but the reason
that the denizens of Q liked it so much was because 'the artist's
lived experience inspired the work'.

One of my pieces consisted of a single line of music, with
cities' names written above each note, where a sharp or flat sign
would go.

'Is this your most recent work?' asked another member of
the Q group. 'The one that Robert liked? It's surprising — it uses
music to reinvent the relationship between real estate and the
legacy of the artist. At first I didn't understand what it meant,
and since the names of Korean cities are written on the notes, I
thought it was your residential history. This piece made me think
about musical symbolism from the perspective of real-estate
investment. But what do the symbols mean? We interpreted it
as a response to the market, to the increase in housing prices. Is
that right?'

Everyone knew that this question had no answer.

Someone else said that she had tried playing the music herself
and, despite the fact that it was in a minor key, found the sound
to be appealing and bright. I had agonised over whether to draw a
repeat sign at the end of the score and ultimately decided to do it.
The group said in unison that it looked both cruel and charming.

The conversation naturally turned to the names of the cities I had written on the musical notes, specifically cities P, A, and C. This was the topic that the group seemed to be most interested in. P, a small city on the outskirts of Seoul, had gained worldwide acclaim as a cultural destination. They said living there, and before that living in A and C, showed off my writerly sensibilities.

Some asked about the trick to making a neighbourhood hip. I couldn't tell if they were trying to make fun of me or were just naive. I replied by asking if such a thing existed. I hadn't had much of a choice when it came to the neighbourhoods I lived in. I preferred to rent on a month-to-month basis rather than pay a large deposit at the beginning of a lease. With a budget as small as mine, you inevitably looked for housing in neighbourhoods on the cusp of gentrification. I lived in neighbourhoods that were no longer being repaired, that were on the verge of being knocked down for redevelopment. A had been that kind of area; new developments were popping up and house prices were surging. When I lived there, a magazine did a profile on me, calling me an 'artist of A City', but prices rose so much that I had to move out before the article was published. The next place I moved to was C, which was comparatively cheaper, and then P. I had lived in P while running my art academy for elementary schoolers, but then the area suddenly became 'hip', making it hard for me to afford rent.

Hearing this story, someone said, 'Now that you're here, Ms An, Q is really going to take off.'

Everyone laughed at this, including me. It wasn't such a surprise that prices had gone up in all the cities in which I'd lived. I had moved around so much *because* the prices went up. Someone else said it would be great if I settled down in Q. He mentioned

Banksy and said that if I wanted to paint a mural, I was welcome to use one of the walls of his house. I said that I didn't paint murals, and he replied that any sort of art would be fine. He was maybe the fifth person in the group? I started numbering them in my head — Q1, Q2, Q3, and so on. Q5 spoke with his mouth as close to me as possible. It reminded me of someone trying to pour the contents from one wine bottle into another, not wanting to lose a single drop. I reflexively moved my head back.

'If you want it, Ms An, we'll move the Grand Canyon here!' the man said. 'So long as you make art about it. If you want a beautiful tree outside your studio window, we'll make it happen. Just let us know. If you want, we'll fill up the dried-out lake. Whatever gives you inspiration, we'll provide.'

'You'd fill up the lake? Is that possible?'

'We can try. It's better when it's filled with water, right? You'll paint the lake, and after the Robert Foundation exhibition, viewers will come to see the point of inspiration for your art. It's better if we're prepared beforehand. I have a story that shows our potential as a creative hub. Have you heard about Q's invasion of Hollywood?'

He was talking about the Hollywood sign I'd seen, the one taken over by Qs. It remained unclear who was responsible for the incident (several groups claimed to have masterminded the stunt), but the Q residents insisted it was them. I wasn't sure if they were serious, because afterwards someone claimed it was a joke. But if it was them, I wondered what they'd have to say about no one being able to pick me up when I was right there — next to the sign! Of course, Q wasn't the Robert Foundation, but even so, my feeling of being othered grew firmer.

Some of the group wondered what materials I had bought, so I took them to the studio to show off my new tools. It was all a bit ridiculous. Maybe this was the price of fame as a Robert Foundation resident. People expected me to come up with a chef's specialty using my precious, fresh ingredients, but honestly, I was at my wits' end. I had disclosed the details of my purchases, but if they asked me more specific questions about my work, I wouldn't have been able to answer. An artist's personality or vision couldn't be summed up by a collection of items you'd find in a small store. I had purchased varnish, though, and that was a bit different from my typical art supplies, so I talked about that with those who were curious.

'I didn't used to like using varnish in my work. But this time I put a few varnishes in my shopping cart.'

They asked me why I hadn't liked varnish.

'Um …well, it was expensive. But thanks to the Robert Foundation, I have unlimited access to art supplies now. And it's all free.'

Everyone laughed and waiting for me to say more. I tried to think of something to say.

'Every artist is different,' I started, 'but I don't like how, when I use varnish, the existing texture and colour gradations get homogenised into a single tone. Even if you paint each part of the piece individually, there's a limit to how much variation varnish allows for. Rather than making the tone consistent, I prefer to allow for the natural personality of the piece to shine through, which is why I haven't traditionally used varnish in my work. But now, come, look over here. You can't ignore the tremendous amount of sunlight here. I was struck by how the harsh rays seem to be peeling the streets of Q right off the ground. So in this case I thought it would be alright to create uniformity using varnish.'

'Varnish is Q's sunlight,' someone said.

'What a cool way to put it!' someone else added.

That was that. But for an entire week after the meeting, all I did was try to figure out how other artists had taken advantage of their time at the Robert Foundation. I found a lot of successes but no failures. This comforted me during the day, but at night I worried about becoming the Foundation's first dud.

I stopped attending meetings with people from Q because they were slowing down my work, but I couldn't stop them from sending things to my studio. The studio filled with documents — informational brochures from Q's government offices, community organisations, and local businesses. The brochures didn't impress me — they just formally confirmed that construction was ongoing. After this path was constructed, then that path was constructed, then after that path was complete, they worked on this path some more. Even though I ran on one of the Robert Foundation's sixteen trails each day, I still couldn't figure them all out.

When I bumped into people while running, they sometimes greeted me like this:

'Ms An, *annyeonghasimnikka* to your art!'

They used this formal Korean greeting to ask how the residency was going. They wanted to know if anything was bothering me, what was inspiring my art, if people appeared in my paintings, if advertisements appeared in my paintings. Some told me that if they were Edward Hopper, they would paint the animal shelter at the end of one of the trails. Apparently, a lot of dogs lived there.

'Why is there an animal shelter *there*?' I asked.

'So people can take the dogs on walks,' they said. 'You should check it out. Recently it's been so hot, though. Don't go during the day.'

'Why should I paint it?'

'If you paint from a certain position, Q City looks especially beautiful in the background. It's the city's best angle.'

The next day, while I was running on a different trail, someone else greeted me in a familiar manner.

'Good morning, Ms An. Did you manage to paint at all yesterday?'

Even the eyes of the CCTV cameras along the trails grew in size as I ran past them. I had no place to hide.

News of the wildfires had briefly calmed, but by mid-August, reports about the fires spreading came in day after day. Deep-sea creatures like oarfish washed up on the shore by the US–Mexico border, and desert cacti wilted and turned grey. The word 'drought' was everywhere, and I started to hear news about the water being cut off. Along with the flames, there was also news that a sandstorm had broken the wings of several wind turbines in the area.

The path of flames included the mall Jun and I had visited. I recalled how everything in that mall — the clocks, the scales, the needles — had been at a standstill. What hour and minute had the needles of clocks been stopped at? After burning part of the building, the fire had continued along the road in our direction. Towards Q, and the Robert Foundation.

In Los Angeles, everyone had paid attention to the direction the fires took, but after arriving at the Robert Foundation, it felt like I'd been cut off from the news. They had failed to pick me up on time because of the fires, but other than that, they seemed wholly uninterested in what was going on. This place felt like a different world. When people greeted me, they said, 'What a lovely day!'

Robert and I walked silently around the Foundation grounds. I could see soft, dry olive-coloured leaves in front of me, as well as various types of palm trees that had been airlifted here from across the world. A hammock dangled from one of the trees, under a tarp placed to block the sun from the user's eyes. Even so, it was impossible to completely separate the Robert Foundation from all the flames and the heat. Inside the campus gates, we came across a bed of sunflowers lying in wait like stalwart enemy troops. Once-yellow blooms had been charred overnight. Their appearance was so gruesome that it took me a moment to realise they weren't kindling. Robert carefully examined the plants. Later, at teatime, he opened up about the shocking encounter.

'Those sunflowers,' he began. 'They look like apple pies. But failures — burnt ones.'

Then he went on about apple pies. He told me about the important of oven temperature and crust density. You wanted the crust to be thin, but if it was too thin, filling would burst out. Robert said that he liked the crust as thin as possible without ruining the structural integrity, particularly when the top of the pie had a classic lattice design. These statements reached my ears through several layers of interpretation, so my initial reaction to the sunflowers had already expired by the time I heard them, leaving a burnt apple pie in its stead.

'Those sunflowers became apple pies,' Robert said. 'Burnt ones.'

'The apple pies were burnt.'

As he repeated the apple-pie story, folding it in half over and over, I gave up on the hopeless task of ending the conversation. Robert had discovered a new topic to fixate on. After he'd folded up his apple pie as much as possible (ignoring the fact that the original story was about sunflowers), his attention moved to the wind turbines that had been damaged the night before. There was a huge TV screen in front of us, showing a heavy sandstorm breaking the turbines' wings. Two of the turbines burned to the ground, sparks flying as if they were being welded. Robert replayed that scene several times.

'They look like candles on a birthday cake,' he said. 'It's a pity that installing wind turbines isn't as light-hearted an activity as placing candles on a cake. They're so similar when burnt. It's regrettable, when you think about the composition. Of course, you can't *only* think about aesthetics.'

I had no fire-safe doors inside me, so if a blaze broke out in one part of my mind, it inevitably spread to another. The wild-fires, sandstorms, burning wind turbines, wilted sunflowers: they twirled around my head, but Robert didn't seem to dwell. He was a flaneur who breezed past with a jaunty gait, avoiding the muddy ground beneath him. And I was a passerby who wanted to shatter his aloofness.

We spent the rest of our time looking at photos of last night's disaster. Sam used a remote to control the speed with which we flipped through the images. It wasn't dissimilar to looking at art in a museum. As we examined a photo of the bruised earth taken by a satellite, Robert said:

'The colour is an irregular mix of earthy orange, marigold, and the Pantone shade Living Coral. The base consists of California Orange and Jamaican Grapefruit, with a splash of Absinthe Green on top. The trees around here turn an unusually mysterious colour when they burn. It's probably due to a difference in the soil and tree species.'

I glanced at Robert's face. He was still wearing the hornlike accessory that connected to the black box. Looking at the TV screen, his mouth upturned slightly. He didn't know I was observing him. Then, as if he'd suddenly realised that I was observing him, his look turned mean and humiliated.

He wore this strange expression for a while before saying, 'It's beautiful. It reminds me of Mark Rothko ... A perfect composition.'

This made me think of something I had read about Robert's facial expressions when he was looking at art. It was in an article about how Robert fell in love with art the way most dogs fell in love with other dogs. What had it called Robert's current expression — the Flehmen response? It could be interpreted as a sign of seduction. But we weren't looking at art right now.

'This isn't art ...' I said uncertainly, not expecting a response. 'It's reality.'

Robert seemed unconvinced. Gesturing at a photo of the red sky, taken by a tourist at a California resort, he said the place was famous for their jojoba-oil massages. He told me I should check it out while I was here.

'Okay,' I said. 'As long as the resort hasn't burned down.'

He seemed to take my words as a joke and laughed. Or, he said he was laughing. He displayed a transcendent reaction to the disaster approaching us. I couldn't tell if this was because he was a dog or because he was super rich. As we conversed, I tried, with increasing urgency, to convey the unfolding tragedy, but he remained unswayed. He just batted at a winged insect on the table with his front paw and continued talking about the topics he was most interested in.

'Anyway,' he said, 'I hope to see colours like these at the incineration. It depends on the firewood. I prefer birch trees because of the sound they make when they burn. Pine is loud, too, thanks to the resin. They both have their charms.'

'About the incineration,' I said.

'I heard that you're really looking forward to it.'

'No, more like I'm unsure about it. The wildfires are moving in our direction. Should we really host an incineration?'

'Are you implying that the fires will hit the Foundation?' Robert asked.

'Not exactly … although I don't want that, either. But we can't say for sure, can we? What I mean is, isn't it weird to start a fire when wildfires are already burning out of control? Of course, I know it's a Robert Foundation tradition, but considering that it's *my* work that is going to be incinerated, it's hard for me to ignore how that looks with everything that's going on.'

I saw Robert's tail wag to the left rather than the right. He didn't look happy.

'The incineration system is like human life,' he said. 'Humans die. Recycling them isn't possible. Humans are single-use organisms.

Living beings are waste destined for incineration, but that doesn't mean we live our lives in fear of our impending cremation.'

Robert drew a line as if to indicate that he was not a single-use organism. Then he twitched, jutting his jaw forward and sharply turning his head.

'It's strange,' he said. 'You still haven't started work on your paintings, have you? You're thinking so much about art that doesn't yet exist.'

I didn't know what to say. It felt like I'd been hit over the head. Robert was voicing a problem I'd been ignoring until now.

'No!' I said defensively. 'I have been working.'

'Good,' he said. 'We'll be going on an inspirational field trip, too, so make sure you prepare for that as well.'

The field trip was a visit to the incineration room. After teatime with Robert, Danny and I began to walk towards the incinerator, or more specifically, towards the Robert Museum of Art — the white building that looked like a roll of toilet paper. From a visitor's perspective, it was an elegant, bright, and beautiful building. When you opened the doors and went inside, a loosely spiralled walkway guided you through the exhibits, and as you looked at the art — feeling like a drop of oil bobbing atop a pool of water — eventually you found yourself at the top. But as I tried to understand the entirety of this building, it became a labyrinth. If the museum was the site of incineration, where the heck did they burn the art? The large circular column in the middle of the museum looked like a chimney, but that was just the elevator. Danny and I rode it up to the observation deck, an open space where you could see in all directions.

Danny asked what I had been up to and if I had been having a good time at the Foundation. I didn't know the exact implication of his question, but I said that I was enjoying myself.

'That's good,' he said. I realised that he hadn't been asked about my paintings, but rather my driving. He must have noticed the tan on my left arm, a result of spending so much time in the driver's seat recently. My driving skills were improving slowly but surely. Danny and I rode the elevator back down to the first floor. I looked behind us and, at last, spotted the incinerator. It looked like a pizza oven. Actually, it was a pizza oven. Danny said they loaded artworks onto a wide shovel and pushed them into the oven.

'We don't incinerate all the art here,' he said. 'If a work is too big, it's hard to burn in this oven. In that case, we burn it outside. Robert decides the location for the burn, but no matter where it is, we always play music. As soon as the fire starts, music comes out of the speakers under all our outdoor lights. Are you working on any pieces larger than three metres?'

'Each of my paintings is a different size,' I said.

'A while ago, we had some sculptures that were over four metres tall and four metres wide. They wouldn't have fit inside of incinerator. So the artist cut off the sculptures' heads.'

'The artist cut them off?'

'Yes, so the sculptures would fit. He beheaded the sculptures in front of an audience. All thirty of them.'

'Thirty?'

The story felt extremely remote to me, considering that I hadn't finished even one piece. I later learned that the title of the group of sculptures was *Möbius Sleep*. After sculpting in a frenzy during sleepless nights, the artist had cut off the heads of his creations for the exhibition.

'Where did the heads go?' I asked. 'Were they incinerated, too?'

'Originally we were going to put the heads back on the bodies for the exhibition, but the artist liked the look of the bodiless heads, so we displayed them separately. He titled the piece *Head Collection*. And that's what ended up being burned.'

'Oh! So you burned something different from what was originally planned?'

'Yes. *Head Collection* just looked so much more powerful inside the exhibition hall. So that's what Robert decided, and the artist agreed.'

'I'm curious — it seems like Robert isn't alone when he chooses the work to burn. Why is the artist present, too?'

'Well, the art is in the artist's studio, so naturally the artist ends up being present.'

'Does the artist not end up influencing Robert's decision?'

'No, it's all Robert's decision.'

'That's why I was wondering. Since Robert can smell fear. Is that reflected in his decision?'

'It seems like you're assuming that he is trying to hurt the artist with his choice.'

'Is he?'

'Are you asking if he watches how the artist reacts to him looking at each piece of art, and chooses the work to burn that way? Why would you think that?'

'Because Robert will want to burn the best piece, considering the meaning he gives to the incineration — right? Of course, he could also choose the piece based on personal taste, but when you consider the close focus paid to the artist's reaction at the incineration event, you'd think Robert would consider what piece the artist values most. He must try to read the artist's thoughts when choosing the art to burn. It's not like he's trying to sniff out a fake, but he can smell how "real" the artist's feelings are for a certain work of art. There's more power in burning a piece the artist really loves, isn't there?'

Danny smiled lightly.

'It doesn't mean anything,' he said.

'Huh?'

'Robert isn't choosing a piece because the artist loves it. The artist loves the piece that gets burned because it's destroyed. In any case, the artist can't avoid fate: the art that he or she loves will burn. It'll happen to you, too.'

Although the incineration was a Robert Foundation tradition, it had started by accident. Soon after the residency's third participant arrived, one of her paintings had caught fire, and the surprised expression on her face had become a big deal. Shocked by the art on fire, the artist was lost for words. Eventually, though, the fire turned her into a household name.

The fourth residency participant suffered a lot. He wasn't told until he arrived that he was expected to burn one of his pieces of art, and he hadn't wanted to participate. The previous artist's creation was destroyed accidentally; burning art on purpose was a bit harder to accept. Eventually, though, he was persuaded by the logic of the Robert Foundation. As the Foundation had expected, the Robert Museum of Art welcomed a greater number of visitors that year. Incinerations had continued ever since. The systematised burnings weren't as shocking as an unexpected, accidental conflagration, but they came to be known as a performance, a symbol of the Robert Foundation.

I had agreed to these terms and hadn't thought they would cause me any problems. I hadn't expected that, as the beginning of August came and went, I would still be at a loss for what to paint. I felt burdened by the deep meaning people here affixed to my every utterance. How could I get away from them? I started to put Post-it notes on the walls of my studio. Pink notes for things I'd said, and yellow for things people had said to me. A few days later, I realised there was no difference between the yellow and pink notes and gave up on distinguishing between the two. Post-its covered the walls like an animal's fur. Only windows and hanging picture frames remained furless, as if they were the animal's eyes and lips. The paper was in its place, my palette was in its place, my chair was in its place, the clock was in its place, and the calendar was in its place. With the glut of Post-it notes, there was only one thing missing from this cramped space: my art.

I started to paint the words written down on the Post-its, but I couldn't depict everything. Did I have too much inspiration? I kept mixing colours, but my hands felt heavy. There was so much oil at the end of my paint knife that it felt like a fish caught in a net. Now that I'd turned my attention to the canvas, I couldn't pull my thoughts together, and eventually I had to throw away the precious pigments. I had several canvases in progress, but none of them were complete. Every time, I would get stuck on a painting, my frustration building until around sunset, when I would give up and would go for a run. The only progress I was making was on my running speeds.

The problem was, it wasn't just me running. One evening, after I passed the two-kilometre mark, a runner beside me struck up a conversation. It was one of the Q residents I'd met — the one with a habit of getting really close to your face when talking. It was disconcerting, but he seemed completely unaware of it. He acted like our encounter was a coincidence, but it seemed forced. I didn't slow down.

He did his best to keep pace with me. He glanced at the watch on my wrist and seemed delighted.

'Ooh, a Garmin,' he said. 'Naturally, since you're a runner.'

He started to talk at length about the superior quality of Garmin products, which led to a discussion of marathon records. The conversation was interesting enough that I couldn't figure out his intentions. I let my guard down and began to walk alongside him. Q5, as I'd started to call him in my head, asked, 'How's your art coming along?'

'It's a mess,' I said.

My acquaintance kept talking, as if he didn't believe me. 'What's it about? The subject matter, the background? Let me know if you need anything.'

I didn't think I had to reply, but he waited for me to say something. Thinking about the emptiness of my canvases, I said, 'Empty ... fields?'

'Empty fields? That's what your paintings are of?'

When I didn't answer, Q5 nodded and asked, 'I'm not an expert, so can I ask about your process, painting fields? Do you include the roads that border the fields? Are there any traffic signs? Or any signs at all?'

'I haven't thought about the details,' I said.

'I'll make a field for you to paint.'

I laughed, thinking it was a joke, then realised he was serious. I quickly apologised. The man was bubbling over with excitement at the thought of creating an empty field.

'I'm thinking about a field I passed on the way here — one that was covered with tyres,' I said. 'There's no need to make a completely new field.'

'But Ms An,' the man replied, 'the field you're talking about isn't in Q. You're supposed to be getting inspiration from our city. We can prepare a field for you. We'll work together.'

'Um, I don't know if we need to do that …'

'There's one place that comes to mind — I think it would be the perfect location for a field. It's currently full of abandoned buildings. A lot of warehouses, too. No one uses them anymore. It would be nothing to turn the place into a field. All we'd have to do is knock the buildings down.'

'Um …' I equivocated. 'If the field is artificial, I don't know if that really counts …'

'Everything we talk about, Ms An, is inspiration for Q,' Q5 said. 'I want to mark this very spot. To commemorate our exchange of ideas about empty fields. I'll outline it, in white chalk.'

'Like when there's an accident?'

'This is an accident. Isn't love comparable to a car accident? What else do you need? It's so interesting to be part of an artist's creative process. Hey, what about those sunflowers over there? They're the symbol of our city.'

'They're nice,' I said. 'Very wild.' The sunflowers on the other side of the path were swollen, as if someone had beaten them up.

'Do you want me to paint the sunflowers?' I asked. 'The ones here?'

Q5 seemed to lose confidence upon hearing my question.

'If you want to, that would be great,' he said, 'but we don't just want you to paint sunflowers. We just want you to follow your artistic eye as far as you can. It's annoying, but people are wondering which "Q landmark" you'll paint. I like sunflowers. You're my muse, though, so I have to ask what *you* think.'

'If I paint sunflowers and then the painting gets exhibited and incinerated, will you turn it into a TV series?'

'If you paint a *broom*, we'll turn it into a TV series. We have high hopes for you.'

'What will happen next?' I asked.

Q5 thought for a moment and answered in a slightly lower voice.

'Maybe we'll construct a museum,' he said. 'A park would be nice, or a library or theatre. We're going to create a space where tourism, shopping, and art all come together. That's Q's new goal. You know, the "Art Highway". Using the momentum from artistic inspiration to tear down the freeway at top speed.'

'And after that?'

'We become famous.'

'What if I don't paint anything?' I asked.

'Huh?'

'What if I don't finish my paintings? Or they're bad.'

'That's not possible.' Q5 smiled. 'Are you feeling unwell?' he asked, examining my complexion a little anxiously.

I told him that I hadn't been sleeping well recently, and he said that he understood the pressure I was facing, that everyone he ran into was talking about my progress. When he saw my dazed expression, he made a big circle with his arms and said, 'My support for you is this big!'

•

As if I were being punished for my confession, I found it even harder to fall asleep that night. I hadn't slept soundly since my first night here. I'd come to realise the problem belatedly; at first I had blamed my sleep troubles on jetlag. I would just barely drift off before being shocked awake by the feeling that the cotton stuffing was falling out of my pillow. When I looked up at *Canyon Proposal* on the wall, the imagery in the picture felt slightly more burdensome than usual. There was a sliding cover next to the poster, or at least I thought there was, so one night I tried to move the embossed plate to hide the poster. That was when I discovered that the piece of plastic wouldn't move. It wasn't a cover for the poster — it was decoration, fixed in place like the collar on my pyjamas. I wouldn't have tried to move it if the poster weren't there, but it was odd to find that the 'cover' couldn't move a single millimetre. I started thinking about the wider version of the photo, *Robert in the Canyon*. It made me nervous. I was inside the frame, and Robert was outside.

If my pillow was a guillotine, was my duvet the blade? When I placed my head on the guillotine each night, the blade moved up and down over my neck, shaving away the hours second by second. By sunrise, I'd almost given up on sleep. The dawn put an end to five or six hours of torture. Drowsiness escaped me little by little, and my eyes began to perceive the wallpaper pattern and dust in the air. When I closed my eyes, my ears heard otherworldly sounds. I'd fall asleep again trying to figure out the sounds, and then everything would grow clear. One sheep, two sheep, three sheep; one wind turbine, two, three, four; one sunflower, two; one Robert, two, three; one artist-in-residence, two, three …

About twenty different artists had slept in this bed, each for intervals of a few months. They had all finished their projects, fulfilled their contractual obligations, and become famous. They made good use of their time in residence. They hadn't all eaten and slept well while doing so. Insomnia was very common. I thought about something Sam had said in passing. A previous writer had found pillow number three too soft, while pillow number four was too hard, and had asked for a different pillow. The Foundation tried its best to source an adequately firm pillow, but in the end it couldn't find anything the artist liked.

'Shouldn't you bring your own pillow at that point?' I'd asked. Until then, I'd thought that my sleep problems were different.

When I realised that there was no difference between my insomnia and his, I felt pressure to get results. The other artist had used his insomnia as inspiration for his sculptures. His sleep was productive, while mine was a pain. His art had vanished in flame; all that remained, in Robert's study, were recordings of artist talks he'd given during the exhibition of his work.

'They gave me a choice of pillows,' he said in one of the talks. 'For me, somewhere between three and four was perfect. Not 3.5 — I wanted a pillow closer to three. But even when I got a pillow around that level, I kept trying to figure out the weight and density of the cotton inside. The pillow I wanted wasn't 3.1 or 3.2. It was somewhere in between. I kept experimenting. 3.15? 3.16? 3.14? 3.141 … Night by night, I got closer to the perfect value: pi. Those digits were like wayward shipping containers blocking me on the road to sleep. That's how I ended up making this sculpture.

3.14159265358979323846264643383 … When you continue down the list of digits, eventually you can't tell what's in front of you and what's behind you. It's like a Möbius strip — there's no end. Huh? That's right. That's why the title is *Möbius Sleep*. Oh, you noticed? The long trail of digits I memorised, yes. At some point, I started reciting the digits to myself, five at a time. I lost myself to the recitation. And that's how I went to sleep.'

I wasn't the only one who wasn't sleeping. In his Las Vegas hotel room, Jun had resisted sleep, practising his lines for an audition. The actor sent me a text soon after sunrise.

'Fate is rather scary, Ms An Yiji,' he wrote.

His first audition had been a flop, but as he was ruminating on the failure, he'd received an offer from another movie.

'It overlaps with some of the things we talked about, Yiji. I really want this movie to succeed. The screenplay is still being written, but the director's Korean. We're working on it together.'

'What does this have to do with me?' I asked.

'The story about the dog who stole a photographer's picture.'

'You're going to make that into a movie?'

'Well, it will be part of the movie. Are you willing to meet with me? Our director wants to meet you.'

'Me? Why?'

They even offered to come to me. But it sounded too similar to the many fruitless meetings I had been having since my arrival at the Robert Foundation, so I refused. Then, of course, Jun pulled out the coupon. The IOU I'd issued a couple of months earlier, stating that I'd help Jun whenever he needed it.

'Does that mean you're using the IOU now?' I asked. 'To make me go to a meeting? Why are you using it so recklessly? You could have at least used it to get me to go on a date with you.'

Jun sounded so serious that I had to take back the joke.

'Why does the movie team want to meet with me?'

'Why do I have to explain?' he asked. 'I'm using the IOU!'

We decided to meet several days later at a restaurant that resembled an island in the middle of a black lake. Fresh asphalt had been laid in front of and behind the restaurant. Even though I ran across it as instructed, shiny traces of black remained on the soles of my shoes. Jun didn't know it, but the director and I were acquaintances. We had done an event together a while ago. It was an art and film collaboration, and we'd worked together as a team. As soon as the director saw me, he apologised for not staying in touch, saying that he'd been extremely busy. We had never been close, so there was no need to make excuses.

I called him *sunbae* because that's what I had called him in the past, but he was really only my senior in age. I'd started my career before him, and we weren't peers. He always called me his *hubae*. He suggested we drink, saying that I had no idea how happy he was that the current Robert Foundation resident was Korean, and a Korean he knew, at that! He seemed to have acquired a large amount of information about the Robert Foundation and its reputation, particularly recent gossip, and he wanted to give me advice.

'*Hubae*,' the director said, 'squeeze out as much Korean-ness as possible. That's your answer. They're probably expecting you to do something along those lines, anyway.'

'I already promised to make art based on the American city

of Q,' I said. 'How can I combine that with something Korean?'

'That's the artist's job. You have to figure it out.'

Seated around the table were the director, me, Jun, and some-one from Q. Apparently I had met the person from Q before, but I didn't remember him.

'I think the person from Q is here to keep an eye on you,' the director said. 'Or maybe not. Q is a little overeager. They're right under the artists' noses. Oh, man — the pressure!'

The director, of course, had nothing to do with Q's 'Art Highway'. Since he said all of this in Korean, the Q resident didn't understand what he was saying, but Jun cluelessly interpreted. Then, Q10, as I has nicknamed him, jumped up and said that he was only here to pay for the meal.

Turning to the director, he said, 'Do a good job on Project Q.' The director shook his head and pointed to me.

'The exhibition has to be a success first,' he said. 'This is for after. Offer our artist here another drink.'

As expected, Q10 took a step back. Suddenly I remembered him doing this before. The neck of an alcohol bottle approached me, and my cup was filled to overflowing.

'I trust you, Ms An,' he said. Four glasses collided in cheers before my eyes.

Moving his gaze between me and Jun, the director asked, 'How do you guys know each other? You're not old friends, are you?'

'How did *you* two meet?' I asked in response. 'Is Jun in one of your movies?'

'We can't do anything without Song Jun,' the director said. 'He's a pillar. We're like two peas in a pod. He's a rare friend to have in a place like this. I was surprised to know he's in touch with you, too. Give me a hint as to what you're thinking about painting. We heard about the empty fields. Are fields important to you? Are they the main subject of your art? It seems like you're not interested in sunflower fields.'

'Really?' I said. 'I wasn't aware of this.'

'I knew it. This is how the world works. It all goes on behind the artist's back. Come on. Let's show off the power of collective intelligence. What if we do something with a tower rather than an empty field? A building structure. We'd be creating a vertical story. I heard there's a tower in the Robert Museum of Art collections.'

'In the museum?'

'There's a story I'm thinking of that would go perfectly with that backdrop. It's one I'm working on right now.'

Q10 had grown quite anxious and asked Jun in English what the director and I were talking about. He felt alienated, unable to understand the information crossing the table in Korean. Anyway, this was what the director really came here to tell me: he wanted my paintings to be involved in the movie he was directing. It wasn't that different from what the people of Q had been pushing me towards.

'The culmination of contemporary art is video, anyway,' he said. 'Look at its impact. If you paint something, *hubae*, that'll become a Q landmark. We'll add a story to the painting and mesmerise people around the world. The process isn't easy. It's too important to be easy. Everyone's survival is at stake. Stay alert, huh? A lot of money is being poured into this endeavour. Sometimes things like this succeed and sometimes they fail.'

He jumped into a description of a project Um Corporation

had done a few years earlier. After he explained that the company was on the verge of bankruptcy, he finished his drink in one gulp.

'Things that seem stable can suddenly start to wobble,' he said. 'The president of Um got involved with a musical and over-invested in a movie version of the play, and then it all fell apart.'

'Didn't you write that musical?' I asked.

'There was one taping of it, but it wasn't a hit.'

The room grew silent. Everything was still. There were work-ers and two big trucks out the window, but amazingly, we couldn't hear anything. They were resting. The asphalt they'd spread on the ground glinted in the sun.

'What's the construction going on outside?' I asked.

Smiling, Q10 said, 'It's construction that will inspire you.'

I waved my hand and told him I didn't need inspiration.

'You ordered a box of pearlescent black paint a while ago, didn't you?' the director said. 'Gossip about that spread all over. Like asphalt.'

'What about it?'

'I heard you were trying to depict asphalt. That's why we're repaving the ground. Like I said, your every move is inspiration for us. People here are in lockstep with you.'

Had all this diligent construction work only begun when I entered the restaurant? It was no different when we left. They were performing for me. We were in an era of excess inspiration, truly. Anything I said leaked to the public, and the people of Q sprang into action. Progress on the empty fields was going sig-nificantly faster than my paintings of them. On my daily walks and runs, I kept coming across wide open spaces that hadn't been there before. A hotel that wasn't even in Q asked if they could provide me with inspiration. There was a field behind the hotel, which they suggested could serve as the background of one of my paintings. Of course, they added, we'd love to be the main subject.

6.

'There's an abandoned airport nearby — what about that site?'

It had reached the point where I was receiving emails requesting 'field location confirmation'. There were three contenders — a sunflower field by one of the trails, an empty factory, and the ruins of a former airport. It was impossible to think this was anything other than ridiculous — confirming which space was going to be turned into a field? — but maybe, like the director had said, I was just old-fashioned. They were creating an enormous An Yiji world, and in the director's words, it was 'not an easy world' to create.

The sender of the email was Q5. Or was it Q8? I was appalled to have eighty-six Q phone numbers saved on my phone. It seemed unlikely that I'd even met eighty-six people since arriving, but somehow I had eighty-six contacts, all beginning with the letter Q. The email, which referred to the Robert Foundation, included documents about each of the three plots of land, one of which had a space for me to sign my name in confirmation. What kind of comedy was this?

Being in the right place at the right time wasn't usually a

coincidence in this city — everything was orchestrated. It was, however, a surprise to run into the dog trainer from the local animal shelter while walking on the trails one day. He didn't seem interested in talking to me, and for that reason, I ended up asking him a bunch of questions. It made it less awkward.

The man ran a dog-walking service on Q's trails. The shelter was actually a two-storey building, located at the intersection of several dog-worthy paths. I initially understood this to mean that these were paths that people could use to walk their pets, but that wasn't it. These paths were for the shelter's dog-rental service. The building contained a total of thirty-nine walkable canines. People who didn't have a dog of their own came here because they wanted to take one for a walk, whether for their own enjoyment or to show off. There were 'photo zones' bedecked with Facebook and Instagram logos all over the trails. Someone was walking a shaggy white dog. It looked like cotton candy hung from the dog's body. Some people held their leashes as if they were casting a fishing rod, their companions dangling like bait. Others ran around holding dogs under their arms like handbags. Some juggled multiple leashes as if they were carrying a bunch of balloons. And then there were those looking on. I was one such bystander.

'Do the dogs ever run away?' I asked.

'Where would they go?' the trainer replied. 'This is heaven.'

To keep heaven running smoothly, the trainer carried a large cane. When I asked if I could watch the training process, he cut me off: 'It's not worth seeing.' He seemed aware that I was the artist involved with Q's 'Art Highway', but was perhaps the only person I'd met who didn't want to be featured in one of my paintings. When I asked if I could paint the dog-rental business, he said sure, if that was what I wanted.

'We're not a tourist attraction, though,' he said. 'We're just a business located in Q. Dog-rental businesses exist in North America, Europe, and Asia. There are twelve cities with rental services like this — even Seoul has one.'

'Seoul, too? I thought this was an exotic foreign concept, but I guess not.'

'We take credit-card payments,' the trainer said. 'It's difficult for anything that exists in the international transaction network to feel foreign.'

He swept his cane over the ground where I'd been standing until a few moments ago. My footprints disappeared instantaneously. Most of the people I'd met in Q made a sort of indulgent expression when they saw me, but not the trainer. He answered my questions, but with a generally apathetic air about him. The overly indulgent people of Q were tiresome, but the trainer's disregard made me nervous. I wrote the words 'credit card' on a yellow Post-it and stuck it on the wall of my studio. It looked like a yellow card in soccer.

I ran three kilometres per day — five at most — on one of the sixteen trails, and at some point I began to feel like I was floating down the trails even after my runs were over. I was like an object on a conveyor belt. I ran to avoid getting eaten up. At least, until I ran into a certain dog.

One day, I was on my run when a red-faced woman came up to me grumbling.

'He pooed,' she complained.

She was carrying a wad of tissues nearly the size of a basketball. A dog-rental employee quickly took the tissue basketball from her. They were filled with droppings, she said. The woman began to explain.

Halfway down the trail, she said, the dog had contorted into a strange pose. As the woman pulled on his leash, poo had pushed out from his behind. The woman found some tissues in her bag and picked up the poo. She kept walking, one hand gripping the leash, one hand holding the wad of tissues. 540 metres, 550 metres, 560 metres … But no rubbish bin appeared, and the woman had used up an entire pack of travel tissues. Holding a wad the size of a basketball, she walked to the shelter. The poo was a time bomb, threatening to drop to the ground at the slightest disturbance. The employee looked at the dog and refunded the woman's money. He handed her several coupons as he apologised. The dog had definitely defecated before the walk, the employee said, so he must be sick. The woman sat down in a chair at the end of the trail. There wasn't any poo on her clothes, but she furiously wiped herself down with wet wipes.

Approaching the frantic woman, I asked, 'Are the dogs not allowed to poo?'

The woman looked at me incredulously.

'The dogs here are a different kind of dog,' she said. 'Don't you know?'

'No, I don't.'

'The dogs here don't behave like that. That's the premise of the rental service. But today *I* had to clean up their poo. You understand?'

'Dogs poo,' I said. 'All of them. Seriously, all of them.'

The woman didn't reply, so I copied her wording: 'You understand?'

She tilted her head to one side and then straightened her posture.

'The dogs here are professionals,' she said. 'You understand?'

The next day, I went to the dog-rental place and said that I wanted to rent the dog that had pooed. The employee took me over to the corner, feigning surprise. The dogs here underwent defecation training, he said, so they wouldn't poo on walks.

'Wasn't there an incident yesterday?' I asked.

The employee assumed an expression of innocence before continuing in a low voice.

'One of the dogs was sick yesterday and made a mistake,' he said. 'It won't happen again.'

'I'm not trying to stir up trouble,' I said. 'I just want to walk that dog.'

It wasn't easy. The dog that had made a mistake was hiding among the thirty-nine rental canines. Maybe they'd already cut the inventory down to thirty-eight.

After a moment, I was escorted to the trainer's office. It was only on the second floor, but oddly induced a fear of heights.

'I heard that you saw the dog,' he said.

The trainer was so tall that his head touched the ceiling. I knew he was tall, but he seemed even more so in this setting.

'That rascal is being punished right now,' he said. 'We'll send him out after his training is finished.'

'Couldn't he have pooed because he was stressed?' I asked. 'He's probably under a lot of stress without anyone realising.'

'Then he'll have to be removed. Many dogs are able to control their bowel movements.'

As the trainer spoke, he tapped his long cane on the ground

with a gentle, regular rhythm, perhaps out of habit.

I took my notebook out of my bag, trying to hide my feelings. All I'd wanted was to go for a walk, but now I was overwhelmed by the events unfolding.

'How do dogs control their bowel movements?' I asked.

'Through training.'

The trainer didn't look me in the eye. The tap, tap, tap of his cane bothered me.

The dogs traded their irregular desires for a regular lifestyle. Just the right amount of food, just the right amount of laxatives, and regular stimulation were enough. Dogs living regular lives under the guidance of the trainer didn't make mistakes. They didn't create unexpected situations on walks. They didn't do things unannounced. They learned — about human speech, the human stride, and human facial expressions.

'Why are you so interested in this dog?' the trainer asked. His footsteps, his gaze, and his cane made me nervous. He stretched his arm out to open the door, and I ducked more than necessary to avoid him. Five, four, three, two, one ... my body grew weak as I descended the stairs, and by the time I reached the ground, my legs were fluttering like Post-it notes in the air. The end of the trainer's cane seemed to wrap around my neck like a noose. The image filled my body with adrenaline. I envisioned a struggle, the trainer hitting his cane against the ground, and the surge of energy left me.

When I returned to the Foundation grounds, I buried myself in the massage chair in the study. As my body vibrated, I tried to determine what was causing this stagnated energy, but I was distracted by fatigue. It was a bit ridiculous, trying to keep my eyes open while I shook in the chair. My eyes made contact with anything and everything across from me: framed photos of Robert and Mr Waldmann, Mr Waldmann and his daughter, Lina, books with long titles, and alphabet blocks that looked like a miniature version of the Hollywood sign. Each block was the size of my palm, and they made up the sentence I AM INDEX. The blocks stood at even intervals and were all capital letters. I am index? It was the perfect sentence for this place. Something Robert might say — the arrogant assertion that one functioned as the reference point for everything else. I closed my eyes, ideas swirling in my brain as I continued to vibrate, and another interpretation came to me. 'Index' in Latin referred to a list of forbidden books. Is that what Robert was?

After I got back to my room, I lay down in bed and turned on the TV. I flipped through the channels, stopping at one for a while before I realised it was a TV channel for dogs, showing a program designed to prevent canine excitement. The screen appeared a little different from usual. The images were positioned as if the viewer were at ground level. Maybe rumours would start spreading about how I watched dog TV. There were no voices — the program was quiet, only occasionally including some non-human sounds.

I passed the time like a bum, before finally turning on my laptop to write emails that I'd long put off. First, to confirm the location for the field. *The field will bring me … calm? Solitude? Quiet? Secrecy?* Choosing the right words made my head feel like it was about to explode.

'You don't have to reply, Ms An,' Sam said. 'Don't worry about it.' This was the first time the Robert Foundation had worked with a local government, she said. Q's overinvolvement was a bit disconcerting, but that was their problem. I, the artist, just needed to focus. She was right.

'Will you do the same thing with the next artist?' I asked. 'Collaborate with a different city?'

'I'm not sure,' Sam said. 'I've heard that this collaboration with Q is an experiment. Maybe we'll continue if it succeeds?'

'An experiment?'

'The Robert Foundation has always been experimental. That's how I ended up here.'

Sam said that she had initially been hired as Robert's groomer. However, she'd only had one chance to groom him, and she'd bungled it.

As I listened to Sam's story, I got a Bballi notification on my phone. The app had been quiet for so long that I'd forgotten that I hadn't turned off notifications again. We were beyond Bballi's reach, but even so my phone was flashing with a notification. When Sam asked what was going on, I explained that it was a delivery app I'd worked for in the past. What once had been my livelihood now simply looked like a phone game.

'It's a coupon notification,' I said. 'The company is trying to promote their entry into the American market, so they're offering all sorts of coupons to riders. You should give it a try — once you download the app, you can get started right away.'

'You think I should become a delivery person?' Sam asked. 'They're already working me to death here.'

'You can just do the safety training, and they'll give you a coupon. I think it's worth ten dollars?'

'Really? What's the app called?'

I was about to tell Sam that the delivery platform's safety training was essentially the same as the Robert Foundation's, but I stopped myself. I wanted to hear the rest of her story, how she'd gone from dog groomer to administrative intern. Initially, Sam revealed the information slowly, but as she grew excited, she started to reveal 'secrets'.

'Dogs have rougher hair than humans, you know? Robert is a papillon — the same breed Marie Antoinette had. Papillons are a long-haired breed — long-haired and short-haired breeds are different. They require different brushes. But Robert wanted his hair to be done like a pinscher. Or, he did at the time. You can see how even now, he walks with a hackney gait, like a pinscher. He lifts his front legs up high. Anyway, I messed up and I was fired. Then they hired me to do administrative work — a different kind of grooming. You don't seem very awake, Ms An. Let me tell you a secret about Robert. He looks sophisticated, but in reality, he has eyebrows like Shin-chan. You know, the cartoon character. You don't? Some dogs have eyebrows. Dark spots of fur, like human eyebrows. Robert covers his with the rest of his fur. If you lift it up like this, you'll see.'

How was I supposed to lift up Robert's fur? Even extending my arm to show him something on my phone would cause the interpreters to turn abruptly into bodyguards. Sam laughed as if I were joking.

'If you're feeling frustrated, take the car,' Sam said. 'Go for a drive. You could take me along, too.'

'Are you okay with that?' I asked. 'I'm a beginner. I have a driver's licence, but before coming to California, I hardly ever used it.'

'It's a good car! I'll help you practise.'

We went to some of the potential fields and drove around, just to drive. The abandoned airport was the best place to practise. When I said that I liked it there, Sam told me she'd come out with me anytime. She couldn't help but feel a special fondness for it, too, she said. She had bought a small plot of land there.

'Because of what I said about wanting to paint a field?' I asked.

'Well, because of the rumours. I bought the land primarily because it was cheap. Interestingly, when the airport shut down, they auctioned off everything inside — the gate signs, the chairs. I liked the sign that said "Gate 2", so I came out to buy it. Then I ended up purchasing land, too. But don't worry, Ms An. How is art supposed to reflect business? I think that has the order mixed up.'

Every word that hit me fluttered precariously like a Post-it note that had lost its adhesive. Sam managed to comfort me, though, in a surprisingly firm yet subtle manner. I felt so comforted by her energy that even when she brought another letter on a silver platter — a letter full of aggression, one that required Robert literacy to read — it didn't upset me.

Her calming effect didn't last long. As soon as Robert saw me, he spat out the following words:

'What's on your mind?'

'My mind?' I asked.

'An empty field?'

'Huh?'

'Has your mind been full of emptiness recently, Ms An?'

'Yes, it's completely empty. There's so much emptiness.'

'The more, the better.'

When I asked the interpreter what this conversation was about, he looked as if he'd just witnessed something disgraceful. When I said I wanted to know the exact phrases being translated, he spoke without moving his lips, like a ventriloquist. *Make Robert a promise. Talk about the future.* But promise him what? I was a mess of confusion and embarrassment. I tried to pretend that I was okay in order to regain my composure, but I could already feel my face turning red. I looked into Robert's eyes. I wanted to know if he was staring at me or completely oblivious. Robert had his eyes closed, as if he were bored. I said that I would finish my paintings soon, but Robert's expression remained unchanged.

We were drinking tea in his beautiful greenhouse. A succulent native to Mexico hung behind Robert like a long braid; beside him, water tumbled down an artificial waterfall. Colourful birds flew around us. From these artificial tropics, Robert proudly recounted his past achievements. His legendary achievements. Apparently he had saved the lives of two drowning aristocrats, found a priceless eighteenth-century antique in a flea market, and discovered that a painting thought to be a forgery was in fact authentic. He compressed the story four times, until it was down to a single sentence: 'I just smelled the paint.' The whole time, I was ripping my napkin into pieces under the table. Long and thin, like dried strips of pollack.

'How did you do all these amazing things?' I asked. I wasn't looking for an answer — it was just empty praise, necessary to keep the conversation flowing — but Robert took my question seriously.

'Every day!' he shouted. Then he explained himself, as if surprised that I didn't already understand.

'I work,' he said. 'What other way is there to accomplish things? How do you innovate if everyone is resting? Everyone says that I'm married to my work.'

'Does your work think it's married to you?' It popped out like a bad joke, but Robert's ears perked up, so I had no choice but to say more.

'Is the marriage dependent upon work's consent? There's so much unrequited love in the world, after all.'

Our conversation would pause whenever Sam refilled our tea, resuming when she stepped away. Robert went on about egregious cases of laziness. As his rant continued, the black box seemed to be emitting some sort of light. I couldn't take my eyes off it. It was just a cube — at first glance, it looked like a napkin dispenser or a speaker. How on earth did it record Robert's violent utterances and convey them in human language? Danny looked at the black box throughout our conversation. An earphone sat in his right ear. Not his left.

'You must be curious about it,' Robert said.

'Yes,' I said. 'It's the thing that lies between us.'

'It's a good tool.'

When I asked Robert why he hadn't commercialised the device, he looked puzzled.

'Why does it need to be commercialised?'

The black box was a sort of Kármán line, Robert said.

'Kármán line?'

'Every day, you get a card showing "Today's Weather". The weather is something you're concerned about. My "Today's Weather" is a little different. I get the weather report for space. The Kármán line is the boundary between Earth weather and space weather, at the edge of the atmosphere. You mourn the dried-up sunflowers every morning, while I look at pictures taken by satellite. We have different domains. That means that our boundaries are different, too. Not just anyone can have my boundaries. They're perfectly tailored to me.'

Robert began to fold what he'd said in half, and then in half again, while I wondered how much the words shooting out of his mouth would have to be condensed in order to pass the Kármán line. To pare down what came from this arrogant, arrogant dog and toss it lightly into space. Thinking about it as the border between Earth and space calmed my dizzy mind. The idea floated in the zero gravity of my head. Big creatures didn't usually tremble. It was small beasts, the Roberts, that were sensitive.

Anyone who saw me and Robert would think that I was enjoying a lovely afternoon with my pet dog ... My reference for the image was a photo of David Hockney's studio in Normandy. In it, Hockney is sitting on a chair in his green garden. His eyes are on his canvas, and his dog Lucy looks into the distance, as if she's protecting him. Lucy is neither his guard nor his patron, but looking at the photo, I wondered if this is what people saw when they looked at me and Robert. There was an advantage to having a dog as my patron, maybe the only advantage: when we were together, what was his looked like mine.

Just then, the sun burst through the clouds, making our shadows more distinct. The floor of the greenhouse filled with delicate shadows that looked like they could be cut out with scissors. Robert's was the largest. His shadow grew wider and wider, hiding his true nature. It swallowed the blank spaces around it like spilled coffee. His shadow continued to widen as the angle of the sun changed. It swallowed a spiky palm tree and was approaching my shadow, which looked, comparatively, like an abandoned pile of crumbs. The black liquid — no, it wasn't a liquid, it was a gas. Before his shadow could swallow mine, I lifted my feet off the ground.

Robert sat at the table like a doll, oblivious to this silent typhoon. He seemed uninterested in me, bored, and yet suspiciously unable to end our teatime. A strange recess, that's what this was. The threads of time continued to unravel for so long that once I had finished digesting my snack in silence, I wondered if we were going to move right onto dinner. I was now counting the number of cacti in view, but each time I counted, the number was different. Cacti of various shapes and sizes helped me to view Robert as just one of many. Finally, I got up. My body, which had been attached to my chair for two hours, just barely separated from it. I had to take a few steps away from the table to reach the herd of cacti.

The plants were solid and beautiful. It was an exotic scene — nice to look at from a distance, but frightening to approach. One of the cacti seemed to want me to draw closer. It had an unusual flower at its top and a columnlike green body. The top looked like a grey mouse, or dried-out foam, or clouds. I decided to call it a cloud in my head. This cloud was covered with tiny needles, as densely packed as stars in the Milky Way. Someone said it was a mink cactus. The mink stood about as high as my collarbone, and when I stepped back, I realised it was shaped like a mink scarf. I tried to take a photo. I stretched out my arm, phone in hand. I just wanted to take a selfie — I wasn't trying to provoke anyone.

I felt a gust of air, and in the blink of an eye, a creature passed in front of me and pressed the button on my phone. It was Robert. He must have leapt off the table like a cheetah. If he hadn't, the distance would have been impossible for him to traverse so quickly. He jumped and licked me aggressively on the cheek. The interpreters got up from their seats simultaneously, and Danny tried to come between me and Robert. For a moment, all sound stopped, and I felt a crack widening in the silence.

Something had definitely broken. When I walked out of the greenhouse, I saw a bird on the ground. The bird must have mistaken the transparent glass for sky and crashed into its death. Robert enjoyed the sound of birds chirping when he was inside the greenhouse, but didn't care much about them dying outside it. He just kept staring at me. I couldn't remember how the meal had ended, but I could feel everyone's eyes on me as I wrapped the bird in a napkin and picked its body up off the ground. The bird was already dead, its body ever so small.

'It's still warm, isn't it?' Danny said. He told me there was a bird cemetery behind the greenhouse. I wasn't sure how many birds had died crashing into Robert Foundation windows, but I buried three more after that first one. Each time one died, Danny or Sam reminded me about the burial site, but they seemed unaware of anything they could do to prevent further deaths.

That was my hazy memory of the day I became one of the subjects of Robert's photography. Everyone around me said this would make things more complicated. They thought that genius dog Robert's photography needed to be protected, and that I'd goaded him into taking the photo. People would often try to get Robert to take photos on their phones, and the Foundation did their best to prevent them, but now it had happened anyway. All because I had wanted to take a selfie. Regardless of my intent, Danny and other Foundation officials considered me to be part of the art, not its creator.

'What, should I frame the picture?' I asked sullenly, wondering what could be wrong with taking a selfie on my own phone. Danny replied lightly that if I framed the piece, I'd have to title it 'Heart on Fire'. That was the name for mink-cactus flowers. Heart on fire.

The Robert Foundation's safety training had clear guidelines for mobile-phone use. 'Do not take photos on your phone in front of Robert.' Okay, but I had interpreted the warning to mean that we weren't supposed to take pictures *of* Robert. I had also read that I wasn't supposed to open my phone's camera when eating with Robert — if I'd followed that rule, this wouldn't have happened. But our meal that day had lasted too long, and Robert was the first to overstep boundaries. Exhausted by his lack of manners, I'd just tried to relieve some of my internal tension, and I could barely even do that.

Danny told me to send the photo to the Robert Foundation and then delete it from my phone. He said it politely, but it wasn't like I had a choice. I looked at the picture once more before deleting it. It was composed like a selfie, but Robert had rushed in like a storm, adding unexpected elements to the image. A strange sense of speed and a fearful expression on my face. I almost looked ecstatic, depending on how you looked at it. The photo was of *my* face, but I didn't want to stir up trouble, so I did as I was told.

It was only after this that I learned that his vision had

deteriorated in recent years, that he barely took pictures anymore and when he did, they were of inanimate objects. Sam explained this all to me, saying that this was probably why people at the Robert Foundation had grown careless about chastising me when they saw me take my phone out. When I asked her what she meant by 'inanimate objects', she clarified: 'things that are dead.'

'Still, everyone wants to be one of Robert's models. Obviously, right? Thanks to you, Robert is taking still lifes again.'

Her words didn't provide much comfort. Especially when I heard about the fate of Robert's photography subjects. One such subject was Rococo, the dead fish from the lake.

'The fish in my freezer?' I asked.

I didn't mean it as a joke, but Sam giggled.

'Oh, Ms An, you're an artist. You're a creature with a best-by date. A fish that's already dead is something different.'

Did that mean that as long as I stayed complacent, I'd end up no different from Rococo? Sam didn't seem to realise the implications of what she was saying. If she had, she wouldn't have told me that Robert hid the fish when the environmental research organisation came to collect it. Contrary to what Robert's letter had implied, it seemed that the organisation had, in fact, come to collect the contaminated fish, but Robert had told them that he'd lost it.

'Look at how he offered you such a treasured item as a welcome gift,' Sam said. 'Robert doesn't skimp on providing artistic inspiration.'

I thought about the 'gift' he'd left on my workbench and exhaled deeply. Sam must not have known the contents of Robert's letters — she was just the messenger. Or else she was growing careless from overwork. What she wanted to say was that, since Robert hadn't put me in the freezer yet, I was different from Rococo. When I asked, deflated, if there was anything else I needed to know, Sam shrugged.

'Look after your belongings,' she said. 'That's what I would do if I were you. You don't want to incite his kleptomaniac tendencies.'

The next afternoon, as I was looking for a missing sock, I received another letter from Robert, asking if I'd go on a walk with him. It was less of an invitation than an order. The letter arrived one hour before the time he wanted to meet, and read, 'Let's spend our time apart and then meet at five.' By the time I read it, it was past four and too late to turn him down. Was our 'time apart' a mere forty-five minutes? I spent another ten minutes rereading the letter. It didn't include an apology, but he did express a desire for reconciliation between us. The sudden change of tone was awkward, but I wanted to know what he would do next.

At 5.00 pm, we met on a walking trail that extended past the Foundation gates. It was a bit unusual that we were walking outside the Foundation grounds. Robert acted rather coldly — he didn't even greet me, which was odd, considering that he was the one who'd invited me on the walk. But the main difference from our typical walk was the leash. A leash was required outside the grounds.

Outside, Robert was one of many dogs. Passersby mistook me for a dog walker. They asked me how old he was and tried to introduce him to their own dogs. Whenever that happened,

Robert looked down and turned to stone. He tried to shut out all sounds. Still, he didn't ask to stop our walk. We continued for over an hour, proceeding into the vicinity like general inspectors. The farther we ventured from the Foundation, the more people we ran into who were unfamiliar with Robert. The chattiest among them was a man who said:

'He's very well behaved. Did you hire a trainer?'

Robert didn't greet the chatterbox, which seemed to surprise him.

He continued, 'I've never seen such a pretty papillon. I heard they're stuck up. They don't smell, either, do they? And they don't shed. My dog is no joke — look at him.'

The man pointed to a dog rolling around on the ground next to a dead rabbit. He looked appalled but said we couldn't forget this was a dog's natural instinct. All three of his dogs had good pedigrees, but they still did things like roll around in the mud.

'Robert is different from other dogs,' I said. 'He's won awards.' I was aware of Robert's uncomfortable expression. The chatty man nodded.

'My Mini has, too. And Fury as well.'

He took my statement lightly. His dogs and cats were award-winning, too. He didn't seem to be teasing. He mentioned another dog that had won awards. A dog from the shelter at the end of the trail, it had grown so popular that the man hadn't seen him recently. The chatterbox said he had rented the dog for a walk twice.

'They've got Boston terriers, Great Pyrenees, Dobermans, Cairn terriers, wire fox terriers, Jack Russell terriers, King Charles spaniels, pulis … Have you ever seen a puli in real life? You can't tell their front from their back. And bloodhounds! Those guys are real sniffers — they flap their ears as they smell. They get a little distracted on walks. There was a papillon, too, wasn't there? You should go check out the shelter.'

Mister Chatterbox stayed with us. He and his three dogs were an unwieldy group, inspiring me and Robert to increase our pace. As we walked, Robert's shadow turned into a dot. Based on its size, you would have assumed Robert was smaller than my hand-bag. But by the time we finished our walk and went back to the Robert Foundation, his shadow had started to grow larger. Like a sponge soaking up water, or an unfurling umbrella. I looked shrivelled by comparison. Small and insignificant, like a drop of water that rolled off an umbrella.

After that, we often left the grounds for walks. We rarely conversed while we walked together, so there was no need for the black box, and Danny didn't always accompany us. We were always followed by one or two security guards, but they made themselves scarce unless strictly necessary. One day, though, Robert and I got separated. The Korean–English interpreter was walking with us, and he somehow managed to drop Robert's leash at the exact moment that a group of dogs from the shelter gathered in front of us.

The dogs were restrained, but they didn't act it. Maybe it was because they moved en masse, but despite the silent trainer in front of them tightly clutching a dozen leashes, they seemed to be charging towards us. The interpreter was distracted, busy pressing buttons on his phone, and when his tether to Robert fell out of his hand, he floundered incompetently. A boisterous wave of dogs rolled around me, and I could barely see Robert in the mess. I heard someone shout, 'Got him! I've got him!' and then 'I've got the leash!' The interpreter sank to the ground and gestured for me to approach. After the dogs had passed us by like a dark cloud, Robert came towards me. A dog's leash rests in the hands of the walker, but you could also say that the walker's wrist is an extension of the dog. The question is whether the neck is being pulled by the wrist, or the wrist is being pulled by the neck. After the leash had been handed back to me, I felt it tighten around my right wrist. Quickly, I grabbed it with my other hand. Robert was pulling me, but when I accepted the situation, my tension eased into relief.

It was passersby who disturbed my nascent calmness. This time, I heard the sound of a radio growing closer behind me. When I turned around, I saw an old man about two metres away, holding what appeared to be a portable radio. I sped up, but the sound of the radio continued to follow me. The volume increased. What the heck … Despite my change in speed, this man and his irritating sounds seemed to maintain the same distance as ever. I wanted to flee before these unknown voices crashed into me like waves. Somewhere between fast-walking and jogging, I took one step, two steps — and still, the old man was right behind. He had begun to run, too. Was this a nightmare? I was responsible for protecting Robert. Where were the others? I was far from the beginning of the trail, but I could see another path stretching out to the right.

'Am I okay? Should I stop at the side of the road?' I said to no one in particular, but then Robert stopped walking and looked up at me. Yes, he looked up at me. The angle made me feel strange. Until now, we'd never been juxtaposed in this way. Whether I met him inside or outside at the Robert Foundation, we were always at eye level with one another. But now that I was looking down at Robert, I thought about how ridiculous it had been, all that accumulated discomfort. My fatigue evaporated. What was this little dog doing? Maybe this was all due to poor interpretation? Maybe deadly errors had occurred when going from Robert language to human language, and then from one human language — English — to another — Korean. Robert frowned, perhaps so I couldn't keep thinking this way. Or, no — it wasn't because of me, it was because of the radio behind us. When I reached the fork in the road, I turned right, but Robert, who was walking ahead, slowed down until I had stopped moving. He was like a rock. Then someone roughly snatched the leash from my hand. Danny.

'There's a person behind us!' I shouted, but when I turned around, the old man was gone. I couldn't see anyone.

I don't know if I can call that day's activity a walk, but my phone recorded my movements, and our trajectory vaguely resembled the shape of the letter Q. The short line turning the O of our path into a Q was thanks to Robert. Even after the walk ended, I could still feel the tension of the leash pulling at my hand, the weight of Robert stubbornly refusing to move. If Robert had pulled with any force, I might have fallen on my butt.

After that day, I never saw the Korean–English interpreter again. Danny said that he had been removed for failing to uphold his duty to protect Robert. His absence was surprisingly conspicuous — his freestyle interpretation had had a greater effect on us than I'd thought. Some might have seen his impact as a disaster lying in wait, but I thought that in some ways, he'd unexpectedly helped me and Robert. For example, when my sentence 'I painted a picture of *sangyeo nori*, traditional Korean casket performances' was translated from Korean to English, it became, 'I'm very interested in traditional Korean supercars,' and Robert was hooked. 'Supercar' was one of Robert's favourite words. He asked me several times about traditional Korean supercars.

'Is the Korean supercar you're painting from a long time ago?' he asked.

At the time, I had painted neither a Korean supercar nor a funerary casket, and I had no intention of doing so. I was so focused on this point that I forgot the content of the conversation.

In response, I said, 'Not from a long time ago — it'll be a modern supercar.'

The Korean word for modern, *hyundae*, sounded like the car brand Hyundai, so the interpreter thought I was talking about Hyundai Motors. Referring to Hyundai rather than modernity wasn't a small incident. The topic of funerary rites had now turned into a new supercar that Hyundai was making. Robert and I had the entire conversation without him realising that we were talking about different things. The story spread quickly.

'I'm sending you materials that will help with the storytelling in your painting,' people told me.

Car catalogues arrived from all over. It was absurd, but once funerals had turned into traditional supercars, and modern supercars had turned into Hyundai supercars, Robert's interest in me had reignited. I wrote notes about supercars on a pink Post-it note.

The new interpreter who arrived a few days later was, surprisingly, Director Choi. He compared the vestiges of the former interpreter to a field of landmines, and said that supercars were one of the mines. He asked what the story was with my collaboration with a supercar company and couldn't stop laughing when we realised supercar was a mistranslation of funeral performances.

'I get it,' Director Choi said. 'I listened to a recording of your conversations with Robert, and I know where the conversation got off track. He made a lot of arbitrary judgements, the last interpreter.'

I was a little embarrassed that he'd listened to Robert's and my most recent meal together, but Director Choi didn't understand why. I had never been told about these recordings. Shouldn't I have been asked permission to be recorded? But they (at this point, Director Choi seemed like multiple people) told me it was in the contract, that I must not have seen that clause.

'I received notice that the first meal could be used as materials for the Foundation,' I said. 'But I didn't hear anything after that. I had no idea that my meals and conversations would be recorded over such a long period of time.'

'The contract refers to "meals with Robert". Usually it's just one or two over the course of the residency, but you've ended up having many meals with him. So, according to the contract, we had no choice but to record. Can't you just think of it like CCTV? That's everywhere. It's not going to be shared externally, anyway.'

'Can CCTV record conversations?' I asked.

'What about black boxes in cars?' Director Choi said. 'We're so used to them that we forget they exist, and they're only opened in case of emergency. We need to replay the records, not just to see the dog's behaviour, but also to see human behaviour. It's for everyone's safety. I was just checking for misunderstandings between you and Robert.'

'So you must have heard what Robert said to me.' I lowered my voice and whispered, 'That it would be nice to have a lot of empty space in one's brain.'

'That was a rough translation. He didn't say anything problematic — the translation caused the trouble. You were talking about the empty fields you could paint, Ms An, and Robert asked his question because he was thinking about empty space. Anyhow, that was a mistake on the part of the Foundation. The interpretation wasn't smooth. This may have caused misunderstandings, but Robert is very skilled, Ms An. He stimulates artists' creativity by criticising and ignoring them. One has to admit that he's a clever muse.'

'… Okay.'

'The situation is like this: imagine you had to deliver chicken to building 3, unit 8, but the chicken still hadn't arrived. So, of course, you get a call from the customer-service centre. Is the chicken on its way or not? This is the situation we're in with you.'

'Director Choi, the Robert Foundation isn't my customer. You aren't, either. People here talk a lot about Jackson Pollock. But his paintings were finished in a single night after his sponsor had been asking about them for an entire *year*. I started to get grilled as soon as I got here. Grilled, that's right. Inside and out.'

'No, that's not what we're doing. This situation is different.'

'Obviously I'm not Jackson Pollock.'

'I'm talking about the contract that applies to you. You have a deadline, Ms An. And even before the deadline, you have the obligation — no, we have an agreement — that you'll update us on your progress as soon as possible. We have to prepare for your exhibition. This is your private exhibition. The Robert Museum of Art is having a private exhibition of *your* art. This is truly a huge opportunity. And Ms An, society is already shaking, thanks to all the meetings you've taken and all the statements you've made. We want to put an end to the rumours circulating about your art.'

Society was shaking? Hadn't they been planning for this from the beginning? I tried to imagine pressing down on my overflowing emotions with a heavy stone. The roiling feelings lost their strength under the weight of the stone and were flattened like a shadow.

'To sum up, Ms An, are you currently painting an empty field?'

'Recently, other than dog walks, I'm thinking of little else.'

It was true. I still couldn't escape the memory of that afternoon. I was fixated on the moment I had managed to grab, from a thicket of canines, the leash for a dog I'd guessed to be Robert. I even had a dream where the leash I was holding so tightly was cut. The leash was cut and I lost Robert, but then I realised that it wasn't my fault: it was actually due to a rip in his collar. Director Choi pulled out an iPad and wrote down 'empty field' and 'dog walks'.

'So shall we walk to one of the empty fields with a dog?'

'No, no, cross out "empty field". That's not what I'm going to paint, Director.'

'Okay, then I'll tell them that you're not painting an empty field. There were rumours that you'd been going to the fields a lot — is this a decision you made after visiting them? I heard that you visited the fields three times in one week, so we had great expectations for those places. We assumed you were going to paint them. There were especially high expectations for the airport. I'll let all the sites know, including the airport, that they unfortunately weren't chosen.'

I hadn't been visiting the fields, I'd just been practising my driving, but I told Director Choi to let the sites know. I turned the conversation to the dog-rental service.

'I've been thinking about painting something based on the shelter's dog-rental service,' I said. 'Maybe something like a "dog of the day" series …'

'Dog of the day?'

'It's like the drink of the day at a café. The dog of the day will be discounted. The dog-walking service is an extreme example of people's desire for instantaneous companionship. It's too much work to train them. People want their dogs to be like instant ramen — three minutes, and they're ready! It's a service designed to provide a faithful — no, efficient — sense of solidarity in a short period of time. So I'm giving it a more instantaneous flavour. The dog of the day: a category created for people who can't even be bothered to choose a dog to walk. Of course, the shelter doesn't have this option, but I'm imagining something pretty extreme.'

'Ms An, are you serious?' Director Choi dropped his pen on his iPad and looked behind him. 'Have you forgotten that Robert is a dog?' He tilted his head. Director Choi did not seem to approve of my idea.

'Ms An, weren't you going to paint the caskets? The ones that got mistranslated as supercars. What does this have to do with funerals?'

'They're connected in context,' I said. 'The dog of the day derives from the funeral performances.'

'The dogs derive from the funeral performances? Are they dead?'

'I mean the idea comes from the mistranslation.'

'Uh-huh … Ms An, are you joking?

'Have none of the artists here painted a dog before?'

'No, no — from what I understand, someone painted a portrait of Robert. But this is different, isn't it? It's the rental service, for the dog of the day.'

'It's not a Robert-rental business. What's the problem? Even if it were, that wouldn't change anything. I don't have malevolent intent, Director.'

Director Choi looked stunned, and his reaction inspired in me a mix of curiosity and fear. I hadn't thought long about the connection between the mistranslations and the dog of the day. They were just two threads I'd quickly tied together under pressure. The longer I dwelt on this impulsive combination, though, the better it seemed. It was a miscalculation to assume that Robert wouldn't like dogs escaping from funeral caskets.

Later, I got a message saying that he was curious about the idea.

My work unfolded for me as if I were searching for a lost sock in a huge pile of laundry. It was all that I thought about, all that occupied my hands. Robert, Danny, Director Choi, and I were sitting in the dining hall under a huge chandelier looking down on us like a spider. There was now one fewer in our party, but there was still the possibility of misunderstandings. Although Director Choi reiterated that we were talking about historical Korean funeral caskets and hearses, and not about Hyundai Motors' supercar, Robert clung to the word 'supercar'. It was conveyed to me that Robert just preferred to say 'supercar' rather than 'casket', so eventually Director Choi started to say it, too.

'I want to escape from this place in a supercar,' Robert said.

This time, it was me who said that we were talking about caskets, but Robert paid me no attention. I pulled up a slapdash PowerPoint I'd made explaining Korean funerary traditions, but he seemed completely uninterested. When I saw the figure decorating the front of the casket, I said how lovely it looked. I became fixated on it.

'There are many types of figures that decorate these caskets,' I said. 'People, chickens, animals like phoenixes. As I've said before, the phoenix is a sacred animal. It appeared not only on the caskets of kings, but also of commoners. It was originally a royal symbol, but the afterlife is egalitarian. The urge to decorate was stronger among commoners. These figurines had different roles, too — some would guide you to the afterworld, others would wait on you, and still others would entertain you …'

I kept talking because it seemed that Robert wanted to keep listening. Now words that I didn't remember existing in my pile of laundry started to come out of my mouth.

I had now received over sixty 'Today's Weather' cards delivered on silver platters. The weather had changed so much during the past two months that it was hard to believe that I'd passed through forest fires — fires that had made car tyres explode — to get here. It had snowed in September, and the next day the temperature exceeded forty degrees Celsius. And it wasn't just here; places all around the globe had broken thermometers. I had read news about the Siberian permafrost melting, and then about people caught in sudden floods. Extreme weather had led to other extremes, inertia dulling the initial shock. I was dulled, too. No matter the outside news, I found peace inside my studio.

As soon as I started to paint the 'dog of the day', time, which had formerly stagnated, started to flow freely and without leaks. The days were long but full, and I returned to the state I'd been in before coming to the Robert Foundation. Sometimes I lost a slipper, a sock, or even a pair of underwear, but I no longer endeavoured to find missing garments. Everything I had done here swirled around me like water being sucked down the drain, and one by one, I finished pieces on which I had previously made no progress. Pressed for time, I stopped running and practising driving. Occasionally I skipped meals.

Without taking a break, I finished five paintings. In the first painting, only the lower calves of a human and dog were visible. I painted a trail of footprints behind the human but no pawprints behind the dog. In the second and third paintings, too, I emphasised the lack of marks left behind by a dog on a walk. However, in these, I wanted the viewer's gaze to focus on a *kkokdu* — a traditional Korean guide to the underworld. Every canvas contained a different *kkokdu*, each with its own meaning. In the first, it was a shredded tyre; in the second, a buzzer; in the third, a K-pop star; the fourth, a credit card; and the fifth, a sunflower. I was able to paint more because I also stopped eating and going on walks with Robert. Maybe I was reading too much into things, but I wondered if the sudden end to the invitations from Robert was because he didn't want to disturb me. It piqued my curiosity about him once more. One day, I caught a glimpse of Robert staring in the mirror as if possessed. Was he looking at his reflection? Or perhaps through it? He seemed to be swimming towards an unreachable point inside the mirror. He must have seen my reflection in the mirror — he nodded briefly in greeting — but he didn't turn his head.

I also saw him chasing two robot vacuum cleaners. At first glance, they looked like three dogs running around on the marble flooring. Robert looked innocent, happy. One night, I briefly left my studio and came across Robert looking very *ordinary*. As I opened the studio door, I heard a rustling sound, but when I turned my torch in the direction of the disturbance, the dog froze. At first I thought it wasn't Robert because this dog wasn't wearing clothes, but it had to be him. What other dog would be around at this time? He quickly turned to look at me, and I saw reddish sauce on his muzzle. In his mouth were the bones from a fried chicken take-out I'd got from town that afternoon. In front of him was the plastic bag I'd thrown away. Chomping on the sauce-covered bones, he looked somewhat surprised to see me, but he gave no indications of aborting his feast. The expression he made right before sitting down was profound, one I'd never seen on him before. I quietly returned to my studio. I felt like I was in a dream. Not in my own, but in someone else's. Did this dream belong to me?

The dog could have died, chewing on chicken bones. The next day, when I ran into Danny, I informed him about the events of the night before. I was worried about Robert's health and mentioned that it was my fault for failing to properly dispose of the bag of chicken. Soon after, Robert's veterinarian visited and fortunately found no signs of chicken bones inside Robert's body.

'This must have been in the plastic bag,' Danny said.

I had seen the dog snacking on the chicken bones, but Danny thought that Robert must have been rummaging through the bag for a very different reason. He held out the bean-shaped button from my shirt. The one I'd mistaken for a tooth. I wasn't wearing the shirt it came from today, so I had no idea how the button had ended up in the plastic bag, but I didn't ask. I just needed to understand Danny's main point — that there was no way Robert would have been eating from a bag he found in the trash.

Danny mentioned that two artists had dropped out of the Robert Foundation residency mid-program. This was so unsavoury that no records remained of the artists' presence. One had left because of a problem with alcohol. The Robert Foundation agreed not to comment further on the matter, in order to protect the artist's image, but said that the situation had been deeply wounding and that they were nervous about something similar happening again. The warnings about vandalism posted all over my room had appeared after this artist's departure, but the problem hadn't been vandalism — it was alcoholism that had put Robert in danger. They didn't want a repeat situation.

Danny had found two empty cans of beer in the chicken bag, too, but that wasn't the only thing he was worried about. I'd got the beer when I'd serendipitously run into the Korean interpreter, before he'd been banished. There was nothing noteworthy about it. But how did Danny know where the beer had come from? I wasn't going to inform him about all my interactions with the interpreter. Not just because he'd been fired, but because of what he'd told me. He'd said, 'If you ever want to know what was said before it got edited, contact me.' When I asked why he was willing to do this, he said, 'Revenge — why else?'

'That walk wasn't the reason I was fired,' he added. 'It was the box — I tried to look inside. They saw that as an even bigger crime.'

'The box?'

'The interpretation box that Robert uses.'

'You looked inside?'

'I did, but I still don't understand how it works. No one understands that thing.'

'What did you see? Tell me exactly what you saw.'

'Just a few napkins. I thought I had opened it wrong. That couldn't be it.'

I stopped my reverie and told Danny I'd be more careful in the future. Danny had a bite mark on his arm. Where had I seen something similar? Oh, on the dog trainer. Of course, they were different people, but some similarities existed. It wasn't just their large frames. They both had low, gravelly voices. No, it wasn't that, either. The similarity that bothered me most was their penetrating gazes. They were also really good at avoiding *my* gaze. Danny asked me a question, and distracted, busy thinking of an answer, I failed to notice him move his arm behind his back.

Frankly, I didn't want proof that the owner of this place, the

Foundation president about to exhibit my art, my patron, was just another dog. But throughout the residency I had kept accidentally catching Robert acting in ways he never usually would. The most shocking incident occurred while I was painting the ninth piece in my series, *Give Me the Dog of the Day*.

I painted this piece on the patch of grass in front of my studio, my canvas lying on the ground. I always went for a walk before breakfast, when sunlight hadn't yet heated up the earth, or before dinner, when the light was waning. The place I'd chosen as my preferred workspace could have just as easily been someone else's preferred spot for an illicit nap. It was mid-September, and I was just finishing the painting when I heard a rustling sound in the distance. Two dogs were responsible for the noise, and I recognised one of them. Robert. He didn't seem to have seen me, but I don't think he would have stopped even if he had. He and the other dog were doing something sexual. The situation quickly came to an end, when the other dog, out of nowhere, flung itself at Robert. The dog began to growl menacingly, and I debated whether I should run up to help Robert while I could. I was still debating this when someone appeared. Again! It was the talkative guy.

The man crouched down, shouting his dog's name, and Robert ran up and jumped onto the stranger's lap. His behaviour surprised both the owner of the lap and the other dog, clearly Robert's enemy. Robert eventually hopped away like a rabbit and disappeared behind a palm tree. The chatterbox led his dog, who was barking like crazy, away from the scene. After everyone disappeared, I slowly walked out of the grass. That was when the worst happened.

Robert had come over to my painting and was pooing. His excrement landed on the left side of my canvas, right where I'd painted the *kkokdu*. It was the ninth *kkokdu*, Rococo, but now it was covered in Robert's poo. Rococo had turned into faeces.

A muddy pawprint would have been one thing, but poo? As I wiped it away with a napkin, I regretted not taking action sooner. I couldn't get the canvas entirely clean. God … I was about to cry. How could there be poo on my painting! How had this happened? I hurriedly brought the canvas and pile of napkins to my studio and spread them out. The more I looked at the mess, though, the more it seemed like this incident, this stain, would put an end to the incineration debate. It was starting to smell. I opened all the windows in my studio.

It was funny, when I thought about it. The idea that you'd paint something only to destroy it. There had to be some commonality between the previously incinerated pieces of art, something that had made Robert choose them. I tried to guess what that might be. What did this mishap mean?

On the other hand — what if I could get Robert to be interested in this ruined painting? Even if I covered the remaining streaks of excrement with another layer of paint, or managed to completely remove it, Robert would still recognise his handiwork. Was it a preposterous idea, trying to use this painting as my incineration offering? Surely Robert wouldn't want another collector to have a piece of art with his waste on it.

For Robert, incineration was a total act of preservation, of immortality. If he really cared about a piece of art, he'd burn it. It seemed to me that this painting could possibly be chosen for the opposite reason, too. Robert cared so much about dignity and class, maybe he'd try to remove not only the remnants of his waste on the painting, but also all possible proof of the accident.

No, Robert wasn't me. He wasn't a human, he was a dog. Wasn't that what the chatty man had said? That rolling around in shit was canine nature, and there was a limit to how much of their behaviour we humans could understand. These thoughts flitted through my brain and filled me with indignation, like the woman I'd run into on a walk a while back, the one who kept saying, 'Don't you know?' Didn't I know? Robert wasn't a normal dog. How could he, a patron of the arts, have pooed on an artist's painting? A painting the artist had worked so hard on?

I lined up the paintings I'd finished on the floor, took a few steps back, and examined them. I was frustrated to realise that the one that Robert had pooed on was the best of them. Poo on a painting … was it supposed to be a mark of one's territory? A streak extended above Rococo like a meteor. Should I try to cover it?

The poo that I'd scooped up with the napkins was now hardening. It was fairly damp in the area surrounding the studio, but the weather that day was extremely dry. The foul smell coming from the napkins proved that this wasn't a dream, that I couldn't just be a passive bystander. Was I going to throw the poo away, or save it?

Jun advised me to use a microwave if I wanted to slow the poo's decay. Microwaves sterilised things, he said.

'Of course, freeze-drying works, too. It would be like making fish or beef jerky. Moisture causes decomposition, so if you remove moisture from something, that stops decay.'

'Should I order a freeze-dryer instead of a microwave, then?' I asked.

'Would an online order even arrive? Deliveries aren't happening these days. Not in this area.'

'Then I'll go to the store and buy one.'

'But if you end up freeze-drying it,' Jun said, 'just know that it will shrink. The shape of the poo will change. Is your goal to preserve the poo, or to maintain its appearance?'

'Um, I don't want the freeze-dryer, then. I'll get a microwave,' I said. 'How do you know all this?'

'I played a role as a genius chemist. I had to do so much research for that role. Of course, I've never seen an experiment like this. Does the dog not eat dog food? That makes their poo dry. It sounds like this guy's poo is pretty moist.'

'He doesn't eat dog food so much as molecular gastronomy … Anyway, don't share this picture.'

The poo didn't have a name written on it, so there was no way to tell whom it came from. I put it in a paper cup and took it to the cafeteria. I was only going to use the microwave for a few minutes, but once I was standing in front of the appliance, I hesitated. Publicly microwaving excrement didn't seem appropriate. The cafeteria TV was playing news about 'zombie viruses' waking up in the melting Siberian permafrost. Maybe microwaving poo would sterilise it, but I didn't like the thought of putting food in there afterwards.

'Do you have any spare microwaves?' I asked.

The cafeteria employee didn't understand my question. In this space, where everything was perfectly arranged, there probably wasn't a surplus of anything, but I still asked if it might be possible to get a microwave for my studio. Soon after, Director Choi appeared and helped me out. A microwave from the cafeteria was moved to my studio. Director Choi talked about how microwaves had been developed as a result of wartime technological innovations. Tapping on the side of the microwave, he said, 'It's an honour for this to be used in the creation of your art!'

'Are you heating up paint?' he asked.

'No, instant rice.'

Director Choi smiled excitedly, as if he thought it was a funny joke. Something about my studio seemed inspiring today. Maybe it was the lights or the arrival of a combat microwave, but that evening my workbench really looked like a battlefield. Aluminium tubes of paint folded in on themselves, paint squeezing out of the cracks. They looked like low-lying soldiers, like casualties, like corpses.

I put the microwave to work at 11.00 pm. I placed the item in a plastic bag, set the microwave to thirty seconds, and pressed start. After taking it out, I set the item on a palette and sprayed it with formaldehyde solution. Next, I scooped it up little by little with a spatula and spread it on the canvas. I layered the concoction as if I were adding petals one by one to a rose, eventually creating a three-dimensional poo shape. The next step was coating the piece with resin. Overnight, the resin dried hard and clear. The poo was still poo, but it had undergone several steps to return to its original resting place.

Now it was time to coat my creation with varnish, the varnish that resembled Q City's sunlight. Varnish marked the completion of the piece. I put off this step as long as possible — it wasn't that you *couldn't* wipe or melt varnish off a painting once it had been applied, but people didn't usually apply it with the intention of doing so. Apart from when I had applied matte varnish to charcoal drawings to prevent smudges, I almost never used the substance. Fear of finality, I guess? But this time was different. I applied two coats of glossy varnish. This last step felt urgent. I used a narrow brush to cover the multilayered, uneven texture. I was careful with the bristles, to ensure that they didn't poke any holes. Maybe I was being paranoid. The finished piece looked like a curled-up soul. Imagine, calling a piece of poo a soul. No, it wasn't just poo anymore. The formaldehyde and varnish were the artwork's real coup de grâce. The new addition covered up my rendering of Rococo, but in doing so, it became a *kkokdu*.

I decided on the title *R's Poo*. I left the painting in my shady studio for several days to dry. I opened all the windows to let air pass through, but when I entered the building each morning, I still caught the odd whiff. The smell managed to pass through several layers of embalming. It was strong enough for humans to smell it, not to mention dogs, but on the day Robert was to choose art for the incineration ceremony, no one who entered my studio realised that part of this piece had started as poo. Of course, I didn't know what Robert was thinking. I took a few steps back so Robert could appreciate the paintings lined up on the floor. He walked up and down the row of canvases with his signature gait. His elegant movements resembled those of a runway model. After repeatedly standing in front of each painting, sniffing it, and moving onto the next piece, Robert finally sat down.

'This must be the piece he wants to incinerate,' Danny said.

He marked the bottom right corner of the painting with a

red stamp that read 'For Incineration.' This was the outcome I'd wanted. I'd succeeded in directing Robert to *R's Poo*. I didn't know it at the time, but Robert was particularly fond of the smell of formaldehyde. I later learned that it was one of his favourite smells. It all helped. I'd managed to protect my other nine paintings.

7.

I'd been cunning. Had Robert chosen the painting because of the formaldehyde smell? Did he make decisions that simply? I hadn't initially placed much stake in *R's Poo*, but when it was chosen for incineration, my doubts vanished. There was something I'd overlooked. It was easy to talk about creating a painting you didn't care about, but once you actually made it, feelings changed. I'd missed that. I thought I could sacrifice one painting to rescue the others, but in the process of seducing Robert with my sacrificial lamb, staring at that one painting longer than I'd stared at any of the others, I had grown attached. Could I really sacrifice it? Was I failing to recognise the real protagonist? The more I thought about it, the more jumbled my mind became. As I wrote my artist's statement, it became clear to me that *R's Poo* was the highlight of my *Give Me the Dog of the Day* series.

> I always choose the 'dog of the day'. The dog
> diligently follows a predetermined path, providing
> appropriate levels of tension and relaxation as we
> walk. It stays one step ahead of the human, but

doesn't stray too far. The dog knows to stop when the
human wants to take a picture or buy a coffee. It's
worktime now. The dog knows it's not time for play.
The dog deals with it, represses all desire for food,
sleep, or defecation …

Preparations for the exhibition were underway. There were
photos to take, frames to decide on, brochures to print, posters
and postcards and other marketing collateral to create, captions
to write — all sorts of decisions to make — but one thing in
particular caught my eye. Ten of my paintings were going to be
displayed, but we only had nine boxes for pieces that sold. There
were also only nine labels to be placed on the silver paper boxes.
The planning team hadn't prepared any spares. There was no
need. One of the ten paintings was destined for incineration.

I was allowed to store my paintings in the studio until the exhibition's opening. I was also allowed to keep working on the paintings.
They were still in front of me. Still, I could hear them slipping out of
my life. It made me feel even more affectionate towards them. One
evening, I bit my fingernails until they bled. One morning, I thought
about how, in order for my one-metre-square canvas to leave the
Robert Foundation campus, it would have to pass through six
different doors. What was I thinking? Of course, the route to the
incinerator was much shorter. You just opened the studio door,
then the door to the museum, which housed the incinerator, and
that was it. I wouldn't have to open those doors myself, either. I'd
do nothing, and when the time came, that would be that. But
I was sketching out another possibility, drawing another line of
movement for my painting.

'Over the past month and a half, artist An Yiji has completed ten paintings in a storm of creativity. Her process began earlier, in a summer marked by a heatwave and extensive wildfires. An's series *Give Me the Dog of the Day* brings to mind roads crowded with people evacuating their homes. Traditional Korean caskets are reinterpreted as supercars. Look at how An uses a Korean funerary procession to confess her desire to escape the here and now. Each of the ten oil paintings in this series contains a *kkokdu*, a "guide" to the underworld. These guides are willing to hop into a supercar to escape this terrible reality, to free themselves from the bondage of endless walks — even if that escape is a path towards death. Modern interpretations of the guides, from a K-pop star to a buzzer, resemble hoodoos — the tall, naturally formed columns of rocks that appear in canyons. The only difference is that An's hoodoos are not worn down by wind and sun. They stay with us, even when crossing the river of death. One such figure appears as a piece of poo. An titled this piece *R's Poo*. As we know, R is short for the fish that the Robert Foundation collected as a relic of the ongoing climate crisis. Rococo's poo will soon be nothing more than the tears of a weak creature driven from our burning planet. What we feel in front of Rococo's poo …'

This is how *R's Poo* was interpreted, by a rather famous art critic. I remembered that he hadn't expressed much interest in me when we'd met at a party in July. Of course, at the time, I hadn't started painting, and everyone I met seemed dubious about my qualifications. Maybe the inferiority complex I felt as a result had served as the opposite of rose-colored glasses sunglasses, keeping me in a perpetual state of disappointment, but his review had an entirely different tone from our earlier encounter. There were so many famous people at that party that I'd felt as ordinary as a streetlamp. A streetlamp devoid of energy, who went outside for a smoke and gave her fellow partygoers weird glances.

In response to my antisocial energy, the critic had said, 'I really loved your painting.'

What a ridiculous thing to say. I hadn't even started my work for the forthcoming exhibition. His words felt like a barb.

'A painting that I haven't painted yet?' I asked.

'I'll love it regardless!' he shouted seriously. I figured he must be drunk, but on the walk home, Danny told me that the critic really *would* love my paintings, that he had good instincts. My wearied spirit felt encouraged.

Now several months had passed, and I was afraid that he'd instinctively known what would happen. That no matter what I painted, if one of my creations was destined for incineration, I would suffer. Fuel for the Robert Foundation's incineration ceremonies came from the artists' minds.

Walking from my studio to my bedroom, I often came across mink cacti. After I noticed them for the first time, I saw so many mink cacti that I wondered if this place was getting overrun by the plants. During the day, they looked like normal cacti, but at night, they seemed to morph into long, spiky blobs before my eyes. I'd even tried to take a selfie in front of them. Of course, that was when Robert had crashed the picture, so it didn't turn out well. It was probably thanks to Danny's flowery language that the incident had felt intensely final, like the last photo of my life. 'Heart on fire' — what was that supposed to mean? At the time, the name had seemed to refer to love, but now it sounded like it signified loss.

•

No one questioned why I kept my paintings in my studio until right before the exhibition. This allowed me to continue to work quietly there. Ten paintings in total — plus a secret extra one. I had started the new painting off the record, one I could keep that resembled the piece destined for incineration. How could I not? I had taken a photo of *R's Poo*, and then a video, but they weren't enough. Was I the only person who wanted to make a copy of the painting to be burned, who wanted to keep it for myself? I was afraid my plan would be misunderstood, so I didn't tell anyone about it.

After I began this endeavour — better suited to a skilled counterfeiter — I slowly grew greedy. I had hoped that as I painted the fake, I'd fall in love with it, too, but that didn't happen. I pushed myself into work that was making me even more powerless. If an artist recreated a specific painting, the second and even third pieces weren't fakes. I'd never thought of them that way. But this was different. I had to replicate my painting with as few differences as possible.

After finishing this second painting, I would stamp 'To Incinerate' on it, but the copying wasn't the hard part. The problem was *R's Poo*. I didn't like to admit it, but poo was where this had all begun. It wasn't *R's Poo* unless the painting contained Robert's poo. The location and shape were important. In order to be the same as the existing painting, I needed to apply Robert's poo on top of the palm-sized depiction of Rococo in my copy. Other poo wouldn't do.

I tried placing the second painting on the grass, where the

first one had been defiled, but all that landed on it were a few flies. I couldn't rely on chance. Eventually, I decided to collect the poo I needed. Robert's was the goal, but I didn't see him poo anywhere. Of course, Robert had a bathroom that he used, and his poo had its place there. But getting his droppings on my canvas would be — how could I put it? — a rare, special feat? I was frustrated to realise that no matter how hard I tried, I'd never truly replace the original. No matter what I did, this wouldn't be *R's Poo*; it would just be a shadow.

My efforts to collect Robert's poo continued for some time. I could tell that the copy painting was drying fast, and I wondered if this ridiculous plan would really be my salvation. Everything here had its place — coffee cups, umbrellas, poo. My eyes were peeled, but I couldn't find anyone's poo, much less Robert's.

Eventually, I walked the trails like a sly hunter, carrying a few plastic bags and some of Robert's favourite cookies in my backpack. Maybe there was another papillon at the shelter. The same breed of dog was ideal, but if that wasn't possible, any dog that ate the same food as Robert would probably have similarly shaped poo, right? The dogs from the shelter supposedly didn't poo during their walks, but I'd witnessed an exception. If need be, I'd grab the trainer and tell him I needed dog poo. I ran towards the shelter.

Now that I'd painted the shelter, I had assumed it would become one of Q City's tourist attractions, but maybe that had been wishful thinking. Maybe they'd been pushed out because of the paintings, or hurt by my depiction. Anyhow, the shelter no longer existed. It was as if the place had evaporated. Q5, the guy I kept running into on that trail, told me that the shelter's management style differed from Q's, and as a result, they'd left. He said that Q was going to start a new dog-rental business, with better management. In response to rumours that the dogs were going to be the same as previous stock, Q5 said, 'The dogs unfit for walks were released before I got here.'

'But where did the dogs go?' I asked.

'I don't know. What's important are the remaining dogs. There's something I'm curious about, though …'

He seemed to want something else from me, so I slunk away.

I fell asleep wondering how I'd get hold of poo, and when I woke up, I continued to wonder. Robert's beloved cookies were harmless to humans. In my quest for his poo, I ate them myself, sniffed them, followed the trail with my body as low to the ground as possible. If not his poo, then anyone's would do. Just as I was tiring of his cheese-flavoured cookies, I did it. I acquired the poo!

I placed it in the microwave, covered it with resin, and stuck the poo to my canvas. I reenacted the creative process so diligently that I even repeated a mistake I'd previously made, where I knocked over a white plastic tub of formaldehyde. After that, I applied two layers of varnish, exactly as I had the first time. I even applied them at the same intervals as before. The sole difference was the owner of the poo. If only I could have forgotten that fact!

At first glance, the colour of the poo was the same as the original. (I was sad to have started using the term 'original'. Oh well.) Its ingredients were the closest to the original that I could find. This should have been Robert's poo. If the desperation of a soul could be measured, the forgery (I used the word, yes, but I didn't mean to deceive anyone) would be much more desperate than the original. But so what? What next? I was running at full speed towards a wall. I felt like I was going to cry. The smell coming off the painting tickled my nose, and I kept sneezing. Outside, I heard a knock.

'Is there a problem?'

It was Sam's voice. I quickly hid the painting behind the door, and Sam asked if I was okay. It was definitely not okay to have someone get this close to me right after a sneezing fit, but I just said I had allergies. Sam nodded and scanned the interior. Ten paintings were lined up against the wall. One emitted the suspicious smell that was still irritating my nose.

'Wow, is this the incineration piece?' Sam asked. 'The one Robert picked?'

She seemed pleased, as if her own good taste had been confirmed. Pointing to *R's Poo*, she asked if it really was poo. 'People have been saying it's made from Rococo's poo,' she said, 'but surely that's not true.'

'This is a secret,' I replied, 'but it's actually Robert's poo.'

Sam giggled.

'You don't believe me?' I asked.

'I want to believe you,' she said, 'but it doesn't make sense. You can't just collect Robert's poo.'

'Can't you get hold of anything you need?'

'There are a lot of things I don't have access to. Anyhow, I like the line you painted over the poo. My favourite piece of poo art is by Manzoni. He canned his own poo. Wait, this poo isn't yours, is it?'

'If I said it was, would you believe me?'

'I'd believe you,' Sam said, smiling. Then she told me that Robert had collected a few pieces by Manzoni.

'Really? Have you seen them? What are they like?'

'They're cans, unopened.'

'Someone opened one once,' I said. 'Did you know that? Guess what was inside? Another can! It was sealed, too. But why does Robert collect art if he's just going to burn it?'

'Well,' Sam said. 'He doesn't burn work by famous artists.' Then she quickly added, 'Oh — I didn't mean it like that.'

I nodded.

'What I mean,' Sam continued, 'is that Robert burns art by new artists to make a name for them, and he collects art by artists who already have a name. We've collected so many pieces thanks to Mr Waldmann.'

'Where are they?' I asked.

'In the storage room.'

Sam didn't know the exact location of the storage room.

'Anyway,' she said, 'you'll become famous, too, when you finish the residency. Then, someday, Robert will buy your work at a high price.'

'I guess that's just around the corner,' I replied. 'Keep your eye on these paintings.'

Sam didn't seem to notice that one of the paintings was different from the one she'd seen the other day. Her lack of reaction convinced me. It told me what I really wanted. I hadn't intended to deceive anyone — I thought I was copying the painting just for myself — but did I still feel that way?

This was my chance. The original and the forgery were both within my reach; all I had to do was switch them. The exhibition

team was supposed to come to my studio the next morning, at
11.00 am. That was when I'd send off the forgery instead of my
original painting — but I couldn't. Was I hesitating because the
new painting wasn't dry yet? No, that didn't explain it. I wasn't
worried the forgery was bad, either. I was anxious about interven-
ing in the fate of the art in front of me. What if I messed up? I
was still hesitating when the planning team came and left with the
original. After all ten paintings had left the studio, I quietly took
out the forgery. It had missed its opportunity. The two paintings
looked almost identical, down to the dead flies stuck to both
canvases.

On the second Friday of October, at 6.00 pm, the exhibition
began. The incineration ceremony was scheduled for 6.00 pm on
1 November, and I had to check out of my room on 4 November.
The gate closest to the museum entrance stood wide open. A series
of small signs guided visitors from the car park to the museum.
Some had flown in from Europe and Asia on Robert's invitation.
Nearby hotels filled with people from all over the world. Even
if it meant they had to come to Q, they didn't want to miss an
opportunity to gather like this.

The dog shelter reopened just in time. They actively promoted
their dog rentals with the slogan 'We succeed whether you like it
or not.' The business was called Dog of the Day. They catered
to walkers' exact preferences: size, preferred breeds, personality,
colour, sex, whether they wanted the dog to be wearing clothes,
whether they wanted the dog to be wearing shoes. Soon after they
filled out a form, the perfect dog appeared. Banners hung at the

waiting room read, 'What kind of dog you want tells us what kind of person you are.'

If you didn't care enough to specify, or if you believed in fate, you could choose the most basic product, the dog of the day.

The opening reception of the seasonal artist-in-residency exhibition attracted as much attention as the incineration ceremony later would. I wore an orange suit and light-blue sneakers. They were colours that said, from a hundred metres away, that I was the main character. But I didn't feel that way. My mind parted from my body and drifted through the museum. Past the emergency exits, hidden stairs, and unknown walkways. When I thought about how little of the museum I knew — whether that was because these spaces hadn't been introduced to me or because they were actively hidden — it became clear that I wasn't the main character of this exhibition. The real protagonist was *R's Poo*. A bodyguard had been hired, and it wasn't me they were protecting. I was far less important than my paintings. Maybe I was the person they were protecting the paintings from. But as the party continued, these thoughts dissipated, and I returned to my body and my orange suit. I even spoke. I talked about how Q had inspired my work, and how I had processed this inspiration.

On the day of the reception, people gathered in front of the pizza oven in the corner of the museum. As people gathered, the location transformed from an unnoticed corner to the centre of the building. I noticed that the formerly dusty oven was now sparkling clean. This was the tomb where my painting would be incinerated. *R's Poo* was one hundred centimetres by one hundred centimetres, and the pizza oven could hold up to 1.5 times that size. It was easy to imagine the scene: *R's Poo* placed on a wide square shovel, pushed deep into the pizza oven. Even when I tried to stop imagining, the inside of the oven showed up in my dreams each night. Paint layers on canvas swelled up like pizza toppings and burst repeatedly until they were nothing but ash.

In the first week of the exhibition, nine of my paintings sold. The tenth, of course, wasn't for sale. The paintings would be sent to their collectors upon the conclusion of the show. Round red stickers appeared under each of the nine paintings to indicate that they were no longer for sale.

There was a different sticker under *R's Poo*, one that read TO INCINERATE. It was an amazing phrase. Visitors asked incredulously, 'This one isn't for sale?' Some asked, 'Can I buy it on discount?' as if it were some kind of joke. Most of the visitors knew much more about the museum than I did. They told me stories that started with, 'The artist at the last incineration …' Apparently, one artist had danced. Some sang, others cried. Later, a woman with red hair pointed at *R's Poo*. She looked like she wanted to say something, so I cut to the chase.

'Please don't say you want to buy this!' I said.

She said it anyway: *I want to buy this piece*. This was her second time visiting the exhibition; I remembered her from her ponytail. She had stood in front of *R's Poo* for a long time the previous day. We talked briefly about the painting, and the conversation went in a predictable direction. I knew the trajectory, down to when she would say she wanted to buy the painting. It was a conversation that had been repeated countless times since the beginning of the exhibition; by now, it was almost a performance. I would point at the incineration sticker and say in a joking tone, 'I wish I could sell it,' and then the other person would laugh knowingly. But this woman didn't. She asked me seriously, 'You *wish* you could sell it?'

'The painting's not for sale,' I said. 'Haven't you been to the Robert Museum before?'

'I've heard about burning the art, but you're really going to do it?'

'Well, I don't have a choice, do I? The incineration is meaningful, and I agreed to it.'

The woman nodded, with a confused look. She drew closer to me and whispered, 'Have you heard? The piece of art that gets burned in the incineration ceremony always ends up being the artist's best work. You might become well known after this, but they say you'll never paint anything as good again.'

'That's sad.'

'Of course it is. P. Wharton regrets not opposing the incineration ceremony earlier.'

'Do you know him personally?' I asked.

'We meet periodically. We've done one individual exhibition, and we're preparing another. He was such a model artist-in-residence. He should have been a thief instead, stealing the piece that got incinerated to keep for himself. Of course, his art is still wonderful, but we all know the truth. His best work is nothing but ashes.'

At that moment, Director Choi approached me, so I brightened my expression. The woman handed me her business card while pretending to take out her sunglasses. The gesture was secretive; my heart rate sped up just accepting the business card. As Choi grew closer, the woman started to give her impression of the piece using flashy and lengthy words. When I told her I only understood half of what she was saying, Choi explained it in simpler language. But my mind was elsewhere. Maybe the woman's was, too. Soon she was gone — the last visitor of the day. When she left the gallery, Choi flipped the sign on the glass door from 'Open' to 'Closed'. It was a two-sided triangular sign; when it read 'Closed' from the outside of the building, it said 'Open' on the inside. My side was open. The closure of one world signalled the opening of another.

The woman did not return to the exhibition after that. The words she'd whispered as she handed over her business card kept replaying in my ears.

'I want to rescue this painting,' she'd said. The word 'rescue' embedded itself inside me. She wanted to rescue it? Because if not, I'd never make art this good again? Was this a curse? After hearing her warning, the paintings hanging in the exhibition hall gained an air of unfamiliarity. It was as if someone other than me had created them.

The woman was an art dealer at S Gallery in London. Her gallery had been making waves in the art world in recent years. Artists that the gallery discovered sold their work at very high prices. S had also turned the auction market upside down when it found that certain 'forgeries' of pieces by well-known artists were in fact genuine. S Gallery had become known as a trustworthy source for verifying art authenticity. When they signed a contract with an artist, they documented everything meticulously. Among their precautions were stipulations on how to deal with damage. Oftentimes, artists wanted to restore damaged work themselves, but S Gallery was so trustworthy that artists allowed S employees to complete restorations for them. Of course, S Gallery didn't match the prestige of the Robert Foundation, but both institutions had attracted attention for their unconventional methods. The difference was that, rather than incinerate art, S spread rumours about it. They were known for their guerrilla marketing events and fearlessness about stirring up controversy. A business that shook up existing authority was now talking about 'rescuing' my art.

Two weeks went by. Visitors tried to imagine me at the incineration ceremony. 'What are you going to wear?' they asked.

I said I'd wear black, until one visitor advised me, 'The incineration ceremony takes place around sunset, and black vanishes in the dark. You should wear bright, intense colours.'

I promised I would. I kept expecting the art dealer from S to return, but she didn't. It felt as if I'd lost my page in an interesting book I was reading.

Once I found my page again, the plot of the book went in a completely different direction from what I'd expected. Jun came to the museum a week before the exhibition ended. Sam recognised him and called him 'Mr Umbrella'.

'It's not over until it's over,' she said. Jun assumed she was talking about the exhibition. I thought she was saying something about my relationship to Jun.

When I told her this, Sam laughed and said, 'I was talking about what will happen to the empty fields.' The abandoned airport wasn't an airport anymore, and now it wasn't even a landmark. I hadn't revived the land Sam had invested in with my paintings. Was Sam the only person I'd disappointed? Exhibition visitors now saw that Q's Art Highway wasn't nearly as speedy — not nearly as impressive — as the people of Q wanted us to think. They could finally see the ridiculous, frightening, and secretive madness that surrounded us. I wanted to run as far from the museum as possible.

Rain started to fall, so Jun and I walked one of the trails carrying our one-time saviour, the black umbrella-slash-knocking device.

'You mentioned two artists who left the Robert Foundation residency before completing their contractual obligations,' he said from under the umbrella. 'One was the guy with alcoholism. Do you know what happened to the other person?'

I shook my head.

After a short pause, he said, 'They ran.'

'They ran?'

'Yeah, they ran away from here. With their art.'

'They stole the art? The piece that was supposed to be burned?'

'That's right. The residency contract has probably got stricter since the incident. No one knows the artist's real name, but I heard they're in touch with an auction house in Hong Kong.'

Rumour also said that the piece had actually been burned in the incineration ceremony, but it survived. Neither the auction house nor the Robert Foundation would confirm or deny the rumour, which meant it had to be true. Several curators clearly remembered seeing the piece at the Foundation exhibition a few years back. It would have been a clear breach of contract if the art had been released into the world instead of being burned.

'But you couldn't sell the art right away after something like that happened,' I said. 'You couldn't even show it in public.'

'You mean because the statute of limitations wouldn't have expired yet?' Jun asked.

'But if the incident wasn't reported,' I said, 'I guess no one would know. The Robert Foundation hasn't publicly responded to this theft, has it? I think the people here are pretending the incident didn't happen because they want to save face. Anyway, where did you hear about this?'

'The movie director.'

'Oh, I don't know if I trust him.'

That's what I said, but the story Jun had told me started to grow in my mind. It moved like the tendrils of a vine, or the legs of an animal. I thought about my contract with the Robert Foundation. How much would it cost me to cancel the contract? Would the damage be financial only? There was a clause that said that if the contract was cancelled, all the works painted during the residency had to be returned to the Robert Foundation. So if you fulfilled your contractual obligations, you'd only lose one piece — to incineration — but if you gave up in the middle, you'd lose everything. Of course, you weren't allowed to sell the paintings if you left early, either. That's what the contract said. This was probably why the previous resident had absconded.

'I don't like adventure,' I said. Jun hadn't asked if I did, but I said it anyway.

'Are you forgetting that we had to cross through forest fires to get here? Remember the dog attacking you?'

'Those were dire circumstances. I don't have a sense of adventure, unfortunately.'

'Why did I tell you about this, An Yiji? Because you're already mid-adventure. Someone told me they wanted to meet you. They specifically said they wanted to meet the artist An Yiji.'

'Again?' I asked. 'Is it another film director?'

'No — did you see the news about the CEO of Um Corporation jumping off a bridge? Well, he did. So now we're not going to be able to get them to fund the movie. We're going in a different direction with funding. Anyway, someone wants to meet with you. I think they'll give you an offer you can't refuse.'

'Are they an art dealer?' I asked.

'I don't think so?'

'Then who in the world could it be?'

'Bill Mori. The guy you told me about. The photographer.'

It turned out that *Bill* was the artist who'd run away from the Robert Foundation. Bill Mori, the photographer who had filed a lawsuit against Robert. I was surprised to hear that he had participated in the Robert Foundation's residency program, much less that he'd run off. The title of the proposed movie, starring Jun, was *Elk with Tyre*, and it would be 'based on the power of truth'. The director had emphasised the power of true stories several times on the day we met.

'If you say "based on a true story",' he'd said, 'that's game over. I only watch *real* stories. Not the news, but stories.'

Jun and the director had found Bill, now the only person who could tell us about Robert in his youth. The lodge manager had passed away. Bill wanted to meet the Robert Foundation's current resident. I didn't know why.

●

I only had one day off during the three-week exhibition. I used that day to see Bill. We met at the shopping mall Jun and I had visited on our way to the Foundation. The mall had been partially damaged by the fires but remained open for business. Driving there was a bit of a challenge, but I managed. In the car park, Jun admired the Lamborghini. He kept glancing at our surroundings.

'Why are you so nervous, Jun?' I asked. 'I'm the one lying to the Robert Foundation.'

'Because I'm an actor!' he exclaimed. 'Are you not worried? I shouldn't have said hello to that old lady earlier. What if she recognised you?'

'We were talking about parking.'

'We shouldn't be interacting with people,' Jun said. 'You stand out too much. Why did you drive such a flashy car to a secret meeting?'

'She's an old lady in the middle of nowhere,' I said. 'She doesn't know anything about cars.'

'Maybe she has a really good eye.'

'Do you think she's memorising licence-plate numbers? All she'll remember is an orange car. You're worrying too much. It's too much.'

'What if, when she turned around, she pressed a button on her glasses frames and started recording us? And why are you underestimating old ladies who live in the countryside? My mother is in her eighties, and she knows all about the newest cars.' Jun chuckled.

He looked a little excited and began to ramble about what we would do if something happened. I gave him a nod, but I still thought it was a little over the top. Jun's phone rang, and he seemed so surprised to be getting a call that when he picked up, he couldn't even give his rehearsed alibi. It was the production company. Apparently, some old lady at the shopping mall had just tagged him in an Instagram post. I found the post and saw that I was in the picture, too.

The caption read as follows: 'This model of car will be released early next year. Only six of them sold worldwide. Lots of trunk space. Good for moving. A car from heaven. This is the second time I've seen it this year. Same owner both times? Two people who speak Korean.'

'We've been caught,' Jun said. He moaned that his first scandal in years was about to break. Still, he looked excited. We walked to the spot where we'd agreed to meet Bill, peering at our surroundings like spies in a movie. Then we saw someone who looked much older than he had in the articles I'd read. He was sitting with a plate of doughnuts in front of him. It was Bill.

Jun described the movie's plot. The main character goes on a trip to a US national park to take a photo of an elk that he's heard is running around with a tyre around its neck. Witnesses say that the elk — who's been dubbed 'Tyre' — has been wearing the tyre around its neck for almost two years, but as it turns out, there are actually several elks with the same strange get-up. No one really knows how long they've been wearing tyres on their necks, but by the time the protagonist gets to the park, one of the 'Tyres' is no longer. The elk ran away when it was first spotted but was eventually rescued by wildlife patrol, who removed the tyre before returning it to the wild. Other travellers tell the protagonist this story. The protagonist exclaims that it's fortunate the elk was rescued, but he can't hide his disappointment. Another character approaches the protagonist and tells him to look on the bright side.

'This means that any elk you see might have been a "Tyre",' he says. 'I don't want to undermine that possibility.'

The main character decides to think this way, too. 'Tyres' are now everywhere he looks. Everyone could be a tyre …

I knew where the story was going, but then Bill said it directly. 'Is it Robert?' he asked.

Bill had been looking into the distance as he spoke, but now he stared at me. He drilled into me with his gaze.

'There are several animals besides the elks with tyres around their necks that could be considered "mascots" of this area,' Bill said. 'There's Brighty the donkey, on the North Rim of the Grand Canyon, and Robert on the South Rim. I've met them all, and I have a lot to say about Robert. Our relationship is an interesting example of how a copyright dispute can play out. I lost half of my life to that dispute.'

He told his story, assuming that I already knew what had happened between him and the Robert Foundation. Of course I knew. There were two things I wanted to ask him. First, how he had fled, and second, how he had sold his art after running away. Bill began his tale at the point where he was making a name for himself as a wedding photographer. Whenever doughnut crumbs fell from his fingers on his plate, Bill pressed down with his thumb and picked them up again. He kept saying, 'I collected all sorts of data. I was meticulous.'

I just wanted to gather information about Robert, but Lina

appeared first in Bill's story. According to Bill, the woman in *Canyon Proposal* was neither missing nor dead. The woman wasn't Lina, but a completely different person.

The woman who'd actually stood in a wedding dress in the Grand Canyon at dawn didn't hate the fact that she had been mistaken for a millionaire heiress. She couldn't reveal herself as the subject of the photograph, because she didn't want her husband to know what she had been doing. Instead, rumour spread that the woman in the picture was Lina, and this became an important alibi for the woman. Later, even *she* came to see the woman in the photograph as someone other than herself. She was surprised by how quickly she believed that the woman was Lina. The clothes she'd worn in the photo were from Lina's dress shop, so all she had to do was keep quiet, and *Canyon Proposal* would belong to someone else. She kept quiet for a long time. That is, until she met a persistent, pitiful man named Bill Mori.

'Of course, I learned all of this after Robert fell in with Mr Waldmann. I even collected transcripts of the woman's testimony from some Las Vegas detectives, from when they interviewed the real woman in the picture. I told Mr Waldmann the truth, I said, look — this isn't your daughter, this was all a misunderstanding. His reaction was completely unexpected. It turned out that he already knew. I don't know when, but at some point he had realised that the woman on the cliff was not Lina, but some random woman living in precarity, running from huge amounts of debt. Mr Waldmann gave the woman money. They helped each other out.'

'What about the real Lina?' I asked.

Bill laughed, aghast. It almost sounded like he was crying.

'The real Lina is so weird,' he said. 'Once you've heard the whole story, you'll feel the same way. Who was the real Lina, anyway? As you know, Lina was found dead in Joshua Tree National Park. She was found with a man Mr Waldmann had disapproved of. I don't know how they ended up there, but there are a few possibilities. There were several people who got lost and died of heatstroke out there that year. That summer was especially hot. Before Lina was found, the authorities discovered the bodies of several drug smugglers. What bothered Mr Waldmann most was the idea that the lovers had *decided* to die. How could they believe that this was the only solution to their problems? Lina's friend and business partner was interviewed several times about whether Lina had shown any signs of distress.

'Anyway, after the story went public, the wedding-dress boutique's sales soared. People were quite literally wearing the story on their backs. That's the part that I focused on. The fact that the subject of this photo, the person who made me both famous and unlucky, was not Waldmann's daughter Lina. That means that the photo Robert took wasn't of Lina, and there's no reason why it would be special to Mr Waldmann. Mr Waldmann's initial feelings towards Robert were gratitude for capturing one of his daughter's happiest moments. What did it mean if that wasn't his daughter in the picture? It meant that Robert and Mr Waldmann had no reason to be together, and that our lawsuit over the picture didn't have to drag on as long as it did. If people knew the photo wasn't of Lina, I wouldn't be as tired as I am. I wanted to get back the time I'd lost. So I collected all the data I'd found on the case and showed it to Mr Waldmann. Do you know how much time he gave me? Five minutes! Five minutes after showing up at Mr Waldmann's door, I was starting my car again. I thought to myself, this man is *choosing* the story he wants to believe. He said it was real, and he made it real. The person behind the story is Waldmann. He made it happen. He grabbed a hold on the rock wall in front of him and just started climbing. Robert was the perfect hold. He used Robert to prove that the woman on the cliff was Lina.'

I thought about the study full of Robert's collectibles. I'd seen some of the accessories found at the site of the cliff photo shoot among them. Sam had even shown me the pieces, one by one.

'What was it like for Mr Waldmann to have Robert picking up Lina's things all the time?' I asked.

'Mr Waldmann was trapped in the story he created,' Bill said. 'He blocked off the exits himself. What he described as Lina's scent lingering on the accessories was probably the smell of the other woman. Or of someone else entirely. Robert faithfully sniffed them all, picking them up with his mouth as a dog is wont to do. One day, Lina's cigarette; the next day, her cardigan; the day after that, her pillow. Mr Waldmann embraced this and decided to remember his daughter in a world he created. He'd moved his daughter to such a comfortable place in his mind. Isn't it amazing? Lina must have only been in the national park for a few days before she died — why would she have left so many things behind? It's because Mr Waldmann had already decided on the resolution to the story. These were Lina's clothes, Lina's cigarettes, Lina's socks. Whatever Robert brought him became Lina's. It became an unspoken rule between the two and made them inseparable. They had no need to separate. They ended up believing the story. Their centre of gravity had shifted, and there was no going back.'

As he spoke, Bill tilted his body towards me, then drew back. The smell of alcohol hit my nose.

'During those five minutes,' Bill continued, 'Mr Waldmann expressed very little interest in what I showed him, but I did feel him glare at me. The woman who was mistaken for Lina appears to have stolen her wedding dress, I said, although she claimed it was a gift. She'd told me that herself, but I didn't believe her. The person who'd actually purchased the dress never got their order — how else can you explain it? This was something only people who knew that the woman in the photo wasn't Lina would care about. Waldmann said that the woman and Lina might have met in person. Maybe my daughter gave her the dress as a gift, he said. She was that kind of person. So I asked, do you think she gave this woman the dress as a gift on the way to deliver it to the actual purchaser? Then Mr Waldmann looked at me with contempt and said, "Someone like you will *never* understand our relationship." That was it. I keep thinking about how Mr Waldmann must have filled in the blanks in his mind after I left. He must have thought about the real likelihood of Lina and the woman posing as Lina actually meeting, and why Lina would have gifted that woman a wedding dress.'

Canyon Proposal and *Robert in the Canyon* were photos intimately connected to the Robert Foundation. Bill's story argued, though, that they told an entirely different person's story. If the subject of *Canyon Proposal* wasn't Lina, then Mr Waldmann had to accept that the end of the story was that his daughter had been found dead in Joshua Tree National Park. Did he accept it, though? Some people lived their lives trying to change the past rather than the future. Mr Waldmann had been one of them. Was it reckless to dream about a life that had already ended? Was it hopeless to try to change the direction of time?

'He must have needed a raft to cross through the darkness,' I mused.

'A fake raft,' Bill shot back.

'Even if it's fake, even if it's made of sparkly sugar and about to melt, someone might still be in desperate need of it.'

'The dog must have been the carpenter of the raft.'

After saying this, Bill quietened for a moment before speaking again in a furious voice.

'I've lost touch with the other woman, by the way. I don't know if she's dead or alive. And the manager of the lodge was killed in a car accident a while ago. You think that was a coincidence? I'm telling you, Waldmann was a scary guy. He was afraid of darkness, so he got rid of everything that contradicted what he decided to believe. I got that within five minutes of meeting him.'

'You had this five-minute meeting with Mr Waldmann,' I said, 'and then you were invited to participate in the Robert Foundation's residency program?'

'That was after he died.'

There was no way to know whether Bill had been invited because the Foundation wanted to support his photography career or because they had ulterior motives. Bill said that he knew Robert was trying to break him. He'd accepted the invitation with the intention of butting heads. After infiltrating the walls of the Robert Foundation (Bill used that word, infiltration), he was surprised by the extreme hospitality he was shown, and grew disappointed and angry once again. Bill clearly hadn't adjusted well.

'Was Robert the problem?' I asked.

'No, I didn't even meet him. But he was everywhere. The space was suffocating. How else could I have felt, sleeping in that room under *Canyon Proposal*? I had nightmares every night.'

By the time the exhibition began, Bill was planning his escape. To be precise, he was taking back what was already his. In the process, he came across the remnants of another world. When he entered the museum through a side door, he found a collection of stone heads, stamped with an incineration notice. He immediately knew that it was the work of the resident before him, the art that was meant to be incinerated. Why were sculptures that had been publicly burned so intact? They weren't even covered with soot — like magicians who used secret escape routes to get out of boxes alive.

Our lives can look completely different depending on the details we add to them. Bill, too, had chosen the details of his life. He had never doubted the incineration ceremony, but the ghostly appearance of art that wasn't supposed to exist had caused him to grope in all directions outside the frame he'd been looking through. Bill's story headed in one direction: where did the art that Robert incinerated end up?

'There was that article about Robert's aesthetics. It's ridiculous. Is everything Robert's decision? What if he's forced to maintain some system of aesthetics in order to get fed? Or he's hit when he doesn't act elegantly enough. What if there's some kind of abuse going on?'

Bill took a napkin out of his shirt pocket. He pressed a stamp onto a drawing of the Robert Museum of Art's side door, which had been scrawled on the napkin.

'This was Robert's seal — his pawprint — at the time,' he said. 'Don't ask me why I have this. There are a lot of rumours going around, but I didn't leave the museum with my art. What I took with me was this.'

He held out the napkin.

'Compare this to all the pawprints on art in the museum,' he said. 'They're not the same.'

Forty minutes passed. Only forty minutes, but it felt like several seasons. When I asked Jun what role he was going to play in the movie, he said 'Driver 2'. It would be his most important role to date.

'So you'll be driving somewhere in a car?' I asked.

'No, I'll be waiting,' Jun said. 'For my boss.'

'And?'

'I'll wait, but the boss won't come, so I'll just sit in my car. The boss won't show up until the end of the movie, so there'll be no reason for me to drive away.'

'What are your lines?'

'I don't have any.'

'You don't have any lines? But you said this will be the most important role you've ever played.'

'I won't need to say anything — I'll have a lot of screen time.'

We walked back to the parking lot.

'What I don't understand,' Jun said, 'is that Bill said that he

didn't take his art out of the museum. He didn't take the incineration piece.'

'Yes,' I replied. 'He was about to steal his own art, but then
he saw the sculptures by the other artist. So he stole Robert's seal
instead. Why didn't he end up taking his art with him?'

I took the napkin out of my bag and unfolded it. Robert's
pawprint was stamped on the paper.

'Did Robert put his pawprint there because he knew what Bill
was trying to do? Or maybe he had no idea. I don't know. But it's
too much of a coincidence that the collection of sculptures was
right there. Does Bill expect me to go look for his possibly burnt,
possibly surviving photograph? I'm suspicious about why Bill
would give me that much detail, down to the museum's side door.
Were you trying to get money from Bill? Am I supposed to go
search for missing art now? I'm not supposed to find some hidden
treasure and drop it from the roof like in a spy movie — am I?'

'Wow, you really are my fan number six. You watched
Hitchhiker. Aren't you curious about the real story? Surely you're
curious about the truth — especially now it's just within reach.
That's how I feel when I'm working on a movie. Some people say
it's silly, but I want to do my part to bring the story to life. Even
if I'm just in the corner.'

'Do you want me to write some lines for you?' I asked.

'Are you the movie director?'

We laughed.

'I mean, you said the director likes real stories. Isn't that why
he wanted to meet me? Now I'm at the scene of the crime. This is
the most useful I'll ever be. I can get the scoop.'

Jun was at a loss as to what I was talking about.

'I'm talking about how to make Driver 2 a more important role,' I said.

'How? By painting me?' Jun asked. 'The exhibition is almost over.'

8.

After I returned to the Robert Foundation and parked, I wandered around for ten minutes. I wasn't just enjoying an evening walk; I'd seen that the lights were on in my room. It was close to 10.00 pm. I didn't think anyone would be changing the pillowcases or towels this late. They wouldn't have gone into my empty room to bring me a snack or say hello, either. The light stayed on for more than five minutes. I kept thinking about the laptop on my desk. Fortunately for me, it wouldn't turn on right now, because the charging outlet was broken. I had to plug the charging cable in and hang it somewhere high up, like an IV, to get the current flowing. If the person in my room wanted my laptop, they wouldn't be able to see anything.

I stood between several palm trees and looked at the square window to my room. I was so nervous that I didn't even think about what would happen if I saw someone inside. Suddenly something jumped up behind me. It wasn't a frog or a grasshopper. It was a dog. The dog leapt upwards like a spring that had been compressed. I fell backwards, onto my butt. The dog looked around, as if it had abruptly been shoved onto a stage. It barked

loudly as its owner ran up to me and apologised. He wasn't from
the Robert Foundation, but he was dressed in pyjamas, as if he
were staying somewhere nearby.

'Look, he's happy,' the man said. 'He's wagging his tail.'

'There are dogs here?' I replied, still somewhat dazed.

'Are they not allowed?'

'No, I've just never seen a dog at this hour. Or a human, for
that matter.'

The dog scrambled his way out of the man's arms and started
to run around.

'Robert!' the man exclaimed.

Robert?

The man threw a frisbee for the dog, who disappeared from
view like a kite whose string had been cut.

'I have to throw this to get him to come back to me,' the man
said. 'He's such a feisty little guy.'

'You said his name is Robert?' I asked.

'Robert! Don't go far. Let's go to bed.'

Looking at me, the man said, 'Yeah, I think one in three dogs
these days is named Robert. It's a popular name.'

At that moment, Sam came up to us.

'Ms An, what are you doing here?' she asked.

I wanted to ask her the same question, but Sam was the one
who had come across a commotion. The dog didn't look in our
direction, as if displeased to have his night-time walk disturbed.
When Sam bent down to pet him, he rolled onto his back. The
dog turned his belly to the sky and wriggled his body according
to the rhythm of Sam's scratches.

Sam chastised the man. 'You can't be here after the museum

closes. Was the gate left open?'

The man apologised and disappeared into the darkness with the dog.

Sam shook her head and said, 'We get so many trespassers during the exhibitions. We're short on staff, too, which only makes things worse. Hey — by the way, I installed the app you were talking about.'

Sam showed me the Bballi icon on her phone screen. She said she had completed the safety training, too. The app's map interface was cute and fun to look at. As I knew all too well, it wasn't very good at calculating the distance between the delivery person and their destination, but Sam commented that looking at the map was a good way to reacquaint herself with the area. Fortunately, she hadn't been assigned any jobs.

'It's just for fun, in this town,' I said. 'You did the safety training? You should have put in my code! Oh, you didn't. A waste of ten dollars. Oh, well.'

The lights in my room were now turned off. It felt as though the window had closed its eyes. I felt uneasy for the rest of the night. I heard knocking in my sleep. A series of knocks. I couldn't tell if someone was knocking on my door or another door down the hallway. But the next door was twenty metres away. When I turned on my bedside lamp, the knocking stopped. I wasn't confident enough to open the door, so I opened the window instead. Sounds streamed in. Grasshoppers, raindrops, fountains, waves, palm trees, dogs howling … I closed the window, and the noise disappeared.

Breakfast the next day was very simple. A few toasters sat on the table, and next to them bread, jam, and coffee. Nothing else. Napkins lay neglected. There was no weather card on a silver tray. I didn't realise until I finished eating that the glass on the grandfather clock — in the hallway opposite my bedroom — was shattered.

Apparently, Robert had charged into a hall mirror in the middle of the night. Sam witnessed it. I hadn't, of course, but her depiction was vivid enough for me to be able to picture it. I, too, had seen Robert standing in front of that mirror, as if he wanted to leap inside of it. Leaning towards the glass as if his centre of gravity was not between his four legs, but somewhere on the other side of the mirror. Sam started to cry. She said that everything was her fault, that she didn't know why this kept happening to her.

When I asked what she meant, she muttered, 'Robert keeps hurting himself.'

'Hurting himself?'

Sam didn't answer right away and wiped tears off her face. Then she spoke calmly: Danny had taken Robert to the hospital last night. They were told that the situation wasn't serious, but Robert needed to rest for a while. He needed stability. Visitors would be coming to see the exhibition today, Sam said, so please keep this a secret. Visitors were only supposed to go to the museum anyway, but, like last night, there was the occasional oddball who roamed the grounds. 'Don't talk about what happened,' she warned.

The mirror that Robert had charged at was shattered, and the corridor, the length of which had been doubled by its reflection, now looked cut in half. The photos of Robert that covered one side of the hallway looked different, too. These were curated memories, and from what Bill had said, it sounded like other memories hadn't made the cut. They had been pushed out of the frame.

Now that I thought about it, I hadn't seen Robert for a while. I hadn't noticed at the time, but he'd missed the reception. Many of the guests at the event felt like they had met Robert without ever coming face to face with him. They'd been invited by Robert, and they thought they knew him. Robert's invitation, Robert's house, Robert's gifts. Every conversation that took place at the event proved his influence. The partygoers probably hadn't given much thought to not meeting Robert in person.

I remembered being told that whenever the lights in the hallway sensed movement and turned on, the CCTV cameras started recording, so I asked to see footage from last night, but I was told that nothing had been recorded. The only character I could think of who wouldn't activate the sensors was Robert. He flitted in and out like the wind. That being said, they probably wouldn't have shown me anything even if there *was* a recording. Considering what Sam had told me, it sounded like this wasn't Robert's first experience with self-harm. Sam said that Robert hurt himself soon after she was hired as a full-time employee, and she'd initially thought it was a test of her decision-making skills. Sam had completed her internship and been hired as an employee around the time I'd arrived in Los Angeles. (Did this explain the lack of communication and failure to pick me up from the airport?) Even if I asked, no one would have given me an honest answer. Sam's explanation of last night's incident differed from the explanation Director Choi gave me.

Choi said that last night, Robert had been working on an NFT project. He'd jumped at the mirror in order to shatter it into ninety-eight pieces. After emphasising the ephemeral irreplace-ability of art, now he was trying sell artwork piecemeal? When I said this sounded like the opposite of incineration, Choi gave an erratic response. He said that Robert intended to donate proceeds to towns affected by the forest fires. Danny looked at me oddly, too, when I asked if Robert was okay.

I was supposed to go for a walk with Robert that afternoon. I thought that if he didn't feel like going, we could skip the walk, but everyone said we had to follow through. Danny talked about how important it was for 'the artist to go for a stroll with Robert', which confirmed that this walk was not taking place for my benefit. The Robert Museum of Art had many visitors, and their eyes were on us.

'Robert needs to rest, so a substitute will go instead,' they told me.

A substitute? They threw out the word very naturally. So now I was going for a walk with Robert's replacement?

A dog that looked exactly like Robert soon appeared. The dog wore the same sneakers as Robert and had the same leash, and our walk proceeded as usual. This continued for several more days. This Robert was so temperamental that Robert in the morning and Robert in the evening were like different creatures, as were Robert in the sun and Robert in the rain. Perhaps because of this, I couldn't tell if the substitute Robert was a single dog or several, or even the original Robert. But it didn't matter. A few days later,

I was so used to the substitute dog that I said, 'I'm a little tired today — can I use a substitute myself?'

At some point, the silver trays that Sam brought me each morning had begun to carry only the daily weather cards. I assumed that substitute Robert would not send me letters like the real Robert had, but a few days later, a thick sealed letter appeared. In Robert's typical style, too. Somehow, I wasn't hurt after I read it. Like Robert, who looked at satellite images of natural disasters and couldn't do anything except comment on the colours he saw, I was now able to distance myself from these sentences full of criticism. I no longer cared if they expressed true feelings or if the words were just decorative.

As we came to the end of October, the contents of the weather cards started to differ from reality. The weather was as volatile as my mind, and the sky changed many times a day. The pond changed just as frequently. It looked like a beautiful stage for a swan in the morning, but after the daily rain it resembled a pile of trash. Green lotuses floating on the water looked like cabbage leaves meant to be thrown out. When evening fell, an unrealistically beautiful pink sky unfolded before me; at night, it rained violently.

As wildfires began to spread again, critics asked whether it was right to incinerate art. They attacked the Robert Foundation and the nearby resort for their waste of water. The Foundation monitored the fires, but what ended up causing damage wasn't fire — it was water. Sudden floods hit several areas simultaneously. The afternoon had boasted clear skies, but as day turned to night, thunder and rain struck. Waterlogged nights continued one after another. The dried-out lake filled back up, and the Robert Foundation's pond was at the brink of overflowing. The land around the pond was permanently waterlogged.

The exhibition was nearing its close, and few visitors came now. Sam said that only on the day of the incineration ceremony would people flock to the Foundation again.

I texted Jun, asking, 'Did you die?'

Jun replied, 'No, don't worry.'

Jun had joined the writing team for *Elk with Tyre*; since then, he said, he had fought with the director almost daily. The two were collaborating on a film based on a true story, but their focuses differed. The director had decided on the Robert Museum of Art as the film's setting, and he envisioned a plot that involved something shocking. After meeting with Bill Mori and sensing the shadiness of the Robert Foundation, he wanted to give me freedom to take the story in whatever direction I liked. Apparently, the director had come up with three separate storylines for my character, but it was all a bit complicated. I didn't like any of the endings he suggested, but they also all felt like realistic possibilities for my actual future. Feeling twisted, I said, 'I don't think any of these are right.'

That was when I thought about my painting. If I wanted a different ending, maybe the secret painting I'd created would allow for that. The director did not know that there was a second version of *R's Poo*, so he'd only envisioned three possible endings. I wanted a completely different story.

'Is your role the same as before?' I asked Jun.

'Driver 2? Yes.'

'It's important for my character to be mobile,' I said, 'so I guess the driver is vital.'

'Fleeing in a Lamborghini — is that the first option for the ending?' Jun asked. 'Or is it the three-hundredth photo-shoot customer who cancels her reservation but shows up again later? Or is it something else entirely?'

'No, the Lamborghini getaway is the fourth option. It's the ending where Driver 2 becomes an important character.'

I needed to think a little more about Driver 2's role in the script, but I clearly saw my role.

The Robert Foundation expected me to play the role of the faithful witness: someone who could testify about Robert, who would strengthen Robert's mythic history. Maybe that was why they'd arranged my walks and meals with Robert. We had never exchanged words, or even eye contact, during the walks; it was as if we were inside a shop window, proving that we were both alive and well. The meals had been a bit different. There, I had felt like some sort of educational assistant. Meals with me were training for Robert's substitute (substitutes?), whether the real Robert had wanted that or not. The shadow that had gradually expanded beneath Robert during our meal several months earlier was now reproducing itself in front of me in a completely different way. It was as if something was growing underneath Robert's chair: a liquid, not a shadow. He was shaking.

It wasn't urine, I thought. Everything happening around me was an amorphous, liquid phenomenon I couldn't define. I just wanted to be done with the experiences of the past few months.

Like the wildfire I'd passed through — I wanted the immense and mysterious problems surrounding me to be over. The acrid smell in my nostrils, the soot on the tip of my nose: they were the price I had to pay for being outside. Bill might have expected that, as soon as I returned to the Foundation, I would go and find the spot where Robert's pawprint had been stamped on the napkin map, but to be honest, I wasn't interested in the truth. All of it felt like distant gossip. What did it have to do with me? I'd be leaving in a few days. Whatever happened to the pillars supporting this place, I'd almost crossed to the other side of the bridge. Whether the bridge I crossed was made of water-resistant materials, I didn't care. But at night, I dreamed about falling onto a pile of napkins stamped with black pawprints. I dreamed about trying to find the napkin Bill had handed me amid a grotesque, catacomb-like pile.

I wondered about Robert's expiration date. If Robert was no longer the special dog people expected, he shouldn't have the right to burn my art. Only the real Robert had the right to incinerate. Considering that I was now eating meals with the substitute Robert, my contract had more or less already been breached.

After going on several walks with the fake Robert, I looked at old videos of the original Robert. There was a lot of footage, starting a long time ago. I didn't know much about dogs, but there seemed to be a subtle difference between the videos. Was I reading too much into it? What if the old Robert was a fake, too? What if I'd never actually met Robert — the first Robert, the one who used Bill's phone to take photos of lovers on a cliff, who snapped pictures of the Las Vegas detectives, who started living with Mr Waldmann? Had that Robert been replaced by another?

Did that mean that my experiences with him were fake? Had I been having fake dinners, going on fake walks, and having fake conversations? Was it a fake Robert who criticised me and would cruelly burn my art?

When I asked people about this, they all reacted similarly.

'Are you serious?' Danny asked. 'If you let something rot, if you let it age and die, it becomes meaningless. Sometimes it's the shell that matters, not the kernel inside. If you frame a picture of the Robert Foundation, people will believe what they see inside the frame. What they see is the truth: the part that doesn't rot.'

I looked at the shark behind Danny. It was a piece by Damien Hirst. When the taxidermied shark started to decompose inside its glass tank, people had tried to slow the inevitable. The shark eventually died anyway. Of course, it was already long dead, but this was a death in a different sense. In the end, the only way to restore the damaged work was to replace its contents. A new shark arrived and was preserved the same way as the previous one.

'Is the second shark fake?' Danny asked. 'The third? No one says they're fake.'

He used Nam June Paik's work as another example.

'Think about *Sonatine for Goldfish*. When I first saw that piece, I was curious about the same thing. It was created in 1992 — has the goldfish in the fishbowl been the same one since then? Of course, as you know, the goldfish has been replaced countless times. Was the only real fish the first one? What about the ones that came after? The continuity of the message is what matters. It's the same with Robert.'

'You mean the first Robert I ate a meal with?' I asked.

'There's no point distinguishing between them,' Danny said.

'Are they different entities, Robert today and Robert from four months ago?'

'I wouldn't say they're different entities. Robert is a continuous world. The appearance of a new Robert doesn't change the *meaning* of Robert. We're maintaining him for the future.'

Maintaining him? What did that mean? It sounded like Robert was a performance. Was Robert just an animal actor in a movie, and whenever he got hurt, a replacement showed up? Even if he was being replaced, the audience wouldn't say the new dog *wasn't* Robert.

Choi explained the situation with a friendlier metaphor.

'What kind of soap do you like?' he asked. 'I like Dial. It's cheap and practical. I had a lot of acne in middle school, and my chemistry teacher told me to try it out. About a month after I started using the soap, my acne went away. I've been using Dial ever since. I don't know how many bars I've gone through. What I do know is that the first bar I bought in ninth grade was Dial soap, and the bar I'm using now is Dial soap, too. It's not like the first bar was the real Dial, and the current bar is Dial number 197. It's all Dial. Ms An, remember when we first met? It was winter — you wore a thick padded jacket. You told me about the Tetris game you play on the train, how if multiple people wearing the same colour of coat are standing next to each other, you can erase them. You said that you wanted space for yourself, a place where you could breathe. Now you're at the doorstep of that space. The exhibition is almost over, and soon you'll be another star produced by the Robert Foundation. Just stay put.'

Stay put, and I'd achieve success. I was in a different position, though, from previous Foundation artists. They hadn't known about the substitute Roberts, had they? I was at a crossroad of strange choices. The Robert Foundation's incineration ceremony was born from a serendipitous accident; maybe that forebode the possibility of another incident. Perhaps the cancellation of my contract, or the theft of my painting. If I wanted the art world's focus on me, it didn't have to come from burning my art. I thought carefully about the quietest and least damaging way to achieve this and decided to call the art dealer from S Gallery. Maybe she'd be able to help me. The dealer answered after only a few rings.

'I knew you'd call,' she said. 'Although you did it a little later than I expected.'

She made an appealing offer. If I sold her *R's Poo*, she would hold a private exhibition of my work at S Gallery in London the next year. She told me that she had already bought five of the nine paintings at my Robert Foundation exhibition. She said, sincerely, that she would help create the 'world of An Yiji'.

I had already walked up to the museum's side door when I called the dealer. It wasn't the most obvious way to enter the museum. As Bill had warned, the door was situated between all sorts of equipment. It was a pair of big iron sliding doors — not what you'd expect for a side entrance. It wasn't an area I would have just come across. The door didn't have a lock, but rather a touchpad that said PUSH. Did I just have to press the button to open the door? It was so obvious that I hesitated. Would an alarm sound if I pressed it? There had to be CCTV cameras nearby; maybe they'd already filmed me fumbling. I probably couldn't use the excuse that I'd pressed the button out of curiosity. I pressed it anyway. The door didn't open. I pressed the button once more, but the door still didn't open. Instead, Sam walked up to me and asked what I was doing.

'I was curious about what this is,' I said.

'You wanted to open the door? It's such a mess over here.'

Sam left, indifferent, and I returned to my studio with my heart thumping in my chest. I felt possessed as I made another phone call.

The art dealer picked up. As we spoke, I got the impression that she had looked into my history. Then she said, 'Museum security can be surprisingly lax. Especially at the Robert Museum.'

'You mean you want *me* to steal the painting? After everything ...'

'You're the one closest to the art. We want you to rescue it so it doesn't end up in the pizza oven.'

I hadn't wanted to be directly involved in the rescue, but the dealer's voice rang repeatedly in my head. It was true — I was closest to the painting. I passed by the museum's side entrance again the next day, and the day after that. I walked by it multiple times until, one day at dawn, I realised that there was a gap between the two doors, a palm-sized opening. How could I not peek inside? I had no idea who'd left the doors ajar, but it seemed like a casual mistake. The incineration ceremony was tomorrow. A bright light was coming from somewhere inside. All I knew was that this was probably my only way to *R's Poo*. I really was the person closest to it.

•

The doors looked the same when I came back from the studio, carrying something in my hand. I touched one of them, but no alarm went off. Next, I gently pushed it to the side and watched it move in the direction I was pushing. It wasn't fixed shut. I had to open the door a little more to squeeze myself through, but there wasn't any problem fitting. I just had to move the door in gentle increments, because it made a squeaking noise each time it moved. The whole endeavour took several minutes. I pushed my body into the building, along with the painting that I'd brought. A square canvas, one hundred centimetres by one hundred centimetres. The future *R's Poo*.

Gradually, the darkness grew familiar. The corridor continued on a downward slant, and light and sound spilled from the other end. Who was there? I seemed to now be in the basement of the art museum, but it was impossible to know how many floors underground. As I walked farther, the light and noise intensified. It sounded like at least two people talking. Someone was laughing, or maybe crying. When I worried I had gone too far, I looked back, but I could no longer see where I'd entered. I had come to find my painting, and now I was trapped.

I kept hearing language I couldn't understand. Anxiety crept in, and I wondered if this passage was separate from the museum's exhibition space. My destination was *R's Poo*; I didn't want to exert extra effort to understand the strange architecture of this building. I didn't want to wander around unfamiliar pathways. After a while, I reached a circular area. I was still underground, but now I could see the sky above me. This place felt like an elevator shaft — why could I see the sky? This space was completely exposed. I was so far underground that I couldn't tell if I was still in the Robert Foundation's domain. I continued to hear mumbling. I remembered what a friend who worked in a crematorium had told me a long time ago. According to the friend, when you cremated remains, they made a sound. Some people said it was from hard items like gold teeth exploding, but that didn't really explain it. Perhaps I could hear the ashes in here. But I didn't understand them.

How long had I walked? I shone my phone's torch, looking around at the unfamiliar world like a scuba diver. All the light landed on was greyish darkness and cracks in various surfaces. At some point, though, I noticed a rounded collection of *something* — a beautiful coral reef of objects. They were faces, the size of my fist, made of stone. As I panned over them with my light, I saw more and more. Could this be what I thought it was? I couldn't read the label, but these figures had to be part of *Head Collection*. It wasn't the whole thing, though; I counted several times, but there were only thirteen heads — not thirty. Next to the heads, I saw a strip of film shining like a deep-sea oarfish and immediately wondered if it was Bill's.

Before I could reach for it, though, someone said, 'Come here. Sit.'

It was a command.

'Here. Sit.'

Two canine eyes stared at me in the dark. Robert. My body shook. It was hard to stand. He stood on higher ground than me. For some reason, he was pulling a cart with his mouth, and inside the cart was my goal: the original painting. Robert smirked when he saw the second *R's Poo* in my hand. He was alone. No interpreter between us. Even so, I understood him — something I only realised much later.

I just barely managed to hold onto the canvas. 'I respect the incineration process, but if you're going to burn my work anyway, why don't you use this painting instead? It looks the same as the original. I'm just worried I'd regret it …'

Robert didn't seem to be listening. Maybe I wasn't getting through to him. In an annoyed tone, he told me that he didn't understand why I would reject the joy of incinerating my art. The real aura of the art, he said, only appears — rises like smoke — when it is incinerated. He asked me to give me a reason for giving up that joy. It sounded like he was mocking me, but he also seemed to want my answer.

'Robert,' I said, 'I understand your concerns. But I'm sick of incineration. I can make a name for my art another way, even if we don't burn it.'

Robert looked at me and said, 'Stop with this drivel.'

He said the incineration ceremony would soon begin. Incineration, incineration, incineration. Robert repeated the word over and over. It was like a gag stuffed in his mouth, incineration. I could almost hear the sound of the oven heating up, the sound of a fire getting ready to swallow the art. Robert said that we would 'save the art' by turning it into ashes, but my heart wouldn't let me do it. What if this was the best painting of my life? I spat out what I wanted to say:

'You're not sponsoring artists — you're using them as guinea pigs! We don't even know if you're the real Robert.'

'I wasn't going to say this,' Robert said, 'but your work doesn't have much personality. The era of art with personality has come and gone, anyway. It only becomes unique when burned. Look at how anxious you are. Your attitude proves the power of incineration.'

I began to cry. Then it hit me. I shouted at Robert.

'*R's Poo* — you know what it's made of?'

'The finest organic paint,' Robert said.

'No, it's your droppings. Don't you remember? This painting is irreplaceable, one of a kind. Are you really going to get rid of it?'

Robert's brow was wrinkled, and he bared his teeth. His tail stuck straight up. This meant that he felt embarrassed. At least I recognised the sign. Robert stood on his hind legs, lengthening his body.

'I don't know whether paintings are replaceable or not,' he said, 'but artists are. If you're so sure about how special you are, then prove it.'

I put the painting in the cart as Robert directed. The original and the copy sat side by side. Robert carefully examined the two works. Maybe I thought I could convince him. I had no choice but to watch helplessly as Robert unlocked the cart and gave it a shove. The cart followed a circular downhill path at high speed before hitting a wall and stopping. I ran after it. Both paintings had flown out of the cart and now lay on the ground.

'Only take one,' Robert shouted from above. 'You have ten seconds.'

He started counting.

'One …'

I stood in a daze until I heard him say, 'Two …', and then hurriedly turned to look at the paintings. I had to pick the real *R's Poo* — that had been my goal all along. But which one was it? I couldn't tell. Of course, the original had Robert's poo on it, but both paintings had *some* sort of poo on them, so they were impossible to distinguish with the naked eye. Three … Four … I reached for the painting farthest away from me but then hesitated for a moment. I still ended up picking it, but that last-minute hesitation was hard to overcome. Five … Six … I ran. I kept running. The exit appeared in front of me like a lie. Seven … Eight … Nine … I couldn't let Robert's words catch up with me. When I emerged outside, I no longer heard any barking. I fell forward, prostrate, just about ready to lick the ground.

It was raining. Lightning flashed, and water fell from the sky as if it had been pierced. The painting. The painting! I wrapped my body around it, but I wasn't big enough. I wanted to cry. This was a mess. I did have an umbrella. I'd brought it for camouflage, but now I could actually use it. I opened the umbrella and covered both the painting and myself. It only took a few seconds, but my clothes were already wet. It was basically pouring. Lightning and heavy torrents. I opened the rear door of my parked car and put the picture inside. Then I went around to the driver's side and cried. I felt a mixture of defeat and regret. Was this even the real *R's Poo*? It was raining so much that I couldn't see. The palm trees in front of me were drenched, shaking in the wind, screaming. The car's windscreen wiper moved like a madman.

Robert had allowed this, so there wouldn't be any problems. I was sure of it … or was I? Would everything work out? There were several hours left until the incineration. If it still went ahead as planned, despite the rain, I'd have to come back here in three hours. I just had to believe that it was the fake painting getting incinerated. I'd be watching a play. But would it be the fake? How could I know that I'd rescued the original? Why had Robert asked me to choose between the two? Why had he given me that opportunity? Was it even an opportunity? Had

I really heard Robert talking? My reflection in the rear-view mirror looked hollow. Through the car window, I saw someone carrying a black umbrella, hurrying towards the museum. It was a woman in an orange suit. Black hair, orange suit, and sky-blue sneakers.

Clearly, I was replaceable. Then I realised that this would be the 'artist' who would attend the ceremony. She would cry like she meant it, would do a better job than I could. I felt lighter. I was the real artist, and my painting was the real painting. The real painting just had to escape quietly, and we'd done that. Were in the midst of doing that.

I sent a message to Jun. Maybe Driver 2 would be a bigger role in the movie now. If the director really wanted the entire movie to come from reality, Driver 2 would be essential to the artist's quick escape. Or, not a quick escape, just getting back what was already hers. As soon as I turned on the headlights and pressed down on the accelerator, a dog rushed towards me. I braked, but the car didn't stop until I was past where the dog had been. I wasn't sure what happened next. The palm trees shook, and all I could think about was how they seemed to be wailing. It was definitely a dog. Had I hit Robert with the car? My body shivered. I just barely managed to open the car door. Outside, someone had already got to the scene of the accident. It was Danny. Danny brought me back to the car and sat me down in the passenger seat while he took the wheel. Amid so much rain that the windscreen wipers had just about given up, Danny drove through the darkness before pulling over. It felt like we'd driven for a while, but we were still inside the Robert Foundation grounds.

'Where did you put him?' he asked.

I pointed to the back seat.

'Robert, I mean. Where's Robert?'

'What was that back there?' I asked. 'Was it a dog?'

'It was a fallen tree,' Danny said. Then once again, he asked me where I had taken Robert. I said he was in the museum, but Danny didn't believe me. I didn't believe it, either, that Robert and I had conversed without an interpreter. It was difficult to believe. I was the one it had happened to, and I could barely believe it. But it wasn't a dream. I could still vividly imagine the scene: the clattering cart, the moment when I picked the 'real' painting.

'Let's get out,' Danny said.

Danny hadn't said anything important in the car. He parked in front of the greenhouse, and I followed him inside. Solid windows protected the inside of the greenhouse from rain and wind, so the plants within remained lush and alive. It was a swamp, a jungle. Every time lightning struck, the plants in the greenhouse seemed to blink.

Danny assumed I knew Robert's whereabouts thanks to a letter. All of Robert's other letters been dictated to Danny, but not this one. Robert had written this one himself. Danny showed me the envelope. It was unsealed, with a familiar napkin inside. This one was stamped with two pawprints. One was the print I recognised from the photo Robert had taken long ago, and the other one looked a little larger. The second print was from the stamp Bill had stolen. The napkin bore the logo of the doughnut shop and the name of the mall where I'd met with Bill. How had it got here? After meeting with Bill, I had placed the napkin inside the four-hundred-page book I'd been given about the Robert Foundation. After putting the napkin there, I hadn't opened the book up again. I examined the napkin. The two footprints on the napkin looked clearer than they previously had. They were the same shape as before, but the second one seemed to have grown in size, like it belonged to an entirely different creature than Robert. Danny picked up the napkin and pointed to what was obviously my handwriting.

'I AM INDEX,' he read. 'What does this mean?'

'What does it mean? Does it have to mean anything? I like to scribble on napkins. I just copied the wording I saw in the study.'

'You're saying you accidentally wrote on a napkin with Robert's stamp on it.'

'Because the napkin wasn't important to me,' I said. 'I didn't intend to do anything with it. The only thing you warned me against was asking if Robert can understand us. You said that was considered arrogant. But why would writing on a napkin be a faux pas?'

'Robert likes to play with arrangements of letters,' Danny said. 'He knows the meanings of different letters from their shape and feel. He doesn't arrange them randomly. Let me ask you something. What did you think when you saw the phrase I AM INDEX?'

'I thought about the Korean translation of "I am index"? And what an arrogant dog Robert was?'

The birds in the greenhouse had stopped singing. The artificial waterfall had stopped flowing. The inside of the greenhouse was silent, while the world shook outside. I couldn't figure out what Danny was trying to say, or what he wanted to ask me. He wanted to know why 'I AM INDEX' was written on a napkin? It was a letter beyond his control, and the words hinted at Robert's whereabouts.

'Is this a game?' I asked.

'I wish. I just hope the letter wasn't a suicide note.'

'A suicide note?'

'We have to hurry up and find Robert, because we don't know what he's going to do. We've looked everywhere — there's not a trace of him. Not in the museum basement, nowhere. Can you think of anywhere he might be? He did the same thing when you first arrived four months ago. He had to write a letter for your arrival, and it must have triggered him. He said at the time that he needed an "extension". And now he's gone again. You have to explain why you wrote these words on your napkin, why you disclosed them to Robert.'

My head throbbed. I AM INDEX was this big of a deal? I didn't know if the line was a shorter, compressed version of something else, or if it had been a single sentence from the beginning. The night after I met Bill, I had sat down in the massage chair in the study, and as I vibrated in place, I realised that the alphabet blocks reading I AM INDEX were no longer there. I wrote the sentence down. There wasn't any particular reason why I wrote it on the napkin Bill had given me. Maybe I'd thought about a new possible meaning to the sentence and wanted to jot down a reminder? There was a colourful memo pad within reach, but it was easier to grab the scrap of paper from my pocket to write on. In my subconscious, everything had its place. The place for I AM INDEX was a napkin in the pocket of my dress. I didn't tell Danny that when I wrote down the sentence there, I'd also thought about another definition of index — a list that tells you where to find what you are looking for.

Robert was a creature that could not die.

According to a provision intended to protect Robert, upon the dog's death, all activities of the Robert Foundation were to be stopped. Danny, however, had a different idea. He couldn't accept that the Robert Foundation would end. If you wanted to grow a tree from scratch, you had to wait thirty years or so; why would it be any different for a foundation supporting the arts? If Mr Waldmann were still alive, Danny said, he would have changed his mind, too. But Mr Waldmann had died, and the only way to keep the Foundation alive was through immortality. This was why they needed substitute Roberts.

Robert had once told Danny, 'When I can no longer carry out the role of Robert, that's when I become a dog. An old, sick circus dog. Incinerate me then.'

Incinerate me. According to the Robert Foundation's narrative, the act of incineration gave the incinerated object a story. It exposed the object for what it was. I was surprised to hear that Robert thought of himself as a circus dog, but I was more shocked to learn that he'd told Danny to incinerate him. What did he think incineration would help him achieve? Anyway, this had all been conveyed to me through Danny, so I couldn't take it at face value.

Suddenly a Bballi notification popped up on my phone. 'Secret!' it read. I was so surprised that I almost dropped my phone. A line of text appeared on-screen.

'Secret! Please collect the item from DEX and do with it as you wish.'

This presented another possibility. The message pulled my mind in a new direction. DEX: that was the old airport where I'd practised driving. One of the prospective empty fields that had been offered to me. I remembered someone from Q telling me that the code for the airport was DEX. It was a discontinued code, now just a useless collection of letters. My napkin note clearly read I AM INDEX, but the alphabet blocks in the study had uniform spacing between them. What if it said I AM IN DEX, not I AM INDEX? I was thinking about the empty airport when Danny reached his arm in my direction, and I stiffened. He opened the door behind me. Noise from the outside rushed in, but the rainfall had notably lessened.

'Go back to your room,' he said.

'What?'

'Go back to the room and wait for Robert to come back. I'll find him.'

I said I wanted to leave. Telling Danny about my conversation with Robert at the museum (he said I'd imagined the whole thing) made me want to take *R's Poo* from the back seat of the car and get out. I didn't tell Danny that it was the original. How could I tell him that I'd brought a copy of the painting to the museum, and Robert gave me permission to take the original? The small amount I'd already told Danny was only partly getting through to him. This was the first time I'd seen him look dishevelled. He wasn't interested in me leaving with a painting. He just feared that the world would find out about the existence of two identical pieces of art. His worst-case scenario was that Robert was found dead, and someone else discovered the body before him. I assured the plants that once I left this place, I wouldn't talk about my experiences here.

'I hope that you can understand,' I said, 'why I'm leaving on the day of the incineration.'

The Robert Foundation had presented me with an opportunity, and I had no reason to dismantle a sturdy, pre-existing frame of support. Bill thought I would be shocked after learning the truth about Robert, but even after reclaiming my painting, I depended on Robert's world to maintain interest in my art. Like Danny, I had expected stability from this world, and Danny knew that. Perhaps that was why, when I asked Danny what he would do if the worst happened, he said the following.

'Someone will have to take responsibility,' he said. 'Sam was the last person to see Robert.'

Danny failed to elaborate on how blame would manifest, but considering what had come out after the interpreter was fired, Sam was presumably not being consulted about her 'responsibility'. Danny had already decided on who would take the blame for the looming disaster: a woman who'd worked her way up from Robert's groomer to Foundation administrator had been caught siphoning organisational assets for personal means, eventually leading to the death of said assets. 'Assets' presumably referred to Robert. When asked if this story was true, Danny said it had to be. No one could get in touch with Sam, and few other people had access to Robert. Sam was the most likely target. A docile wildebeest. This was why Sam would be the person responsible.

The birds in the greenhouse fluttered their wings in unison. I heard a mysterious melody. Danny had asked me if I wanted to play any particular music for the incineration, and this was the song I'd requested: 'A Day in the Life', by the Beatles.

Danny looked around. We walked outside into the rain where, despite being dampened by the weather, music was playing from speakers in the streetlights. Lights flashed to indicate that the incineration oven was in use. Director Choi hurriedly ran towards us, without an umbrella to protect him.

'It's not the incineration ceremony!' he shouted. 'Something is wrong!'

9.

The incineration ceremony was cancelled. The Robert Foundation didn't even have to announce the cancellation, because few outsiders had come through the downpour. No one saw the woman in the orange suit. No one saw Robert in the museum. They were like misprints, pages that would soon be torn out of their book. But the incinerator was lit, and something had gone inside it.

Director Choi was afraid he would find bones in the oven. No one found bones, but they did discover what might be considered part of Robert's body: the black box, folded in on itself like a fortune cookie. The interpreter had said it was empty, but now there was no way to verify the claim. The box was dead. Danny busily made phone calls. I was looking for something, too. For evidence of *R's Poo*. Even though I had chosen the original painting, I was conscious of the one I'd left behind. Maybe that was the real painting after all.

And the painting I believed to be the original — maybe it was, maybe it wasn't. Either way, it was the one I had chosen, and I left the Robert Foundation with it. No one chased me, but I ran like I was being chased. It felt like some sort of poisonous gas was chasing after me. The Robert Foundation was expanding, faster than I could run.

The last thing I saw before leaving the Foundation was the stepping-stone path, made from ten stones that were now in complete disarray. They looked like the teeth of someone who'd been beaten up. The path was like the skeleton of an extinct animal, on display in a natural-history museum.

Bballi sent me another 'secret' request. I couldn't be the only delivery person in this area; how had no one else taken the job? I wasn't in a position to work as a rider, but it felt like the request was aimed at me. I pressed 'accept'. I had no idea what would be waiting for me at DEX. I didn't even have a car. I couldn't hop into the Robert Foundation's Lamborghini anymore. Now it really was Driver 2's time to shine. Jun waited for me at the entrance to the Robert Foundation. He said that I looked like a big umbrella walking towards him, with a canvas shield, as the canvas and umbrella were the only things I carried and they hid me from sight. As soon as I saw Jun, I relaxed.

'Let's go to DEX,' he said.

'Where?'

'DEX. The airport near here. I'll show you around.'

When I'd first arrived at the Robert Foundation, in the ripeness of summer, I had practised driving there. I'd spent a lot of times driving in circles around the empty lot, until my artistic endeavours began to gain momentum. Sam was the only person who'd gone with me. She was also the only person to tell me about the airport's history.

'Aren't you going back to Korea?' Jun asked. DEX was in the opposite direction of the airport in Los Angeles. Our priorities were probably out of order, but Bballi continued to make pleading requests on my phone, so we decided to head towards DEX. What would be there for us? What were we supposed to collect? Usually the app gave me information about my jobs, but there was no information this time. If I AM IN DEX was the correct interpretation of those blocks, did that mean we'd find Robert there? That he hadn't ended up in the incinerator? But Robert couldn't have got to the airport by himself. I called Sam, but she didn't answer.

As we drove, I turned to the painting I'd rescued. It looked unfamiliar. I called the art dealer from S Gallery. The phone rang for a long time, but the dealer didn't answer.

'Isn't it dangerous to pick up a mystery package?' Jun asked. 'We don't know what it could be — it might be drugs, or firearms.'

'No,' I said. 'I have an idea of what it might be. The pick-up location is Gate Two, and there's only one person who knows where that is.'

It was someone who, long ago, had bought the sign for Gate Two at auction, who had until recently gone with me to the airport under the guise of driving practice, but who really used the time as an excuse to blabber on about the history of the place to me — someone who said that things weren't over until they were over, who was now writing a story anew. The Robert Foundation had thrust her into a position of weakness, but Sam probably knew Robert's whereabouts, and she wasn't answering her phone. I imagined arriving at the airport only to see Sam holding Robert in an embrace. Would that Robert really be Robert?

'What was that movie with "Truck" in the title?' Jun asked. 'A Spielberg movie.'

He started to talk about a scary movie that began with a truck chasing after the protagonist.

'Why are you asking about that now?' I asked.

'There's a car like that behind us,' he said. 'I tried to let it pass us, but it won't. Is it Driver 2's job to decide what to do?'

Jun slowed down like he was going to stop. Through the side mirror, I saw the approaching vehicle. I could only see the front, but that was enough to tell that it was huge. I kept calling the art dealer, but she didn't answer. I sent her a text, but still nothing. I was nervous. The truck eventually passed us.

We reached DEX, slow and steady, after nightfall. Someone was standing at the spot where I'd practised turning. It was Sam. She stood next to something that, at first glance, looked like my carry-on suitcase. Just as Sam raised her hand in greeting, the art dealer finally called me back. I gestured for Jun to stop the car. For a moment, we forgot about Sam and her luggage. Over the phone, the art dealer sounded tired. I delivered the news.

'I rescued it!' I exclaimed. 'I have the painting!'

The dealer didn't seem to believe me. That's impossible, she said.

'I have it,' I said. 'The original. The first painting … Hello? Can you hear me?'

After a moment of silence, the dealer spoke.

'That's not R's Poo,' she said. A painting without an expiration date wasn't the real thing.

She hadn't expected me to actually take the painting, she said. She repeated that if I rescued a painting that was supposed to be incinerated, then it was no longer authentic. When I asked why she had told me to take the painting and flee, she replied she had meant it in the moment.

'I'm sorry,' she said. 'I had a change of heart.'

'What do you mean?' I asked. 'Say it again.'

I mumbled like a person possessed. Through the phone, the art dealer spoke slowly but firmly.

'Only the art that burns is real,' she said. 'Only when it's on fire does it have the power to move souls. In that sense, if you run from the flames, you're no longer the real thing.'